I0738226

Blythe of the Gates

Leah Erickson

For Mary Mulkerrin Erickson

One

Covered in cracked, brown leather and very old, the box had rows of hammered brass tacks along its edges, the lock held shut with a heavy latch of blackened metal. Only the Magician was allowed to use the key, and he kept it in his breast pocket at all times.

Luna knew about the faded red velvet lining. And she knew how the antique metal hinges creaked when he opened it. She knew about the ancient smell of mildewed newspaper, the smell of trapped life, the smell of time passed by …

"Luna. Open your eyes and look at it!"

Why the Magician did this to her, she did not know. Some nights when he was in a particularly wicked mood, he'd take the box down from the top of his closet and make Luna look inside, even though she turned away, and shut her eyes to it.

This made him laugh. "Girl, I am your husband. Listen to me! *Look* at it."

But it was unbearable, to look straight into it, because it *hurt*. Looking straight into the thing was like looking straight into the sun; when she shut her eyes, she saw pulsing blood, red and floating orbs …

"Look."

To look inside the box was to feel dissolution, deep down in her very center, spreading out and out until she had no more edges to her.

But once she did look, it was so hard to look away again.

Two

Luna hardly noticed what was around her. The woven wicker seat she sat on, the advertising cards lined up on the wooden rails above the windows. COCA-COLA. GOLD DUST WASHING POWDER. OLD NORTH STATE SMOKING TOBACCO. The women's wide-brimmed hats as they bobbed and swayed with the motion, the dust particles that floated in a beam of sunlight. She sat on the trolley clutching the strings of her small embroidered pouch. A faint, private smile played about her lips and made her look like a woman enjoying a pleasurable daydream.

Her favorite time, these secret mornings when she took a ride to the Brooklyn Navy Yard; she felt full of excitement and buoyant hope when she saw the trolley approaching her stop that morning, dark green with gold gilding, one headlight trained like a single eye searching her out. These trips were her own, no one else's. She usually told the Magician that she was at the fruit or the fish market.

A little boy in woolen knickers ran up and down the aisle with a toy zeppelin; he toppled into her as the trolley rounded a corner and she was not even annoyed.

"There, there," she said and pulled him upright. He

looked into her eyes for a moment, face small and grave as an owl's. Then he ran back to his mother.

She wore a long tweed hobble skirt with a narrow band that clinched at the knees, and her thirteen-button boots with the small heel, but she felt exhilarated enough on arrival to step down to the pavement with a little hop in her step. Though she was twenty years old, sometimes she still felt as jubilant as a child. Especially on mornings like this, wearing her rabbit trim coat and wide-brimmed hat trimmed with dark blue plumes. The cold air stung. January. There were still banners in the street saying NEW YEAR 1911 that swayed back and forth; the wind always blew at the Navy Yard.

She didn't mind. She was only there to stand and look, to take in the view. It was her spot where she could stand at the tall metal gate that had ribbons of ice flowing down it. She touched the wire links, and although she wore her leather gloves, the thrill of the cold spiraled right through to her fingertips, down her spine.

Beyond the fence, she had a view of the battleship USS Connecticut in dry dock. Farther back yet, the steel gray sea, the endless sky, and a view of the Brooklyn Bridge. From this far, everything looked so still, save for the billows of soot blowing from the smokestacks, the tiny bright flutter of nautical flags, and a scattering of gulls flying, their cries refracted through the air so that they echoed a tinny delay by the time they reached Luna's ears.

The way this scene came together was a kind of music; each detail scattered, and different notes united in harmony. The sun illuminated it all, threw bright cold reflections and dazzling fragments of a rainbow that haloed things if she looked in just the right way.

Her lover, Sean was one of the men working on the

Connecticut, giving it a refit. The men working the shipyard looked small and featureless from where she stood. But still, knowing *he* was there made the blood hum in her veins, bringing her alive in a way she rarely felt in her everyday life. Even more so than in those stolen moments when Sean held her in his very arms.

The breeze lifted the brim of her hat playfully, and she had to clutch it to prevent it going windborne. The gust could probably take her, a small woman, away if she jumped into the air and surrendered to it.

The wind made her eyes tear, burned her cheeks, and pulled loose tendrils from her dark hair, loosening its pins; she gripped the wire gate and stood on tiptoe, her eyes closed, and gave in to the current that flowed through her.

Up the stairs she hurried, a rustling paper bag in one arm; her eyes strained to adjust to darkness again. Lit by a single bulb that hung from the ceiling, the air in the stairwell to their apartment felt close with the smell of cooking odors.

Pausing to catch her breath and steady herself, she opened the door.

"I'm back," she called and pulled off her gloves on her way to the small kitchen.

The Magician said, "Humph," from the front parlor.

In the paper bag were potatoes, a half dozen rosy blushing apples, and a bundle of carrots, vibrant with the dirt and grit still on them, and frothy green tops that stuck up out of the bag like plumage. She unpacked onto the countertop, and touched gently everything with her fingers as she listened, still, gauging the mood in their small rooms.

"I-I got some lovely apples. I could make a pie or … or a tart? I saw nothing good at the fishmonger's, but I—"

"Luna, will you come in here, please?"

Her heart stilled, and then suddenly started up again with a loud, irregular gallop, like that of a crippled horse.

But when she went into the parlor, he did not even look at her. He held a large piece of paper, unfurled from a large cardboard tube, now propped in the corner.

"Come here, girl, and tell me what you think of this."

He turned the key of the rose-colored globe lamp and then knelt at the edge of the coffee table, smoothing it with his hands.

"Oh!" It was, she saw, the new poster for the act: COSMO, THE INCOMPARABLE, in large yellow letters at a dramatic slant across the top.

She stared at the picture below, at the illustration of the Magician wearing white tie and tails, hair center-parted and combed back, gleaming, his hands held out, god-like. Levitating before him in a silvery dress, filmy and insubstantial as smoke, was Luna, eyes closed, dark hair loose and swirling as though she floated in water.

"I, um …"

"*Well?*"

"I-I like the design in the background." The background was an inky midnight blue, with silver stars and a silver half-moon with a beautiful woman's profile on it, smiling a mysterious close-lipped smile.

"But look at *me*." The Magician flicked the paper with his finger. "It looks nothing like me."

"Oh, but I think it does …"

"The mouth is too soft, and the brows are too faint."

In truth, the illustration *did* soften him. In real life, he had heavier brows, more thunderous. His nose and chin sharper and more thrusting. His mouth, though small and full-lipped, had a hardness about it, even when in a good mood. And his hair never stayed down neatly. It was thick and unruly and spilled forward from his deep widow's peak.

"I think it is quite nice." Her eyes lingered, uncomfortably, on her face in the poster. The illustration made her look beautiful but dead. It was eerie, as if she were watching herself asleep. Something she was not supposed to see …

"Come to, girl. Speak sensibly. Finish your sentences."

"B-b-but it's only our first poster. There will be others—"

"Our *first*, yes. But our most important, that's the problem. I've worked hard on this act, harder than I've worked on anything, and every detail has to be perfect. If we are going to take the act on tour one day, first I have to conquer New York! I will not fail. I will not be *laughed at*."

"But darling, we *are* at the Beaumont Theatre, three matinees and three evening shows a week, surely you can say—"

"Surely, nothing! Even though we are the best there is, if we don't have proper billing, then it's all for naught. I want to strangle that printmaker. Shoddy work and he ripped me off, charging me not what he quoted." His eyes darkened, and he pursed his reddish lips grimly. "Someday he'll get what's coming to him."

A compressed stillness overtook the Magician at times like this: an inert force that felt as though it sucked the air from the room.

"Oh, now, darling," she fluttered, voice high, chest tight, eager to distract. "The new stage dress I am making for myself is coming out *so* nicely."

"*White?*" His eyes darted back quickly from the void and trained intently on her face.

"Y-yes. White." This came out in a whisper. It threw her off when his whole attention focused on her and she tended to lose her train of thought.

"Like the one in the poster?"

"Yes. Sort of."

"Well, I would like to see it on you."

"It will be ready, I think, tomorrow."

"Well, it had better be. We open Saturday. And I don't think we've rehearsed nearly enough."

The rehearsals. They had felt endless, and just thinking of them drained the life right out of Luna. *I just won't think about it.*

He rolled up the poster, a pensive look on his face.

"Well, anyway," he murmured after a while, "best get to that pie."

Three

They had been married one year and courted only two months.

Luna had just recently come to America from Ireland when she met the Magician. She, her father, and two of her sisters had come through Ellis Island. After the voyage, the week spent in foul-odored darkness in steerage, an almost hallucinatory vision greeted them when the steamship pulled into the harbor at last: the Statue of Liberty beckoned like a benevolent goddess. Luna squeezed onto the open deck with so many others, dazed and speechless with wonder.

The registry room itself at Ellis Island was a dizzying, reeling place that had continued to haunt her dreams ever since. It was high ceilinged, cathedral-like, and echoed with thousands of different languages. Mothers in embroidered blouses and sheepskin vests, with their babies in slings. Men in tunics and turbans. A Dutch woman in a large white bonnet with wide, strange wings on the side. A bearded priest with a tall, black, cylindrical hat. Unreal.

All of them, packed together, lined up on hard wooden benches. Luna had struggled to take it all in. The whole process took five hours, but it felt like days. Years. In fact, Luna had wondered if she'd died and entered another plane of existence, reborn as an entirely different person by the time she and her family took the ferry to Manhattan.

Those first chaotic months she'd lived with her auntie in Hell's Kitchen in a dark, rickety tenement. Wooden floors that sank in the middle. Stifling air. Mice. She and sister Lil to a single bed, Mary Catherine on the floor.

Luna found employment as a seamstress in the Garment District. Down 9th Avenue she walked all the way from 34th street, a scene she found difficult to adjust to. The glittering mica of the pavement, the speeding trolleys and wagons, and the rumble of the elevated train. The jumble of billboards, and paupers on the street selling things spread on blankets. A man had a small chained monkey that danced. It wore the china head of a doll, its wide painted eyes studying her from beneath the stenciled-on eyebrows. Its lips like a tiny pink rosebud.

Sometimes, with so much to take in, it made her lightheaded, like being on the steamship all over again, tossed back and forth, unsteady on her feet. Frightening, but exhilarating to a girl who had lived her whole life on a farm in County Clare.

The tailor's shop where she worked was long and narrow, with racks of garments in the front and rolls of fabric stacked on shelves along the sides. She and two Russian ladies worked at tables in the back. She had her very own Singer machine, painted with leaves and medallions in gold and red, a faceplate engraved with grapevines.

The turning of the bobbin, the thrust of the needle, the repetitive hum and solitude of the task soothed her nerves and let her mind run free. As she pushed the fabric along under the presser foot, she had time to remember her homeland. The rolling hills and pastures. The cliffs of Moher at sunset. The white brick house and the soft sound of her chickens cooing and settling when she put them into their coop at night.

Did she dream it, her whole life? Because it felt as though that dark, rough ocean voyage had erased the all realness away. A story from a picture book that had happened to somebody else.

One day, deeply involved in the task of hemming a pair of trousers, she was aware of being watched. She looked up to see a tall young man at the front of the shop, and though the sun through the dusty window backlit him, she made out his strong dark brows, lips unnaturally red as though rouged, and black hair so thick, his Derby gave the appearance of perching on the very top of it. Thought unable to see all of his face, she felt the bright beam of his attention on her. It flustered her for a moment, and she had to rip apart the crooked seam she had just sewn.

She kept her head lowered but watched him covertly as he sifted through bolts of fabric stacked near the front counter. And he, too, looked at her from the corner of his eye. He looked foreign. But princely, in a long wool overcoat with a velvet collar. His posture regal. Imperious.

Slowly, in this roundabout way, looking at the wares, then back up at her, he made his way to where Luna was. She looked down, cheeks burning. Would he say anything to her? He was close enough now that she could smell him, a mix of lilac water and sweat. His coat, though sharp, was shabbier up close. A bit of the lining had ripped and flapped outside the hem.

She dared not look at his face. Her eyelids trembled, her heart leaped.

He stood right in front of her. He said nothing but did something curious: right at her eye level, he made small gestures with his hands. Smooth, graceful gestures. Reminiscent of an oriental lady she had seen on screen at the Nickelodeon once. But down low, covert, *contained*, so she was the only one to see. She let off on the pedal; her machine stilled.

His hands, long-fingered and expressive, slid over each other, shuffled, cupped, and out of nowhere, he produced a long-stemmed white rose which he laid on the sewing table next to her. Her head snapped up, shocked, to look him in the eye.

Despite his impassive face, his eyes burned hungrily into hers; he doffed his hat, made a little bow, and walked out of the shop, the bell tingling in his wake.

Luna's heart beat so fast, it made her dizzy. No one had seen what had just happened. *Had* it really happened?

It took her some time to recover herself as she finished the seam she had been working on. Summoning the courage to pick up the rose, she saw that it was not real, but made of spun sugar.

This made her laugh to herself, delighted as a child. After looking around to see that the Russian ladies were not watching, she took a tiny bite; the sugar melted on her tongue deliciously. It had been so long since she had had a treat.

Though it did puzzle her: had it not been a real rose when he offered it to her? She swore she remembered the dewy white petals, the rich fragrance, the way it trembled on its thorny green stem. Perhaps she had been mistaken.

Her work finished, it was time to go home, and she picked up the rose again to find it was now made of glass. In her shock, it slipped through her fingers and landed on the hardwood floor, where it shattered with a bright sound into delicate shards.

This cannot be.

Luna ran out of the door, ran all of the blocks back to Hell's Kitchen. Her Granny had warned her about coming to America. She had said though God might not visit very often, the devil was around every corner, and she would never know what form he could take.

Surely the man in the shop was a trickster of some sort? Had she not been such a besotted fool and looked more closely, would she have seen cloven hooves? It was a relief to get home, back to the crowded walk-up. She closed the door of the room that she shared with her sisters, took her rosary from out of its little wooden box and wrapped it around her hands, though she could not find the words to pray.

Anxiously, the next morning at work she took her place at her sewing table at the back of the shop. The other ladies smiled at her; did they know something? The owner of the shop gave her a pile of mending to do. Everything seemed normal again; the clatter of needles, the spinning of bobbins, the sounds of the horsecars trotting outside the front windows, the occasional sputter of an autocar going by. The strange, harsh syllables of the Russian lullaby the woman next to her sang as she worked.

Luna was relieved to be going about her typical day, just like most others.

But part of her watched for the young man again. Although he had unnerved her, he was the first person who had really *looked* at her since she had arrived in this new strange city, this place that was not yet her home. He was the first to see her.

And it had felt so good to be seen.

She refused to admit to herself that she was waiting for him until he finally did come back. The shop was busy, the owner taking orders from a flock of customers, but she noticed right away when the young man entered, as she knew he would.

He wore the same wool coat as the day before. The same Derby. He did not have hooves. He had an ordinary pair of high-button shoes, worn-looking at the heels, but polished. He could not be the devil if he did not have hooves.

This time, he came straight to her desk and doffed his hat. "Miss? I am in need of your assistance."

His voice was deep, theatrical, full-bodied. Her hands shook just a little, so she hid them on her lap. "If you'd like, sir, the shop owner can help you when he is done with his other customer—"

"But it is you I wish to deal with." Pious eyes, but a hint of a smile about his lips.

"But I just work here in the back. I'm not supposed to—"

"From Ireland, are you? What a lovely brogue."

"Th-thank you."

He flicked his eyes in either direction, then leaned in and said confidentially, "I need you to make something for me."

"I mostly do mending, sir. I am the newest one here. Miss Sonia is the one who—"

"It is you I will work with. I insist." Smiling now, broadly, he looked straight into her eyes in a way that made her feel lightheaded.

"What is it you need, sir?"

"A cape. An opera-style cape that I can wear over a suit."

She stood and stepped out from the desk, and went to the set of large oak drawers containing the sewing patterns. Mr. Russo, the owner, still held up with another customer, looked over at Luna and nodded gratefully.

"Well now, just a few moments, please, I know I've seen one." Her vision swam, and it was hard to read the handwritten tabs. But at last, she found the paper envelope containing the pattern for an opera cape.

"Did you have an idea, sir, of what type of fabri—"

"Yes. A light wool. Lined in midnight-blue satin. With gold spangles shaped like stars."

She laughed, lightly, as though he had made a joke.

At that, he scowled. But just a mock scowl. "You see, my dear, it is for my work. I am a magician. I work in costume."

Luna's eyes lit up. "Oh! How exciting. I-I never met a magician before."

"Well, now you have. Did you like my little trick?"

"Trick?"

"The rose." He smiled again, head tilted to the side as though he found her baffled expression endearing.

"Oh, yes. It was very … clever." So he was not the devil, after all. A heavy mantle of dread lifted from her shoulders. Now she was giddy from the unexpected turn of the afternoon.

"Well, I can show you more tricks some time, if you like, miss." Now he held her gaze for a long moment, before looking down again at the sewing pattern. His lashes were as long as a woman's, she noticed, almost brushing the tops of his cheeks when he looked down.

They went over to the bolts of cloth, and she showed him several weights of wool; she showed him the blue satin, a midnight hue that she thrilled to run her fingers over.

"So, this will do, sir?"

To look into his eyes was like looking down a long corridor, lined with shut doors, with no end in sight. She felt hypnotized, compelled to run down that corridor and not look back.

"Yes," he said at last. "This will do nicely. Very nicely."

Luna rolled out the piecrust, hands caked with flour. The Magician sat in the front parlor, head in hands and stared at the poster, lost in his ruminations.

She had not really known him when she married him. And she did not know him after all this time. All she knew was that he was a cruel and capricious man, prone to slapping and punching her if she did not do what he wanted, the way he wanted. Meek and quiet at all times, she hoped to avoid his anger. Her life had shrunk to surviving day-to-day, hour-to-hour, minute-to-minute.

She missed the tailor shop. After the wedding, the Magician made her quit and take a job as a cigarette girl at the Orpheum, while he performed his act on stage. But now, she was to be *part* of the act. The Magician's assistant. The Beaumont Theatre! Her stomach lurched to think of it. Everyone went to the Beaumont … the size of the crowds. All eyes on her. She dreaded it with all of her being.

Lost in these fearful thoughts, she traced a finger through the filmy layer of flour on the countertop and gazed out of the window at the icicles that hung from the pane, glistening like daggers.

Four

He had had an identity before he became the Magician, but one made of ash, blown away on the winds of time.

His name had been Jack Friday because someone left him at the door of the Foundling Hospital on a Friday. Ridiculous name. It shamed him even to say it.

He had become the Magician at the age of twenty, and until then, his youth had been harsh, and as slow-moving as a glacier. Now twenty-one, things were finally changing for the better. The whole world would cede and open to him, where once it had been closed tight as a fist. He knew it in his soul, in the marrow of his bones.

Yet still he remembered the cow's cracked teat that bled in his hand on a winter morning so cold the snot froze below his nostrils. Hellscape of cold, a dizzying blue sky, the cock regarded him with one crazed and preening eye, and the farmer slapped him hard on the ear with his big red hand because there was blood in the milk.

The first time that he had ever been in a theatre was at the age of nine when they sent him off on the Orphan Train. He and the other children took their turn on the stage in each town, walking and turning side to side, in the hope that someone would pick them for adoption.

Though he didn't know then that he would one day be the Magician, he felt an affinity with that amplified space, the hushed expectancy of the rows of seats, the majesty of the velvet stage curtains. Some of the other children grinned or sang or danced, but he, a boy of nine, steely and tall for his age, stood impassively, arms crossed, looking straight back at all of them. Even then, there were intimations of the power that would one day be *his*.

The farmer and his wife chose him at one of these theatres and took him to their farm in Michigan, where he often slept in the hayloft and worked sunup to sundown. He was a city boy, and the wide-open country spaces and its animal life frightened and repelled him. For seven years he withstood it but knew that someday, when he was ready, he would return to New York.

He had been happier when he lived at the Foundling, sleeping in a row of brass beds with the other kids. He had his little gang of boys, all younger, who looked up to him and did whatever he said. And how he had loved the Sisters who cared for them and drifted through the halls in their long white gowns and wimples, skirts swaying; so like earthbound angels with large, folded wings. Why did they send him away? Put him on a train with a nametag and a sandwich in a brown bag? He would never forgive them!

The notion of escape fortified him through those harsh Michigan years. Escape, and revenge.

One spring day, the year that Jack Friday turned sixteen, he walked down the dirt lane into town, a rucksack across his shoulders. The farmer's wife had sent him to buy coffee, cornmeal, and a bottle of nerve tonic. A breezy day, the wind stirred the tall grasses, a few fleecy clouds raced through the sky. His mind on nothing, really, besides the pleasure of getting away from the farm. Taller than most men at six foot five, and though wiry, he was strong from years of farm labor. The farmer hesitated to lash him now; he could draw himself to his full height and fix the old man with an unblinking stare until he backed down and lowered his eyes, muttering, "Never mind. Worthless."

But that day he walked the lane with his empty rucksack in a lighthearted mood. He picked up a stick and trailed it along a cow fence, the rhythm of a train striking down its tracks. *Out, out, out of here. Soon.*

He heard a horse and buggy race up behind him, but he did not turn. Let them pass. But the driver pulled up on the reins as he approached.

"Here now, boy! Take this, would you?"

It was a one-horse buggy, old and creaking. The man who drove it was red-headed, with a swollen red whiskey nose. He had the look of an old pervert about him. And the boy smelled the drink on him from that far away.

He held out a piece of paper in his fat fingers. With a look of distaste, the boy took it from him. It was a flyer for a circus.

FORENZI BROTHERS
GREAT AMERICAN CONSOLIDATED SHOW!
AERIAL ACROBATICS
RECKLESS REDMEN ON HORSEBACK
MARVELOUS CURIOSITIES...

The boy broke off reading and looked at the illustrations. Ink drawings of clowns, fancy ladies in costume, monkeys in frilled collars.

"Come to the show, the field behind the Town Hall. Five cents. Tell your friends. Post that thing up, ya hear!"

The buggy was already past him, kicking up a cloud of dust when the boy looked up again.

"Hey!" he called, but the driver did not turn back.

Left behind in the sudden silence, he peered again at the faces of the clowns, grinning rapturously. A Chinaman with inscrutable eyes and a long trailing mustache, hands tucked into his sleeves, gazed back at him. A snarling tiger. It looked like a block print; the bright colors overlapped the black outlines, the vibrancy too much to contain.

To lower the flyer and look back at the dirt road and tall grass and the cow fence was to see it all anew; he saw it as a man might look at a quaint scene of his past, soon to be vanquished to memory.

Something deep inside lit him *up*, and he walked faster, and then ran, just for running's sake. He crammed the flyer into the rucksack, and he raced, free as the wind and the clouds above. Every once in a while he tipped his head up to the sun, a blazing ball of fire too bright to look into, but he dared to anyway.

His legs brought him to the field behind Town Hall, where from far away he saw rows of garish, painted wagons aligned to the side, and four enormous poles already erected stood tall enough to puncture the breezy blue sky itself.

Without even thinking, he ran boldly up to the men preparing to pull back on the ropes to raise the canvas tent. Each rope attached to a circus horse that stood at the ready.

"Let me help," he said, not smiling, but drawing himself up to his full height, and looking at the foreman down his nose.

Handed the reins of a gray-spotted mare, he waited for the signal to pull forward.

The tent's billowing red-and-white striped fabric caught the wind of the spring day like the sails of a great ship, grandly exiting the harbor.

Five

For four years, he traveled with the circus, hammering spikes, nailing together wooden bleachers. From town to town they moved, an eight-wagon show. He didn't mind the work. He welcomed the repetitiveness and the silent camaraderie of the crew as they set up and broke down, again and again and again.

In the downtime, they would share dinners of roasted meat and tinned beans around a campfire. He developed a fondness for drinking spirits from a flask the men passed around. He lost his virginity to one of the acrobats, a Russian girl who wore a costume of velvet bloomers with a wide sash and an embroidered waistcoat. He wondered at her compact body and lithe muscles she used to lean all the way back and lift herself up onto her own hands, making the crowd cheer. Remarkable. Her eyes were large and solemn, and she didn't bother him with much talk. He liked that.

True, it was a no-count circus. Not grand like Barnum and Bailey's, but a threadbare group, shabby. Most of the men were runaways like him. Some were criminals evading the law. The one exotic animal they had, a tiger, was rheumy-eyed and lethargic. The freaks and curiosities mostly hoaxes.

One thing the young Jack Friday had a flair for was pickpocketing among the throngs of crowds. Older members of the crew taught him how, impressed by his natural talent. He knew how to pick his target, the kind of self-satisfied man in a silk hat with a good gold watch chain across his portly belly. As soon as the man was transfixed, and leaned on his walking stick as he watched the Red Man standing astride a galloping steed, the Magician knew just how to press against him as though by accident, and quietly, with smooth dexterity, slip his hand into a pocket and take his money-purse.

By and by as the group lived and traveled together, day in and day out, Jack Friday developed a fascination for one performer in particular: Cezar the Great. An old man, as sorry and worn out as the pathetic Bengal tiger. And *yet* …

Cezar performed a magic act, but the "act" was said to be the real thing. He levitated objects in the air, sending a handful of rubber balls spinning high above his head like a constellation of planets. He made fire shoot out from his fingertips. A swarm of bright blue butterflies poured out when he removed his raggedy top hat. He once hypnotized a woman until she writhed, spoke in tongues, and her eyes rolled back in her head.

Treated differently from other members of the circus, Cezar slept in his wagon instead of joining the camp tents. Jack Friday at first thought this was merely because he was old, but it dawned on him that the others were afraid of Cezar. One of the female clowns always crossed herself when she passed Cezar. Most people averted their eyes when they dined with him and gave him the best piece of meat.

Cezar's magic was not a trick, his fellow crewmen told him, it was a dark power. It made others superstitious because undoubtedly such a thing wasn't right. Not from nature. But what could they do? He amazed the crowds. He was a great draw. And if anyone crossed the man, they feared they would be cursed.

And yet the man looked so ordinary. Yellowish-gray hair and beard. Bent-backed. Short, with long, dirty fingernails. Thick Romanian accent. Slow, shuffling movements when he walked. Most often in bed, smoking from a carved wood opium pipe, when not performing.

Jack Friday intended to find out how such a slovenly creature radiated such power.

"But where did he learn magic? Surely he was taught somehow," he said to the other men one night as they sat around the fire, passing a bottle of dandelion wine from hand to hand.

"He didn't learn it," Sergei the tumbler said, the fire illuminating his lumpy face. "It comes from the box."

"The box?"

"The box of light he keeps hidden. He keeps a box of light and a book of Sanskrit. Those are his secrets."

"Have you seen them?"

"No. I wouldn't go near that Romanian devil or any of his things. My cousin Alexi saw it. Not a month later, he caught TB. He lives in a sick home now."

Jack Friday intuited that he should not bring up the subject again. But his attention was as fixed on Cezar as the gaze of a raptor: he would wait and bide his time.

That time came when he saw Cezar alone one day, sitting on a wood bleacher watching the men spreading sawdust through the center ring. Jack Friday watched Cezar for a few moments. Then he sat next to Cezar, took something from his pocket and held it out to the old man, down low, fingers cupped, so no one else could see.

It was a silver match safe, carved with a Greco-Roman design of a satyr having an orgy with three nymphs. The boy had taken it from a man's coat pocket. It was one of the most unusual things he had ever stolen. Certainly the dirtiest. The most favorite thing he owned.

The old man was slow to notice Jack, and when he did, he lowered his eyes to the thing proffered. Then he took it in one yellow-taloned hand and held it up to his pearly pale eyes.

He didn't exactly smile: it was more of a leer. But it was as close to a smile as the boy had ever seen.

Cezar grunted and said, "Lechery does not become the young," and gave it back.

But the boy pressed it back onto him and said, "It's for you. I stole it from a fat rich man in a checkered coat."

This time Cezar peered more closely at the boy, as he pocketed the match safe. After some interminably long moments, he sniffed. "Kid pusher brought you in? Why you still here? Thought you'd be gone by now."

"No. I'm staying. I'm seventeen now, and I'm not a kid."

The old man shook his head as though bothered by a fly, and then turned away again.

But the boy persisted. "The other people here say things about you. Are they true?"

Cezar looked at him again, raising his eyebrows. "This place is full of half-wits and fools. I doubt it."

"They say you can place a curse. Can you?" He laughed at this, one short, harsh syllable. But this only encouraged the boy. "They say your magic is real and that you must not be crossed."

"They can say what they want. I take no notice." Cezar

yawned then. The old man's pale and blind-looking eyes were red-rimmed. Must be from smoking dope, the boy thought with a thrill.

Jack Friday pursed his lips, and tilted his head to the side, as though considering an idea. Then he said, "You know what, Cezar? I don't care what they say, either. I'm sick of the whole lot of them. And I am offering you my services as an apprentice." He did his utmost to remain calm and nonchalant, but his eyes slid furtively to gauge the old man's reaction.

Cezar's face slowly broke into a wide smile, revealing many very small crooked teeth. He laughed. Laughed and laughed as though the boy had made a joke! Jack Friday did not smile; he crossed his arms high on his chest and looked Cezar levelly in the eye.

"Do you hear it?"

"Hear what?" The boy lay back on the built-in bench running along the inside of Cezar's wagon. The space was minimal, space just for the bunk, the bench, one built-in set of drawers and a tiny cookstove with a pipe chimney.

Smoke filled the room, so thick that his eyes stung, his senses dulled.

"You aren't listening hard enough." The old man took his turn on the opium pipe; on a small folding table a sticky black lump hissed and bubbled on a tiny oil lamp, the vapors inhaled through a long wooden flue. More of the tarry lumps dwelled in a small silver box inlaid with a jade stone on top.

The smoke itself had a wonderful floral smell, suggestive of incense. He remembered the smell of incense from the chapel at the Foundling Hospital, where he sang choir songs at Christmastime; he took another hit for himself, lost in old memories. In his mind's eye, he saw the rows of little Foundling girls dressed in their little white smocks on Christmas Eve. Like cherubs.

The smoke tasted a bit like jasmine tea, a bit like licorice, smoother than smoking a rolled cigarette. And it gave him a wonderful cozy feeling, like waking up in a snug, warm bed, covers over his head. Without thinking of what he did, he crooned:

"O sisters, too, how we may do

For to preserve this day;

This poor youngling for whom we sing,

By, by, lully, lullay—"

"What the hell are you on about, boy?"

"That's the "Coventry Carol." I sang it in choir at the orphanage." Oh, the nativity scene, and the spiced oranges they gave out! The Sisters in their wide wimples, each as beautiful and mysterious as the Sphynx. A heaven to him, now forever lost! Why, why did they send him away? He would *never* forgive …

The old man snorted. "Don't be quoting no religious nonsense in my quarters, boy." But he said this gently, his eyes closed, with no accusation; the boy studied his fascinatingly ruined face, like craggy outcroppings of stone, tufty eyebrows like dead grass. Some were amused that the youngest member of the circus troupe had befriended the oldest; most found it unnerving, and now cast the same wary side eye at both of them.

But the boy was eager and hopeful to learn the old man's secrets. He wanted to see the box of light that everyone spoke so fearfully of. But so far it had not been mentioned.

"I can see you, you know," Cezar was saying, "even with my eyes closed."

"And what am I doing?" he asked cheekily, a smirk on his face.

The smirk died away when Cezar snapped, darkly, "Being a fool. Now be quiet, boy, and be still! And then you will hear."

Hear what? he wanted to ask. But Jack Friday did as he was told and said nothing. And there was nothing. *Daft old badger, his brains are fried.*

But then … slowly …

He sensed something at the very edge of his hearing. It wasn't the usual late afternoon circus sounds of joking and small talk, and horses snuffling as they were fed and washed down. This was a different sound, quiet and hushed but steady, there, underneath it all.

It had a rhythm to it. A rushing beat, blood-warm, passing through a vessel, bringing life. *Whoosh whoosh, whoosh whoosh, whoosh whoosh.*

And the more he noticed it, the louder it became. The boy who would one day be the Magician grew very still. On the verge of feeling frightened, he gripped the edge of the wooden bench with his fingers.

"You hear it now, don't you?" the old man said, a smile in his voice, from the bunk, where he now lay on his side.

Damn him. "I …" Louder, *louder.* It overwhelmed him because he did not know if the now thundering was from within or without. Pulsing vibrations felt as though they and the little wagon were being swallowed up by an enormous unseen creature, and the sound was the sound of its insides. The beast assimilating them. Jack Friday whimpered a little to himself.

"Relax, boy, it won't hurt you. You simply hear what is always *there.*"

No one said anything for some moments, the two of

them akin to unborn twins, floating in a womb together, soon to be birthed. The boy couldn't tell where he left off and the old man began. *It's the dope!* he tried to reassure himself.

The only thing that helped quench his panic was to little by little just surrender to it. Accept what was happening. His mind, no longer on alert, meandered. *Was this what it was like, to be in his mother's womb*? He had never known his mother and had been left at the Foundling with his gnawed off cord still attached, and oily blood covering his body … on that unholy Friday.

"Don't worry, you won't die!" Cezar shouted at him now, reminiscent of two men in a storm-tossed boat, their voices drowned out by the din.

"Is-is that the sound of my *mother*?" the boy bleated. The fear resurfaced. He tried to beat it down. The very walls of the circus wagon, those rough-hewn wooden boards, shuddered and pulsed in a most repulsive way.

Cezar laughed, but unkindly. "Fool, it's the sound of the earth turning – of time passing. You hear life!"

The boy laughed, too, at the profundity of it all, smack in his face, as the very corpuscles of his body spun and spread apart, until he was air, until he was everywhere and everything at once.

They laughed, they shouted, they stretched their arms out to each other. Off in the distance, under the noise, he heard the cry of the blind Bengal tiger, keening for meat.

Six

Jack Friday vowed to himself that he would never smoke opium again. To see and feel too much was a frightening thing: it might split him wide open. He convinced himself that none of it was real. Not only would he give up dope, he would also quit spirits.

He wanted to keep his mind bright and hard and focused. He wanted power, not to feel like a bloody babe in the womb.

Jack watched Cezar closely when he performed, amazed at how the shuffling dope smoker transformed, larger than life, before an audience. It was as though he metamorphosed into an entirely different person. The audience watched his every move in tense silence. And he could do *anything*. Not only levitate objects but levitate himself, relaxing a good six inches above the ground for minutes at a time, arms spread Christ-like, a rapt and almost ecstatic expression on his face. And always a new trick to deliver the unexpected. Scarcely believing his eyes, Jack trembled when Cezar emitted plumes of smoke from his fingertips that evolved into ethereal, fairy-like creatures that danced and frolicked around him like mincing demons. With a snap of his fingers, they dissipated into smoke again, and the audience burst into applause.

Jack stood by the side, Cezar the Great's faithful assistant. He took to wearing an embroidered vest with a wide silk sash that he borrowed from Ania, the acrobat. The circus owner told him that he looked exotic. "You look like an Arab," he said. "We should tell the audience that you are an exiled Saudi prince!"

So he played up that dynamic, striding tall and imperious as he took away Cezar's cape, or brought in the props. And people did look at him; he relished their curiosity. And he thrived on the attention.

In truth, he didn't see Ania as he made love to her in the privacy of her tent, too focused on his own sensations, and his feeling of intransience. He felt like a god.

"What do you think of, when you look that way?" Ania asked once afterward in her deep Slavic voice. "You are different now. Something is wrong, I know. Did the old man put a spell on you?"

In answer, he slapped her, quick and hard. She never asked again.

He hoped that in exchange for his devotion, Cezar would one day gift him with a lesson in magic. But for Cezar, the magic was something not to be discussed.

There came a day when Jack Friday obtained a flask of vodka from Ania's brother, said to be so strong and pure, "it will make your teeth rattle." He took it to visit Cezar's wagon.

"That is good stuff," the old man said, nodding, after taking a long draw. "Goes down like water."

They passed the flask back and forth, the boy only pretending to drink as he watched the old man sink lower and lower on his narrow bunk like a sack of potatoes, until he lay horizontal, one arm dangling over the edge, and his words slurred.

The time seemed right, and Jack asked, "Please, Cezar, tell me how you learned your magic. *Please.*"

Cezar, his mouth hanging open, turned his eyes up to him and wagged a finger. "There is. A story. To *that.*"

The old man straightened himself up again, into a semi-sitting position. "I was just a boy. Not so much older than you. Living in Romania. Beautiful country. Rolling green hills. Mountain peaks in distance. Like painting." He made his fingers into an unsteady frame shape. "I grew up in small village. We keep sheeps and goats, simple life, you know?"

The boy nodded, lifted the flask to his lips in pantomime.

"In our village, there was a house out on edge. Thatched roof, like all others. But in bad repair. This was abandoned house. What we called *house of bad luck.*"

"What was wrong with it?"

"A man stayed there. They called him ghost. A bad spirit. An omen."

"How did they know he was a ghost?"

Cezar paused and rotated his head around, slowly, clockwise. This seemed to orient him enough to go on. "Romania, in parts, is different, cut off from rest of world. We are still the land of folk tales and fairy stories."

"But those are not real."

Cezar held up one finger with its long, curving nail. "There, they are real. Embedded in the land is legend. He was a cursed man. Tall and thin and pale. People spat on ground when he walk past. Men cross themselves when he come to scythe the hay with the rest of us. Bad luck."

Sounds like the way people treat you, Jack thought, but

he screwed his face into an expression of deep interest and asked, "But why?"

"Why anything? Man's mind is broken. Eyes twitch in sockets. Unnatural movements. He bring bad luck wherever he go. A blight on the sheeps." He looked down, silent some moments, swaying a bit. "Back then, I was open-hearted boy. I feel *sorry* for the bad spirit. I bring him food in the night. Black bread, cabbage stew. I leave it outside back door. But one day I get *bold*. I knock, then open door to leave the food in kitchen.

"I see him, eye to eye for first time. He was waiting for me. Such a tall, thin, strange man with a long black beard. Locking eyes with him, I feel confusion. I forget who I am, what I am doing. My brain slowly as broken as his. He was a devil that had power over me. He could do things, things that were frightening, *unnatural.* These things I will *not* tell you!" He suddenly wheeled to look at Jack Friday with a fierce expression. Then he slumped down again. "I think I am at the bad luck house five minutes. I learn I was there five hours."

Here the old man raised his eyebrows, with a wry smirk. The boy handed the flask back to him. Cezar needed no prompting to go on with the story, the boy's silence enough.

"It change me, meeting that bad spirit, that shadow man. He took a hold on my soul. I couldn't keep away from him after that. He showed me a box. A box with something unspeakable in it. The box was his power, he said. The box gave him power over all that was nature. He sent me to the heavens, a star system once. I saw other planets. He make me disappear and reappear. Having me as his slave made him stronger.

"Well, I know he is bad, I knew he is harming my mind

and blackening my soul. One night I know I have to do something. I kill a goat and smear the blood on his door. The villagers see that as serious, a true sign of the devil, they come into his house and grab him and take him away from the village. I mean, *away*." He chuckled darkly. "Meanwhile I went back to where he keep the box of magic, in a cabinet. I take it for myself." He laughed again, which turned into a wet cough. He pounded his chest. "Ever since? I am nobody's slave any longer. I am master of *myself*."

Cezar hoisted himself up, then knelt down and reached under his wooden bunk. He pulled out a box, covered in old cracked leather with brass studs hammered along the sides.

He ran his hand along it, fondly, but did not open it. After several silent seconds, he looked up at the boy, brow furrowed.

He stood up, leaned close to the boy as though he were about to tell him something of great importance. Jack felt something lift in his heart. *Finally. He is going to share his power with me. Because he sees me as his son, he sees that I am special … Father and son, conquering the world, together.* And it was as though he could hear the *sound* again, of the earth vibrating on its axis. Faint but insistent. A deep planetary heartbeat bringing everything together, perfectly. Or was it just the beating of his own humble heart, inside *him*?

But instead of opening the box, Cezar pulled a small folding knife from his pocket. With astonishing swiftness, he opened the blade and pointed it at the hollow of the boy's throat.

"Don't you ever go near box, child. Or old Cezar cut you but good."

Speechless, the boy looked at him with wide trembling

eyes. Why?

Then the knife was back in the pocket, and the old man, stronger than he looked, grabbed the boy by his shirtfront and pulled him to his feet. "Now, you get out of here, you little worm."

And before he knew it, Jack was on the hard ground outside the wagon. He lay there, dust on his palms, and looked up at the empty blue sky, alone.

Seven

The circus traveled to another town the next day. It was a windy place that felt like the end of the world. The gusts were strong and whipped around bits of newspaper, old letters, and other debris. Both hands of a large clock tower in the middle of downtown permanently pointed straight up to twelve o'clock.

The men struggled to raise the great striped tent; the wind wanted to carry it away. Mostly children, queer-looking children who did not laugh or run or clap, came to watch; they just stood and watched with great blank eyes of dull-witted astonishment.

The whole way down in the wagon Cezar was unusually talkative. Neither mentioned the day before, the vodka, the box of light, or the incident with the knife; it seemed as though Cezar didn't remember it. Most likely he didn't, considering how drunk the old man had been.

If he noticed Jack was quiet, he said nothing.

The work of the day done, the tent raised, the wooden planks assembled, Jack and the old man retired together to the wagon as they did most nights. The boy even prepared the opium pipe for Cezar, with a flourish. He knew just what to do; he had watched so many times. The movements, the gestures were as familiar and intimate as though they were family, and this their ritual.

Great jets of smoke streamed from Cezar's nostrils. Twisting and rising in the small space of the wagon, they looked not unlike the smoke creatures he conjured onstage. Angels and devils hovered all around them. "You know, boy?" he asked at one point, droopy eyes bloodshot and focused on him only blearily. "You are different from the others. Maybe, we are alike. Not strangers to misfortune, but sometimes, the strongest ones…"

But he nodded off.

With no time to lose, the boy moved the little table aside, quietly. He stood over Cezar for some quiet moments, and then removed the wooden pipe, carved to look like a bamboo stalk, still clutched loosely in the old man's hand. Then, with the deftness born of much practice, he slipped the knife from Cezar's pocket. Mother-of-pearl handle, a beautiful thing, and he couldn't help but admire it. He flipped the switch and knew just what to do; he'd bled out the pigs for the farmer, from when he was just a boy of ten; he could do it easily, with a tune in his head. *O sisters, too, how we may do, for to preserve this day …*

The blood spattered on his shoes and looked like a scattering of rose petals.

Done, he wiped his hands, wiped the blade on Cezar's shirt, and took what was now his. He held the box of light to his chest as though embracing it, and ran away from the circus for good.

Eight

Luna took a deep breath and parted the beaded curtain.

Sean had said that liked her best this way, dressed in her underthings, her dark wavy hair let down loose around her shoulders. He watched the slow removal of her corset, with all the hooks in the front and the lacing on the side. The chemise, the drawers, the black lisle stockings held up with garters.

"Wot?! *Oooo-eeee*! Ya are my Celtic *goddess*," he said, from where he lay back on the bed, arms behind his head. "All other men should *weep* in envy. I may be kilt stone *dead*, she did!"

She found herself blushing, still not used to behaving in this way. As lovers did. Losing her nerve, she drew back behind the curtain.

"Come out, ya! Come to ya Seany boy! Give us a kiss!"

And she did come out again, reluctantly, and to cover up her embarrassment, ran to him and leaped onto the bed.

It wasn't often that they had these stolen afternoons together, on days that Sean did not have to work at the Navy Yard. He had taken her out to go motoring that day. She had asked where he had gotten the Model T, and he smiled mysteriously and said, "Someone owed me a favor."

She did love his smile, and the way it spread generously across his broad face. Freckled from working at the boatyard, he had the same Irish fair complexion that she had. He wore his pale red hair combed straight back, though it liked to stand up in a cowlick in the front. This gave him an off-kilter, madcap look that always made Luna smile.

For the motoring adventure, she had worn goggles and an English walking hat, pulled down low, so no one could recognize her. Plus, she knew where the Magician was that day, and where to avoid him – he was negotiating his terms at the Beaumont.

It was her first time in a motorcar. It was not like a train, not like a trolley. More like a horse-drawn carriage, but not having a horse in front felt so strange and exhilarating. And the car itself was lovely, a dark midnight blue with brass headlamps and a sliding canopy on top. Sean had driven fast and recklessly through midtown, dodging buggies and pedestrians and other puttering motorcars as Luna closed her eyes and screamed in terrified pleasure. She had never had so much fun.

Then back over the bridge they came, to the set of rooms he kept in Bay Ridge. Consumed by such a delirium when they made love, Luna feared she would leave her body entirely. And his body was so new and different to her. While the Magician was tall and thin and effete, Sean was muscular and solid. Wrapped in his large forearms made her feel safe from harm.

Always careful to use a sponge soaked in vinegar, she dared not become with child. The Magician had not made love to her since the first few nights of their marriage. He was a prudish and meticulous man in the day-to-day, though he did keep a cache of pornographic photo cards in a box that she found once, images of men and women doing such shocking things that she hastily put them back, slamming the lid on the box and vowing never to look again.

Luna lay in Sean's arms, eyes idly sliding over the patterns in the frost-covered window. "I wish I could stay longer," she said as though to herself. Now that it was quiet, panic had set in. Everything had happened so *fast*, like the dizzying motorcar trip. She didn't recognize herself anymore. Taking such stupid risks. Getting herself into this situation with no solutions. No solutions that seemed right, anyway.

"Why don't ya leave 'em then?" Sean propped himself on one arm to look at her. His pale eyes had a merry squint to them, even when he was serious. "Mealy-mouthed punk don't deserve a woman such as ya." Sean had met the Magician only once before. It was also the first time he met Luna, when they had gathered for a family dinner at the apartment in Hell's Kitchen. Sean was a close friend of James, one of Luna's cousins. The two were close as brothers. They were both in a group called the White Hand Gang, and did much business together, though they were vague about what the business was.

The first time Sean laid eyes on Luna, he held them pinned there, looking up at her intensely as he bowed to kiss her hand. Flustered, she had looked away first, but later peeked at him again and again from where she sat against the wall in a straight-back chair. It had been a warm day, all the windows open, a breeze stirred the hem of her poplin dress with the sherbet stripe and sailor collar around her ankles. She studied him covertly through the wall mirror so no one would see her staring.

"I don't like 'em, ya know," he whispered now in her ear, playful, but menacing. The bed springs creaked.

"That much is obvious," she said, giggling. His breath tickled her ear.

"He looks to me to be a goddamn wop, a *dago*." he said, these words in a low hiss, into the hairs at the nape of her neck.

"Well, there's no saying what he is," she said, pulling the covers up tighter. Sean hated Italians, and she tried always to avoid the topic. "He was a doorstep orphan. He could be anything."

"He could be a fookin' scarecrow-hangin' corpse if I had anything to do with it." He was on top of her now, tickling her, but his words alarmed her and she stilled.

"Sean, don't even think of it. Please. He has the devil in him. He's more powerful than you know."

"He's a two-bit carny if I ever saw one. Best belongs playin' children's tea parties."

"Sean, I'm telling you, his magic is real."

"Well, if he ever hits ya again, I aim ta make *him* disappear."

"*Don't.*" She pushed back with one hand on his chest, drew back to look him straight on. "Promise me you'll just keep your space from him. He's dangerous."

Sean sighed. He was still smiling and reminded her of a panting dog that wanted to go after a rabbit. "Well, take notice I am goin' down to the Beaumont and see the show meself."

"Good. Come. Just be discreet."

"And I'm not comin' to see that poncy fraud. I'm coming to see my love, the beautiful magician's *assistant*..."

She sighed, with a winsomely sad smile. "At least I do

have a lovely dress I made, with spangles."

It had an empire waist, cap sleeves, and skirts of gossamer that shimmered with reflected light. Ages, it had taken her to make it, and it did make Luna proud that she had created it; it was the fanciest thing she'd ever done. But the sense-memory of the shimmering fabric under her fingertips stirred up something else in her, too. A sense of dissolution of self. A sense of no pull of gravity to anchor her. A sense of abject, helpless fear.

"Hey now, darlin', why are you lookin' that way?"

The kind, baffled solicitude in Sean's face was enough to send her into wild tears.

"Luna. Tell ya lover what's wrong."

"I … I just don't like to think of the show, is all."

"But ya have done *plenty* of rehearsin', ya will do fine."

"But it's not that, exactly. It's just …" How to explain what was too abstract to put into words? "It's just, you don't know the kind of things that he does."

"Does he hurtcha? In the *show*?"

"No. He doesn't hurt me. But he works his magic through me, and it just …" It just infected her soul, her pure Catholic girl's soul. The magic contaminated her. Deep down, it shamed her to know she wasn't a good person anymore. That's why she was *there*, acting the whore, doing things she knew had no good end. She was going to hell, anyway. But she couldn't tell Sean that, or he wouldn't love her anymore. And if she did not have Sean, then she would have no one. "It just makes me very tired."

"That pug-faced simp! I'll knock 'em to drobes."

"Please don't get angry, Sean. It's okay. We're here together now, aren't we? Let's not ruin it by discussing such things."

"Well, okay then, if that's the way ya are wantin' it. But

I am comin' to see ya, Ol' Sean will be watchin' from afar, ya know that?"

"Yes." This somehow made it more bearable, to imagine being held fast in her lover's gaze. It made her feel less afraid. A little.

But as she rested her face again on Sean's broad chest, she had a sense of her wholeness unraveling. And soon it would be for a whole audience to see.

Nine

The Beaumont. She remembered the first time she had seen the place. It was a raw spring day, wet and damp, and she had worn her new long, fur-trimmed coat and her picture hat with red silk roses that trembled in the chill breeze.

She had ridden the trolley over the bridge into Manhattan, her excitable young husband sitting by her side, quiet but not unhappy looking, tightly wound in anticipation of ... *something*. He refused to tell her what he was taking her to see.

He led her down Sixth Avenue, through the blocks crammed with vaudeville shows and signboards for the new moving picture theatres. Until suddenly he stopped, gripped her by the arm and gestured for her to look.

The Beaumont Theatre, she had to admit, was impressive. Arches and marble pillars surrounded the front. Stained-glass windows and gargoyles on either side of the entrance.

"My goodness, it looks almost like a ... a church!" Except for the placard in front, with its list of performances and times, and ADMISSION TEN CENTS, she didn't add.

"Better than a church. Soon, this will be our new place

of business."

"Ours?" She had grown to like being a cigarette girl at the Orpheum. Even though it was small and shoddy compared to the Beaumont, she liked the people there. Everyone was kind and the regulars knew her by name.

"Yes. Ours. I had a meeting some time ago with the man who runs this place. He admires my work. He said that I am a *genius*." At this, he paused and looked into her eyes, significantly. "He expressed great enthusiasm in my coming to work for him. With *one* stipulation."

"What is that?"

He smiled as though she were a silly child he was pulling a prank on. "The condition that I find myself a beautiful assistant! People like couple acts. A beautiful woman brings in the crowd more."

"But I—" She had only watched him perform from far away. The stage light that surrounded him seemed a world unto itself, a line of demarcation that she couldn't cross. It was *his* world, the only place where he seemed happy. "I don't know what I would do …"

"That is for *me* to explain." He took her gloved hands in his and smiled. When she didn't smile back, his eyes hardened. "What's the matter, girl? Doesn't this news thrill you?"

"Well, it's a bit unexpected I guess."

"There is nothing for you to fret about. I am in control, and I have everything in hand. I have a lot of ideas, *good* ones. Don't you see? We'll be the greatest magic act in New York! And one day we will go on tour. Ride a luxury steamer train. We will be stars."

She looked into his eyes: he radiated something that seemed almost like love. Almost like happiness, a rare thing to see in him. He was her husband, but she did not know him. At City Hall where they married, with only her father and sisters in attendance, she wore her dead mother's white lace and held a small bouquet of orange blossom, and she wished always to make her husband happy. She wished to make the dark and troubled young man see her, *love* her, and they would begin a new life, together, leaving sadness behind.

Marriage hadn't turned out that way, so far. But standing in front of the Beaumont in the fresh rainy air of Sixth Avenue, the wind catching at her hat, she tried to beam back his rapture into his eyes. Maybe it will all be okay, after all, she thought,

But to be inside the theatre was an utterly different experience from being outside.

The stage. The hot, bright light of the stage, from which she could not escape. All around her, the audience in velvet seats, on balconies and in private boxes. Like the theatre of a surgeon about to perform a procedure on a patient. And she, in a way, anesthetized.

And so the act began.

At her cue, she joined the Incomparable Cosmos onstage, where she walked from one end to another in her beautiful white dress of which she had been so proud, but now she felt like a girl in a nightgown, living some dream or nightmare, but unable to wake up. Unable to run from the stage and down the short flight of steps, down the halls lined in red brocade silk, through the marble and brass lobby, until she was *free.*

She could not do that. She moved from one end of the stage to another, turning, spinning, waving with one flat palm as though she were royalty, in just the way that the Magician had shown her.

And then, when the applause died down, she stood in the bright beam of a spotlight. With grand and imperious gestures the Magician beckoned her to come forward upstage and stand before him. One by one, he pulled long stem roses from his sleeves, red ones, which he gave to her until she held a dozen. But as she clutched them, smiling, he made a swift movement with his hand, and the petals all loosened and swooped, alive, through the audience like swarms of bees to gasps and incredulous laughter, then enormous applause.

He approached her for a tender kiss on the lips. Then he stepped back, and she opened her mouth, and a tiny black bird emerged from her lips. Its small dry feathers and the skittering of its feet meant she had to control the impulse to gag, but the little fellow stirred and took flight, somewhere toward the high molded ceilings of the theatre, and she looked after it with a blank expression as it flew away, and now the applause showered down over them like a hailstorm.

Again she bowed and curtsied, her face smiling, still and serene. But when Cosmo led her to the table, something in her always changed. Her inner vision choked and narrowed as though she saw and thought only through a dark tunnel.

Because the table was where her soul wanted to leave her body, to follow that little bird. But she forced herself to lie supine and inert as a sarcophagus as the Magician opened a case of silver knives and held it forth, walking the stage for the audience members to inspect.

He set the case on a small table, and selected the longest of the knives and held it up so the stage lights glistened down its length.

"Be still, my darling," he said in an overly loud, yet

tender tone. "This will not hurt you."

He drove the knife into the center of her chest and the audience not only gasped, but also some cried out in terror.

Though it was true that Luna felt no pain, the coldness of the blade invaded her insides. Her eyes, huge and trembling, stared straight up ahead but saw nothing. Her body shuddered at the invasion. *Saint Michael the Archangel, defend us in battle, be our protection against the wickedness and snares of the devil …*

In this way, shuddering and silently reciting the prayers of her girlhood, she endured as he drove five blades into her torso, the handles protruding like arrows in the hide of a fallen gazelle.

Silence reigned in the great hall when the Magician held a hand up, sweeping the audience with a grave look, then thundered, "Behold!"

With a brandish, he pulled each of the knives out of Luna, and then held out a hand to help her up. She twirled to show them that her dress was still white, with no blood and no wounds, the applause deafening, but she was beyond hearing it.

Next, the Magician led her back to the table and helped her lay back down. He stood behind her, to face the audience for some long, dramatic moments, gazing at them intensely.

"My darling wife, you will ARISE!"

Her eyes closed, she heard the hush, a white roar, the sound of hundreds of still and silent people. The sound from the inside of a seashell.

She clung to the energy of their focused attention on her, because it was the only thing that made her feel safe. Only dimly aware in her consciousness that her lover was out there, somewhere. He, his love, the memory of their shared afternoon now seemed as far away as the moon.

The terrible force of will of the Magician overrode all this: *he* was inside her now, deep at her very core. Suffusing what was once *her*, Luna. Unable to breathe, it was as though someone had gently but firmly clasped a hand over her mouth.

Luna heard the murmurs as, little by little, she rose off the table, her long gossamer skirts grazing softly against its edges as her body lifted up. And up.

Weightlessness: an indescribable feeling. There was nothing to do but give in to the terror and blankness of it.

She remained horizontal for most of her ascent. Halfway, she dared to open her eyes, just a little, and looked around her. Hanging above the stage from hidden beams were large, glittering cutouts of a half moon and stars. She idly noted the way they swung back and forth, stirred by the air from vents placed high on the wall.

She remembered her old home and that pebbly beach where she liked to collect driftwood as she imagined the force that held her up was like the sea, the green Irish Sea. There were so many secret places that she liked to go to as a girl, and she tried to go there *now*. The grassy moors. The old village graveyard where she visited her favorite headstones, ones for children with angels and little lambs that were friendly to sit by; more afraid and ashamed to be afraid, of her mother's headstone, too new and immaculate looking, the earth still fresh and dark where it had been dug.

Did those places still exist? Sometimes it seemed as though they vanished when she crossed the ocean to this new country. Was she still Luna Mulkerrins of County Clare? Was that still her family, father and sisters and cousins, somewhere in the faceless and unknown crowd below? Would they judge her if they knew her true thoughts and deeds?

At the highest place, the Magician gently rotated Luna until she was upright, high up like a Christmas angel, and she held her arms straight out as instructed. She hovered there, and the audience not only applauded but cried out and whistled; it was the grand finale of the show. An ocean of upturned faces, all directed up at her. She concentrated fixedly on a crack in the plaster ceiling and a small drift of spider web. She was so alone, so high up.

Slowly, slowly, she descended, weak and lightheaded as though deprived of oxygen. She trembled the whole time, her muscles shuddering in a quick involuntary fashion that she would feel later as a general soreness. The lower she got, the more the warmth and effusion of the unseen thunderous audience enveloped her because all she *could* see now was red, her vision flooded with blood red, the color of the velvet that lined the Magician's box.

Her feet in their ivory satin slippers touched the hardwood of the stage. Gravity, her friend! The pull of it a shock, it was something she never noticed or appreciated until it was gone, that strong invisible pull each body feels to the planet. She whispered a silent prayer of thanks, held fast again.

Her legs wobbly, she feared she might buckle and fall. Relieved, she walked gracefully to the front of the stage with the Magician beside her, who held her hand up in the air in triumph. They made a bow together.

Finally able to focus, Luna stole a glance at the Magician, surprised by what she saw: a look of rapturous wonder suffused his face as he let the applause wash over him in great waves. Covered in a light veil of sweat, a little pale, he trembled too from the exertion to keep Luna aloft, so high and so long, with his willpower. The magic didn't always come easily. But in spite of his fatigue, he looked exuberant, like a man who had just burst through the surface of a body of water, diamonds of droplets sparkling in the edges of his hair, his eyelashes, long as a woman's.

She had never seen him this way before. In awe, electrified. Reborn. He did not turn to look at her, though. He gazed around, and up, into the balcony seats at the audience and the standing ovation.

At last they walked offstage; she feared the noise had deafened her. The staff working backstage smiled and held arms out to her as they mouthed … something … to her. She heard only the rushing of blood in her ears. And she saw the expression in their eyes shift from jubilance to confusion to fearful concern as, finally, her legs *did* go out from under her, and she surrendered to sweet gravity once and for all as the floor came up to meet her.

Ten

In the following days, a review appeared in the arts section of the newspaper:

> Cosmos the Incomparable put on a dazzling opening show at the Beaumont Theatre on Saturday evening. His feats of the impossible astonished the audience, culminating in the levitation of his lovely assistant to the very rafters of the house. No one is able to ascertain Cosmos's secret – he uses no wires, no strings, and no trap doors. The mysterious Mr. Cosmos, in our interview, stated that he was raised a Romanian gypsy, and that magic resides in his lineage. "Reality itself is malleable," he told our reporter, "depending on our perception of facts. Whatever we perceive, can become real. The impossible becomes possible."

Before long, enough word had spread that their shows were packed nightly. The Magician renegotiated his contract, and earned, to them, a staggering amount of money. Enough to buy as many fine new clothes as they wanted, to go out for steak dinners in restaurants with candles and linen tablecloths and waiters in uniform.

Best of all, they were able to move to a new place in the city, a handsome Greek revival row house on East 4th

Street. Though the halls were narrow and the ceilings low, it was scores better than their old walk-up, with beautiful moldings above the entrance. Ivy grew up the bricks, and though the windows were grated, at least they did not look onto an airshaft.

And for a while, Luna truly believed that things might be different. The Magician didn't hit her as much. Though he still seemed distant and preoccupied most of the time, his attentions to her were usually benign.

As she walked the streets of her new neighborhood, in her fitted bottle-green velvet jacket and ostrich-plumed hat, she admired the drift of cherry blossom in the air, the sound of the old women speaking Yiddish from their stoop and the way it carried through the fresh air. How could she not be grateful for her good fortune, a blessing, willed from God? How could she not try to be a better person, someone *deserving*?

For a little while, she even thought to give up her lover. It had mortified her so, to have Sean see her from the audience that first opening night, prostrate like a floating corpse.

She had seen him the next morning, a Sunday, when she joined her family for church at the Holy Cross. Still feeling unwell, it was as though her feet scarcely touched the ground. Though she knew he would be there, she was too demoralized to take care in how she looked: threadbare shirtwaist, plain face with no rouge.

As the family stood on the steps of the church after the service, Sean had approached her where she stood, apart from everyone else.

He doffed his flat cap, and asked quietly, "Did ya see me in the audience last night?"

Unable to meet his eye, she looked instead at the winter

sky, at the sun blazing from behind a thick wall of clouds, a V of geese honking dissonantly.

"Luna? Are ya well?"

"I can't complain."

Concern washed over his broad, freckled face. His humorous mouth set straight and grim.

"I can tell ya didn't like it," he whispered.

"Why would you say that?"

His expression now hard, he reached out a hand and held her chin between his fingers, tilting her face up to his.

"Stop it," she whispered. People were glancing over. She moved up the church steps, away from him.

"That pug-faced wop," he hissed. "He married ya, just so ya could work in his show."

"Sean, *don't* make a scene. My father is watching us."

"I don't care," he said now, levelly, though there was a dark flush to his skin, and his eyes flinty with anger. "The man was making ya miserable last night. Does it cause ya *pain*? When he does what he does?"

"I can take care of myself."

"Did ya feel it, when he plunged the knife into your chest?" An altar boy passed them, his robe fluttering in the wind, his round, puzzled eyes set on them as he descended to the street.

"No, I didn't feel it, I didn't feel a thing."

"Then why are ya so sad?"

"I don't know!" Dangerously close to tears, she pulled her hat lower over her face, ducking her head.

"I'm gonna kill that wop wonna these days. Soon."

"Sean please—"

"And I'm gonna take ya away, to marry me, and we're gonna be happy, and ya won't never have to do any a those evil things again."

"There is no way out, you *know* this—"

"And ya know *this*! I love ya, Luna."

At this, the tears did come, and her brain brimmed over like a boiling cook pot, and her chest cracked open with the burden of her heart. Powerless to control herself anymore, she clamped a gloved hand to her mouth to stifle her cries as she ran away, blind, into the streets of midtown.

The rattle of streetcars, trotting horses' hooves, the keening call of the day's headline by the paperboy: all her senses jangled and confused as she plunged down 42nd street. Far in the distance, she heard a man shouting, "Luna! Luna!" But she did not turn around; she loved him, but she did not deserve him. She loved him, but she was too ashamed to have him look at her. After the night before. Humiliating, to be held frozen, aloft, dangled like a freak for all to see.

That had been back in early February when ice lingered in the wind. But now it was May, and birdsong woke her every morning as it drifted through the open window.

On impulse, she decided to catch a trolley, to cross the bridge to Bay Ridge. (But was it really *impulse* that drove her to pick her finest new clothes that morning, and to rouge her cheeks and lips carefully, and to pomade the ends of her hair until it curled charmingly around her face?)

It was a Wednesday, Sean's day off, the day they most often planned their trysts. But there had *been* no tryst in the past months. She had only seen him in passing at church on Sundays. Which was not to say that she did not still want him. She simply wanted to atone for her sins, to be clean again.

But now, here she was, boldly going to him unannounced, practically leaping off the trolley and rushing over the cobblestone sidewalk as quick as her ten-button boots would allow.

When greatly anticipating seeing him, sometimes she would count down in her head to distract herself from her excitement. Fifty, forty-nine, forty-eight. Forsythia blazed against the sides of the tenement buildings, the sky so blue it hurt.

Twenty-five, twenty-four. She passed a butcher hurrying down the street in a bloodied apron, his hair disheveled. Even this detail was steeped in beauty on such a fine day; he pantomimed tipping his hat, though he had no hat, and his eyes did not quite see her.

Nineteen, eighteen, seventeen. Only one more block to his building, so very much like all the other buildings down that street, but different, and special, a halo about it, because this building homed her beloved.

Five, four, three two … Now she was at the entrance. The door stood ajar with a brick to let in the breeze. She rushed, breathless, up the crabbed stairway, three flights, until she reached his very door. Then she took a breath, rapped softly, and held her breath in her throat.

And then he was *there*, filling the doorway, a big man, a shipbuilding man from Galway. Youngest of a family of six children and the only boy, he adored his sisters. He worked hard all day and sent money home. Still always keen to grab a pint and be rowdy, and go to his meetings with the White Hand Gang. He was twenty-two, a *good* man, and he loved her.

The way he looked at her when he opened the door, she was sure she would never forget. The joyous surprise, the open vulnerability in the eyes of such a large, rough-looking man. He picked her up in one fell swoop and carried her to the bedroom, beaming at his good fortune.

"I always feel safe with you," she said, breathlessly, as he lowered her gently to the edge of the bed, unbuttoning her boots before setting them side by side neatly against the wall.

"As well ya should," he said, smiling. "I will always take care o me girl."

But then nothing more was said as he lifted off her ostrich plume hat and unbuttoned her bottle-green velvet jacket with the nipped waist, and already her soul, which she had struggled so hard to shrink and purify, expanded like an overblown rose.

"So why were ya not seein' me?" he asked later. A shaft of sunlight shone through the pink tips of his ears, as he leaned over her on one arm, bringing out the rosiness of his cheeks, the tip of his nose. Each freckle in his milky skin was like a star in a constellation showing her the way to happiness. She marveled at the sight of his beauty; it had been so long.

"It's hard to explain. I didn't hate you. I love you. I just didn't like myself very much."

A look of unfeigned puzzlement swept across his face. His transparent eyebrows puckered. "But what is there not to like about yaself? Everything about ya is so dear and lovely." He nuzzled her neck.

She arched her head back, closing her eyes. "Thank you, love. I feel better. Now."

"Well, I'd wait for ya like a dog on a chain. But I still don't get ya meanin'. But what was *wrong*?"

"I don't want to talk about it anymore."

"Ya are still doing the shows? Nightly?"

"Yes. I have to. We're sold out. There have been talent agents coming to the show. And ... and a German crown prince. And someone said Mary Pickford was in the audience the other night." She realized her voice was getting higher, stammering and a bit giddy.

Sean studied quizzically. "Well, *my* goodness. A prince and Mary Pickford. Ya don't say."

She had forgotten his contempt for royalty, and celebrity in general. She struggled to change the subject. "Well, I just mean to say … well … I'm glad we're making money, at least."

"But ya hate it. What ya do."

Luna hesitated for a long second. "I'm getting used to it now."

"Ya don't look very convinced to me."

She sat up straight and ran her fingers through her hair, agitated. "Well, okay, it was a bit draining for me in the beginning, performing the act. But the more I do it, the more I can tolerate it. I just go somewhere else in my head." It was true that when the Magician plunged the silver knife into her chest, she felt nothing more than a little jab. The smallest contraction of her muscles resisting.

"Don't be mad at me, Luna. I want for us to be honest here."

"I am being honest. I do it five days a week. It's a job like any other. Like working at the tailor shop, or selling cigarettes." In truth, she missed both her old jobs. At least she interacted with people and didn't have strange things done to her for the titillation of a faceless crowd. "It isn't so bad."

"Even when he raises ya in the air, all the way to the ceiling, with your poor little dance slippers danglin' down?"

She reddened. "Stop it, Sean. Don't mock me. It hurts."

"I ain't mockin'. Just sayin'. Makes me mad to see me

girl displayed in such a way. Like a split between Christ-is-risin' and a little bride doll on top of a weddin' cake—"

"But I am no such *thing*! I am a professional entertainer!"

"Ha! I got ya! I was waitin' to see how long it would be before ya crossed your arms over your chest like ya do when you've had enough o' me."

She smiled, though she stayed turned away. "I have never had enough of you, Sean."

He grabbed her up into his large arms and pulled her on top of him. She stroked his upper arm, where he had a tattoo of a regal ship with many masts ballooning in the wind, a mighty wave swirling beneath; his other arm simply inked with the word *Mum* in calligraphy.

"I just want ya to be happy," he whispered in her ear.

"But I am. I swear it. I have money now. So as I see it, we have more options."

"Such as?"

"I-I can get us a room if I wanted. A nice one. Maybe someday if we are really rich, we could have our own little apartment, a secret, just for us—"

"Luna. Ya can't have things both ways, darlin'."

Wounded by the sudden seriousness in his tone, when she looked at him, she saw no trace of humor in his expression.

"Sean, why are you cross with me?"

"I'm cross with ya because I can see ya are not happy, and no amount of money or good press or Mary Pickford is going to make up for it."

"I am doing the best I can in … in the situation I am in, as you can *see*."

"Christ, girl, ya have no children. Yet. Get away from the mongrel before it's too late."

"But it's ALREADY too late!"

"No, it isn't."

"If I try to leave him, he'll kill me."

"I won't let him lay a finger."

"But, you don't understand. His magic is real. He could curse me, he can levitate me and hold me fast, he could give me a wasting disease …"

"He ain't that powerful. I know a huckster when I see one."

"Sean! Sean." He got up and put his clothes back on. "I came back to you to feel right about things, and for you to judge me this way—"

"I'm not havin' it, Luna. I see the marks on ya back."

"They're fading, and he doesn't do that as much. Can't you accept me as I am? What do you expect from me?"

"I want ya for myself. And if I have to pop that mealy-mouthed faggot, I'll have no compunction whatsoever. I can get me boys on it right off. The White Hand boys always stand strong together."

"Sean! I don't even want to know about the White Hand. Leave your gang out of it. Those men scare me. My cousin, Patrick, told me some of the things they do. I told him you would never partake of such things. Promise me that's not who you are. Promise me." Her tears were in earnest now.

Sean came back to her, stroked her dark curls and rocked her back and forth. "Luna. I'm sorry to make ya cry. I don't mind waitin' for ya. Ya are a smart girl and brave girl, and I know ya will make the right decision. In the meantime, tell ol' Cosmos the *Incomparable* to watch his back, aye?" He put his finger by the side of his nose and winked.

Eleven

Alone, when Luna was at the shops or church or visiting with her family, the Magician liked to sit at the head of their dining room table, beneath the Tiffany glass lampshade that bathed his face and hands with shades of brilliant red and blue. He folded his hands beneath his chin and looked forward, intently, like a man watching events unfold from a great distance.

He often remained frozen that way for hours, with brief expressions flitting across his face, a smile here, a frown there, until the sun cycled through the sky and the blue and red crossed the room and faded into late afternoon pallor.

He had to do it: it was the only way to release mental strain. He emerged from his trances rejuvenated.

Where he went in his mind during these sessions, it was hard to say. If he concentrated hard enough, he felt he could transcend dimensions, his spirit lifting right out of his body until something, a powerful cord attached to his solar plexus, pulled him down again.

The Tiffany lamp and its wash of bright colors reminded him of being bathed in the light of the stained-glass window at the Foundling chapel.

"O sisters, too, how we may do/ For to preserve this day …"

"He's a bright little ragamuffin, the most clever boy in the ward …"

"There is blood in the milk, boy!"

"That is the sound of the earth turning …"

All these competing voices from the past, echoing in his head, making him feel all sorts of ways, happy, sad, humiliated. Didn't matter. He was taking all of it and refining it inside the fire of *himself*. A fire that was violet blue, like a gas jet, soldering all that feeling into something new: power.

For the first time in his life, he had real power, aware of it most acutely when he was on the stage, listening to all of their gasps, their cries, and their cheers. It invigorated him. More than that, it was life *itself* to him.

Sure, magic also took a lot *from* him. He was still new at it. To produce miracles drained the marrow from his bones. But the applause brought it back again, tenfold.

Stealing the box of magic was the wisest thing he had ever done. It had changed everything. He kept it beneath his bed, so its essence would seep into him as he slept. He wanted it always to be near to him, in fact, a part of him. He was the box. The box was him.

And he had Cezar to thank. Cezar, that poor old fool, wasting his life away in that fleabag circus, sucking an opium pipe into oblivion. True, the Magician hadn't *had* to slit the old man's throat; he could have left him in his drunken stupor. It just felt necessary at the time. *Right*. Like a sacrifice to the gods. A sacrifice to the man he would very soon be: a person of consequence.

Sometimes he could still see it in his mind's eye, the blade going into the neck, craggy and creased as a turtle's.

Drawing a bright bead of blood at one corner, and then the torrent. Oh, the gurgling sounds Cezar made, his mouth gaping and moving like a beached carp! Bleeding out a man was so different from bleeding out a pig!

But there was still much he needed to learn. He had no idea what the power meant when he first acquired the box, carrying it through train stations, holding it in lonely railroad apartments and anonymous boarding houses. It wasn't until he got to Albany that he dared even look to see what was *in* the box. Pitiful, hidden in the cloakroom at the train station, people bustling about just feet away, but he had to peek, just once; he was still a boy with a boy's impatience.

What he *saw*, turning the key, popping the iron lock and opening the cracked leather box just a sliver, nearly turned his mind inside out. He spent the rest of his train journey looking out of the window in a daze, but he didn't see the trees and hills blurring past, only the inside of the box. Which contained the inside of everything. Past, present, future, all at once in a light so blinding that it had burned upon the insides of his eyelids.

For a long time he felt different and knew he *was* different, but he couldn't say exactly how. In the city, he took a day job pushing a broom, and contemplated the box and its secrets at night.

The first bit of magic he accomplished was to raise himself in the air. Just two inches, and he sweated and shook when it was all done, and dropped to the floor in a heap. But even as he lay there, on the splintered floorboards among the clods of dust and odd bits of string and a lone mousetrap, he felt like a god.

He wanted more. Eventually, he willed and conjured other things, able to light a candle, just with his mind. Make a flower bud open, bloom, and then wither to dust in the space of a minute. Although slow going and challenging, he found the secret of the box: nature would realign itself with his will. And the more in tune he was with the object, the better it worked. He had to commune with the flower, or the flame, or the very force of gravity that wanted to hold his feet to the floor.

So he practiced, looking at a thing and feeling its essence. If he could feel the life force and inner being of a honeybee, then he more easily turned the bee into a spark of ember, or a piece of thistledown, or a tiny silver bubble. If he *felt* his way into it, he could make it whatever he wanted.

So it began with rubber ball tricks done on street corners, until he was skilled enough to pick up a few stage jobs here and there. Back then, he called himself by his true name, Jack Friday; he would not give himself a stage name until he was magnificent. He kept his job as a janitor at the department store, but entertained on the side, at children's parties or women's tea parlors.

Spiritualism was the trend. He did not know how to speak to ghosts. Because, he realized, he didn't believe in them, or an afterlife, or any such fatuous nonsense. But after a while, he learned how to conjure the smoke creatures he had seen Cezar create. Delicate, drifting, though thinner and longer-limbed than Cezar's, and with a tendency to dissipate faster. But still, he was not displeased with his work.

"These are the spirits of ancestors past," he would intone to the ladies in their pearls, swishing their feathered fans. Sometimes they fainted dead away.

It was a rush, acquiring new skills, becoming better and better. But he knew there was a next step to be taken. He wanted, knew he *must*, be able to feel his way into the inner soul of a human being. And not just any, but a woman. A beautiful woman.

There was no shortage of beautiful women on the streets of New York. But in the beginning, he didn't know how to pick the right one.

A lot of them were aloof. They did not notice him at all, walking right past him on the street, long skirts whispering, under the secretive shade of a frilled parasol. They were opaque to him, as devoid of inner life as a woman from a page of *Collier's*. Women like this made him feel small, the *opposite* of powerful, and were not a worthy investment of his time.

Then there were those who *did* notice him but did not seem to care for him. Alerted right away by the pierce of his gaze, they looked up. It might be, say, a woman with cool ash hair and skin like porcelain, glass drop-earrings catching the sun as they swung to and fro. Her pale eyes trained right onto his, in shock and incredulity.

And disgust.

Just because he was tall and thin, and his clothes the slightest bit raggedy? But he was still coming up in the world! He knew he was a handsome young man, everyone had always said so, even back at the Foundling Hospital. Now he looked like a Turk in a picture show. What right had she to crinkle her smooth brow that way? He saw the slight sneer on her lips. Well, he wouldn't want her, anyway. She was not the right one for him.

But the more he remained aware, the more he noticed another type of woman, typically younger, more vulnerable. Usually she did not have a fine hat or a fancy parasol or any jewelry whatsoever; she had worn shoes, and a dress of the past season's cut. She looked around with wariness, like that of a lost child. Or a beaten dog.

She was most likely a girl with no father to protect her. A

lost girl. An immigrant girl.

He sought out these girls, recognized them, and practiced his effect on them. He wasn't one to smile naturally, but he quickly trained himself to do so, a small smile, a kind smile. Almost paternal.

And these lost girls looked back at him, but not in disdain. They regarded him straight on, in wide-open innocence. With just the smallest degree of apprehension.

That was a good thing. The fear connoted respect.

He knew he must make the next step, of *approaching* one. But how? He saved up some tricks to impress them with. Small, easy, charming tricks. Disappearing coins, fresh flowers produced from thin air. Remove his boater to have a hummingbird emerge, bright as though freshly painted with a child's brush.

And then one day, he saw just the one. He was in the tailor's, looking at the fabric bolts, planning a stage costume that he would have commissioned when he had the cash, and he *almost* had the cash.

She was at the back of the shop, one of several women working at the sewing machines. The other two were older, old enough to be his mam. But this one was young, deliciously young.

Dark wavy hair, a bit damp around the temples. Pale skin, but ruddy around the cheeks and nose. Small, light-boned, dressed in a proper skirt and shirtwaist, but no other adornment. He visualized lifting her easily.

Surreptitiously, he watched as she fed a seam into the machine, deep in concentration. But then she looked up at him; pale green eyes, like a cat's, and rather large. She looked for a long moment, lips parted slightly, startled to be the object of his attention. Then hurriedly looked down again, and he saw the blush coloring her all the way to the small tips of her ears. She glanced up at him again, and he saw something else: a daring in her eyes. A light of adventure in their green fire. Just a flicker, but alive nonetheless.

He thought it was mostly Italian girls who worked in the Garment District. He couldn't quite guess where *she* might come from. Just that she wasn't American; he knew it without even hearing her speak. He leisurely fingered the tweeds, the linen blends, but all the time his mind whirred in anticipation. Yes, yes, she was the one.

He walked over, close to her worktable. Willing his magic forth, he produced a white rose, and laid it on the table next to her machine. He saw her bite her lip in consternation; he had mercy on the poor girl, and backed away, smiling benignly.

He knew he had to be careful in his approach, to think it through. So he left the bustle of the tailor shop behind and walked into the cold daylight, but he had gladness in his heart, and his step was light. Fate herself, he divined, was intercepting in his life, and guiding him. *Friendly* fate. Time, for once, was on his side.

And so he went back not long after. He knew she had spotted him as soon as he walked in the door, by the subtle change in posture. Her narrow shoulders just perceptibly hitched up, and locked, a tenseness about her. But also giddiness, as though she were a child playing a game. Hide-and-seek as she waited to be seen, to be found.

He smiled to himself, in anticipation. Already insinuating himself into her. Slaving away in this dull dark room, she was radiantly full of life. Positive energy emitted from her like a glow. He even saw her try to suppress a smile as he stood over her. Yes, it was all a child's game.

"Miss? I am in need of your assistance."

Twelve

A day out. He knew he had to take his wife out for a special day because she had been a good girl, flawless in her evening performances. The audiences adored Luna. He would reward her. Also, more importantly, he had a question to ask of her.

He decided on a carriage ride through the park. It was spring, after all. Though the pollen bothered his nose, he figured she would enjoy such an outing. He took her out at dusk, when the street lamps were coming on, and settled a rough blanket around her lap and asked, "Isn't this nice?"

"Yes, it is," she said, smiling about her mildly. But still, there was something distant in her eyes. And had been for some time – weeks – now that he thought about it.

She wore a very becoming dress of mint-green, dotted Swiss, with a draped skirt that ballooned right above her ankles. That was the style, hemlines coming up. Also, part of her hair she wore loose at the back. Only the top was piled up on her head. The pale green dress, the twilight, all of it made her look somewhat aqua-washed. As though a reflected ocean light played over her. A sea-maiden from an Impressionist painting. She looked not at him, but straight up and ahead, at the arches of branches swaying over them.

"I'm glad you think so," he said. "I am very proud of how well you have taken to the show. The audience adores you, you know."

"I think they just like me well enough," she stammered.

"Not true. I would say you are the true star."

"You flatter me."

"I am sincere." At this, he took her by the hand, something he normally did not do. She looked at him for one shocked moment, and then arranged her face in a smile.

"I have some ideas I wanted to share with you, Luna, about the future."

"Oh?" A hesitance in her tone, though she still smiled.

"Yes. Regarding the show. Before long we will be coming up on six months. I am considering perhaps, changing things around a bit."

"Change? How?"

"I wanted to introduce some new flourishes. Run up some new posters."

"Oh, but everyone loves what we do now! The reviews—"

"The reviews are yesterday's news! To be competitive, we need to outdo ourselves. Keep them coming back for more. For what is different and *new*."

To the sound of the horses' hooves, and the cries of children running the streets in the chill of the damp spring twilight, the lamps just coming on glowed golden and flickered uneasily in her vision. Luna drew the rough-hewn blanket higher up around her and pulled it tight. Then, in a small voice, "If you think so. But are you thinking of something I would be good at?"

"Well, I can tell you this much. I have already thought of a name."

"A name for what?"

"A name for the act, of course. An act must have a name if it is your very own, and something no one has ever done before. I could patent it."

Luna said nothing, but her lips gently parted in a way that happened when she listened deeply to the thoughts running through her mind.

"Luna, I have decided I will call this new act 'The Gilded Moth.'"

"Oh!" Said as softly as the sound of a handkerchief dropped to the floor. And she could not bring herself to ask him the inevitable question.

"Wouldn't you like to know what it entails, dearest?"

Her lips shaped the word *yes*, but nothing came out.

"It is a disappearing act. You will be wrapped in bolts of silk. Beautiful, gold glistening silk. Or, I don't know, gossamer of some sort. Something diaphanous and lovely. Very slowly, it will unscroll and wind all around *you*. And underneath you will wear a new costume. Something very becoming. Something in white, I think."

She nodded her head now, in short, automatic movements, like a palsy. They passed a little girl with large, downturned eyes standing on the walk selling bunches of violet nosegays, and who looked after them blankly. A horse whinnied in a shivering way, shaking the bells.

The Magician looked at her for a long beat. "Once you are fully and tightly wrapped, there will be a brief organist's interlude …"

He searched out her hand again, under the woolen blanket, but this time could not find it.

"And then? Do you want to know what happens next, Luna?"

"Wh-what is that?" She smiled a vacant smile.

"Why, you disappear! Right into thin air. It will be astounding!"

She stared straight ahead, compulsively blinking as though she had something in her eye. But she said nothing for some time. And then, faintly, "Where will I go, when I disappear?"

The Magician turned all the way toward her. Funny, she usually drove him over the edge with what he called her nattering, her daftness, her childish ways. Having to tell her the same things over and over again, until forced to strike her for her own good. But he had no desire to strike her now.

The way his wife looked, as though she stared into the abyss of her demise … it actually made him feel tenderly toward her.

"Where would you go? Well, I guess that will be difficult to say. You will exist on the physical plane of existence, of course!" he laughed suddenly, loudly, as though he had told a funny joke. She did not smile.

"I would say, Luna, that when you disappear, you are still there, in a … philosophical sense. Your spirit would remain. It is just your physical body that would momentarily … dissipate." He made a vague gesture with his fingers, waggling them in the air like the legs of an insect. "You would not have to worry. I have made things disappear, many times. And brought them back."

"But not people."

"Not people, no."

"Not *me*."

"No, that is true, darling. But come, now. I think you

would enjoy it, once you were used to it. To exist, but not. To escape this time and this place, and *yourself*, even temporarily, I think would be invigorating!"

Her wan face filled him again with tender pity, so much that he kissed her on her brow, which was cold but damp, and very pale.

"Come on, darling," he said, smiling. "You are an Irishwomen. I know the Irish believe strongly in the other realm. Fairies, changelings, and whatnot. Maybe when you disappear, you can go to visit the little people!"

Thirteen

Her new little sewing room was at the back of the apartment. It had one narrow window that threw an oblong of light slantwise over her sewing table as she fed the fabric into the machine. Not white after all this time, but a brilliant tangerine color. Silk.

Though lovely, it was difficult to work with, because it frayed easily at the edges, so she tried to work fast after cutting the pieces from the pattern. Also in this small room, the mechanical clacking of the sewing machine tended to overwhelm, to fill the air completely. The stirring and rattling of gears deep within her bones buzzed her delicate brain, making her see things blurrily.

Her new dress for The Gilded Moth act would be floor length, with a silken overlay on top, meant to resemble wings when she spread out her arms, creating the illusion of full wingspan. Each would be painted into delicate segments, an eyespot right in the center.

Luna tried to lose herself in the process of making the dress.

Clackclackclackclackclackclackclack

Her foot on the pedal drove the gears, spinning and

whirring. Just as the thoughts in her head spun and whirred, spun and whirred, endlessly.

How did this all come to be? Her life was moving too fast; things were happening before she could process them. Out of control, it was.

Ireland, its green hills and stone walls, now a disintegrating vision. The little white cottage and her beautiful chickens all at the far end of a vortex. A vortex that had carried her across an entire ocean and landed her *here*, in a room that resembled a prison. Where she had to construct her own burial shroud.

Clackclackclackclackclack

He intended to make her disappear, and she felt helpless to stop it.

She could run, couldn't she? But where would she go? Her family was relieved to have her gone, and who could blame them, all living in that cramped tenement, damp laundry strung across the room, the air heavy with the friction and constant resentment of human bodies made to live in too close proximity. Her father had been hunched and dead-eyed since his wife's death, and the voyage over had finished him off entirely. He would not save her. He could not.

Sean wanted to make her his wife, but he could not take her in now! She was a married woman. Her family would disown her for being a whore.

And maybe I am a whore. Who deserves the harshest judgment. Maybe I deserve to be put upon that stage, humiliated, night after night.

But to disappear … who was to say it would be temporary? She was twenty years old. In spite of everything, she was still in love with life. Even when things felt at their worst, she knew deep inside that some better, brighter eventuality would come to find her. She loved the feeling of blood pumping through her veins, even when terrified. She loved the bustling streets of her new city. Searching out her place, her destination, whatever that might be.

Best of all, she loved her dreamy private times visiting the Brooklyn Navy Yard, looking out at the great warships in dock, knowing her love was among those men. Yearning for the riches of the future.

Ripping out a crooked hem with her seam ripper, she vowed that it could not happen. Luna Mulkerrins would *not* disappear. Happiness would find her. A solution, in whatever unseen or backward way, would present itself.

She buried her face in the tangerine silk, letting it absorb her hot indignant tears.

She tried to stop it, she did. She had gone to the Beaumont herself, wearing her most serious shirtwaist and gray skirt. For she wanted to be taken seriously. She had walked through the showy marble foyer through a small side door, up a flight of stairs to where Mr. Klein kept his office.

"Mr. Klein, did you know of … changes to occur? In my husband's show?"

"Why, yes, there was some discussion. Excellent discussion if I may say so!"

"So this is something you approve of? I just thought … we are doing so well as we are …"

He looked at her. He was a very slight yet still very tidy and stylish old man in a velvet waistcoat and sleeve garters, with a twinkle in his eye and a tight-lipped smile.

He stood up and rummaged in a storage closet, then brought out something rolled in a cardboard tube.

"*This* just came back from the printer! Your dear

husband has not even seen it yet."

It was a poster. Showing a moth with its wings outstretched against a starry night sky. The wings were stylized in sleek geometric design, flame-colored with bold black outlines. Very modern, different from the florid art nouveau posters she was used to seeing.

But the moth had the head of a woman. A lovely woman with wavy dark hair falling in tendrils around her pale face, a slender halo of light above her head, her face tilted up, as though praying.

As though beseeching. As though suffering some unknowable pain.

And down below, also sleekly stylized, staring fiercely with hands poised in the air in front of him, was the Magician.

COSMOS THE GREAT
PRESENTS
HIS NEWEST SENSATION
THE GILDED MOTH!
AMAZING! SPECTACULAR!

Mr. Klein chuckled, not unkindly, as he thought she was overcome with the beauty of the thing as she ran out of his office, one hand over her mouth.

Twenty years old, and soon to turn twenty-one.

The Magician had arranged a birthday dinner for her, at Barbetta, a restaurant not far from the Beaumont. Not only for the two of them but for her family as well.

"That's wonderful of you to think of me this way." She mulled her words carefully. She knew if she seemed ungrateful he would be angered, "But isn't that a very fine place? A *fancy* place?"

"It is the very best." He smiled triumphantly. "All kinds

of show business people go there. Actors. Directors. Playwrights and critics. It is about time we joined their ranks. We are just as good as they are!"

"Yes, but the money—"

"We have enough money, silly girl. You just are not used to it yet."

"But isn't this the kind of place with serious waiters, and rules of dress and … comportment?"

He smiled fondly at the word comportment. "Yes. That is exactly the kind of place it is. Elegant rooms. A wine library. And a patio garden that is to die for, like something from a grand villa estate, I am told. I'm keen to see it myself. I reserved one of the drawing rooms, just for us and your … family." His lips twisted ironically at the word.

"B-but you see, darling, that is just the thing. I don't know that my family will feel comfortable in such a place. They have no fine clothes or fancy manners."

He kissed her on the forehead with a smack. "Yes, I agree, it will be amusing, won't it? To see them struggle to know a salad fork from a shrimp fork?"

"But it is unkind to laugh at them."

"Don't worry, my love. I know that you come from a family of rubes, it is no secret. The experience will take their breath away. Don't you want them to know how far you've come? I think you worry too much. I think they will find it to be elucidating. The beauty will *stagger* them."

"Well, I suppose. If you think so."

Fourteen

The Magician had ordered her a new dress for the occasion, one he picked himself out that was of the newest design. It was midnight blue crepe de chine, with a wide Asian-style sash that tied under her bosom. "It is what the ladies are wearing in Paris, darling."

And she *did* feel beautiful, even regal, as the Magician helped her step down from the cab that let them out at West 46th Street. Housed in a brownstone, Barbetta had an unobtrusive, tasteful sign on the front.

"It doesn't look like much from the outside," the Magician said ushering her forward, "but just wait."

And truly, she was overwhelmed upon entering. Downstairs was a gracious dining room, with heavy gold drapes, chandeliers, and roses in crystal vases set on gilded tables. Candlelight flickered from long white tapers, amplified and reflected in the mirrors, the crystal pendants, and the tinkling wine glasses of the patrons sitting at the white-draped tables. The headiness of it all made her feel as though she might swoon; some of the diners glanced up at her, curiously, and she quickly looked down again.

The mâitre d' led them upstairs to a different area, to the

room they had reserved, the Garden Room. Smaller, with a fireplace, it had a long table set for ten, again with roses and crystal and white candles. He seated the Magician at the head of the table, Luna to his right, to wait for their guests to arrive.

The Magician examined the wine list, printed on creamy cardstock. "We will have the 1895 Bordeaux."

The wine arrived promptly, and the Magician sniffed the cork. He nodded for the glasses to be filled. Luna sipped from her glass, and very quickly felt the blood rush to her cheeks; alcohol tended to make her flushed. But she smiled with genuine happiness and love in her heart when her father and two younger sisters came into the room.

Lil and Mary Catherine! The two people in the world who always made her smile, especially now that she hardly saw them anymore. She rose from her chair and rushed to embrace each girl.

At seventeen, Lil was set to become engaged to one of the boys who worked at the docks. Her thick red hair piled up with pins, she wore one of Luna's hand-me-downs: a blouse with a high lace collar. Nice, but so out of fashion. Luna felt a wave of shame for even thinking such a snobbish thing and hugged her tighter.

Mary Catherine was fifteen, with plaited dark hair and a wide-open smile. She looked around the elegant room in open astonishment. She had made her dress for the occasion, with a narrow red stripe and short, tucked sleeves. Her arms were so slender that her elbows seemed slightly bulbous. She still had the foal-like look of a girl not yet grown into womanhood. Luna's heart swelled with love at the sight of her.

Their father, reluctant to enter, hung back. He allowed Luna to kiss him on the cheek and gravely shook the

Magician's hand before he took his seat.

"Good to see you, Joseph, old boy," said the Magician magnanimously. "I trust things have been well with you?"

"Aye," he said. He was a small man, with thick curly hair, just turning gray. But his piercing eyes and his jaw jutted forward in a particular way made him look somewhat pugnacious. A quiet man, but formidable.

"And you are still working … in construction, is it?"

He looked at the Magician fiercely, waited a beat, then said, "You could call it that."

"Brickwork still?"

Luna held her breath. She knew he had lost the bricklaying job after a fight with the foreman, and no one liked to speak of it.

"No. I am a digger now."

"A digger?" The Magician languidly swirled his drink around his mouth, closing his eyes to savor it. He motioned the waiter over, gesturing at her father.

But Luna's father did not swirl the wine. After the waiter poured his glass, he drank it down, hard and quick, then said, "Aye. Layin' down gas lines. Diggin' ditches for cable." The wine glass looked absurdly fragile in his large, callused fingers with their dirt-blackened nails.

"Profitable work, is it?"

But he did not have time to answer before more guests arrived, Auntie Tess and the boy cousins, with the usual bustle of greetings as they sat down, the wine poured, exclamations made. Everyone was there now. Though this was Luna's whole family, the room felt oddly muted compared to the other times they gathered together for celebrations in Hell's Kitchen. These dear people all seemed diminished, small and drained of color in the imposing room.

"I have taken the liberty of ordering the first course," the Magician announced, as a team of waiters bustled in with silver domed trays.

As the silver domes lifted, the Magician smiled. "A quail's egg appetizer. I think you will find it delightful."

The women made small utterances of admiration, but Luna's father looked at the dish dubiously: a mound of fried onion, nestling a bowl filled with something yellow, tiny speckled eggs tucked in artfully all around.

"Wot t'hell is this?" he growled.

"Quail's eggs," the Magician said louder, and slower, than before. "A delicacy, Joseph. That is a cheese fondue in the center."

"Don't look like any kind of egg from *my* chickens. These look no-count. Too small."

"They are much prized."

"I think ya been cheated, boy."

"Excuse me?"

But her father motioned for his glass to be filled again and paid no more attention to the queer-looking appetizer in front of him.

It was mostly the ladies who made conversation, speaking of Lil's new job sewing flags at the Naval Yard, Mary Catherine's new school. Letters from home about what was going on back home, in Doolin, the village they had left behind.

The boy cousins spoke in their gruff, quiet way to each other and ate the quail's eggs hungrily, not paying much mind, as though it were pub food. The Magician gazed up and down the table, as though he were not a participant in the scene, but an amused observer. Although his eyes did flare with impatience when he saw no one had touched the fondue.

The waiters came to clear away the dishes and he said, "Next they will bring us the rabbit."

"Rabbit, la?" That was young Cousin Patrick. "They skinned a rabbit just for us, boss?"

"It is roasted with herbs here," said the Magician, a grim set to his face.

"Fact o'god, like?"

The Magician glared at him, as the other cousins sniggered.

"Patrick, please." Her cousin was only a few years younger than her, but Luna tried to sound like a stern parent. She turned to the Magician. "He doesn't mean anything. It's just … just a bit funny because we ate rabbit a lot when we were young."

Cousin Georgie, thirteen, broke in, grinning widely. "Our mam would send us out to shoot a rabbit when there wont nothing else to eat. T'was Patty who was best at it! He would shoot 'em out behind the privy!"

"And I used to skin 'em, too. Scrawny old things they was," Patrick said.

"Only thing to eat besides a moldy potato was a damn scrawny rabbit! So hungry some days I could go mad! *Mad!*" Georgie was small for his age and wore a man's suit jacket that was enormous in the shoulders and dwarfed his head and thin neck.

Patrick turned a keen look at the Magician. "Sorry to rattle ya, like. This is a fine place. And ya are a fine man. A gentleman. Ya ever skin a rabbit in your life?"

The Magician looked at him with a small, inscrutable smile on his face. "I can't say that I have."

"Well, I guess ya pulled a few rabbits outa a hat, right." His eyes were merry with mischief. "Ya got those hands. Long, elegant. Clean. No savagery for you!"

"No. I am not a savage, it is true." The smile died down a bit, the eyes remained steadfast on Patrick's freckled young face. Seventeen, already working the docks with the men. But he had a gap in his front teeth that made him look younger than he was.

"You're educated-like, right, master?"

The Magician paused. "I am self-educated."

"Ya know the good life, la? Read the papers. Eat quail eggs and keep your mustache clean."

From the way the Magician held his drink paused to his lips, Luna knew to put an end to the conversation, immediately.

"Ya never killed no rabbit, my good man? Never heard it scream? Oddest thing, it is. Sounds like a woman when it screams—"

"Patrick, enough." She tried to smile benignly. "I would like to enjoy my lovely birthday dinner without such talk."

"Screams like *EEEEEEEH!*" Patrick made an eerie sound, shrill, high in his throat. And just as he did, the staff came in again, bearing plates for all. In one synchronized motion, the waiters lifted the domes with a clang.

Each plate was like a work of art, arranged just so. An elegant portion of rabbit meat studded with green herbs. A spray of asparagus, fanned out across the plate, with a stylized drizzle of sauce over the top.

"This looks wonderful," Luna said, to cover up the tittering coming from the boys; she saw Mary Catherine's flicker of a mischievous glance exchanged with Patrick.

"I'll bet their hairy wop chef shot it out back a the loo."

"Patrick! Stop it now!" She hissed, but it was too late, the teenagers were giggling in earnest. She turned to the Magician. "He's just a boy," she whispered.

"It's no excuse," the Magician said, icily, "for being a

rube."

"A *wot*?" The boy was still smiling.

"A rube. An uneducated rube. And you have no excuse."

"I ain't lookin' for no excuse, master."

"Well, I'm not offering you one."

"I won't take no offerin' from a lily-white-handed layabout like yourself." Still the smile, but a trifle of menace in Patrick's eyes. He was only a boy, but already had a taste for booze. And fighting. He idolized the men in the White Hand Gang. And Sean said the boy could fight like a grown man. And he had been putting back plenty of wine.

The Magician put down his cutlery and wiped his lips with his linen napkin. Then smiled tightly. "I have seen more in the world than you think I have, Patrick."

"You do magic tricks for foolish rich folk, la. Don't sound so rough to me."

Her husband suddenly pounded the table with a fist; Luna jumped.

"I'll thank you to shut your mouth, boy. I came from just as rough circumstances as you did."

"Aye?" Patrick raised an eyebrow.

"Indeed. If you would like to know, I was born an orphan, left off at the Foundling. I had nothing. They sent me off on the Orphan Train when I was too young to have any choice in the matter."

"So wot?"

"So, everything! I went out into the world with nothing. I was taken advantage of by cruel people, out to exploit a young boy. And do you know what?"

"Wot?"

The Magician's eyes blazed now, his full red lips compressed in a straight line. "I *bettered* myself."

"Goody for you."

"I struggled. And I worked. And I made something of my bad fortune. Reality can be what you dictate it to be." He tapped his fingers on the table, to underscore each word. "Reality will reform itself to your will." He paused, looking each guest in the eye, turn by turn. "Someone taught me that once. It was a wise lesson."

Silence except for the sound of cutlery. The chiming of a crystal glass. The smell of melting wax and roses made Luna feel faint.

Auntie Tess cleared her throat. Luna was touched to see her usually harried-looking aunt dressed so carefully in her burgundy dress with a cameo at her neck. Auntie Tess had worked as a laundress for years, her knuckles permanently roughened and red. But she looked stately at this table, with her graying blonde hair pulled up in tortoise combs.

"My darling Luna," she said, "Disregard my cheeky son. This is a most wonderful dinner, and I hope you're having a happy birthday."

"I am, Auntie."

Tess smiled warmly at her, and Luna wondered what it would be like now if her mother had lived. Would they sit together at a table like this? Would she be proud of Luna and this dinner in this fine room?

Or would she think she was a fraud, out of her element? Oh, nothing about this evening felt *right*.

"We save all the clippings in the paper of your show, Luna. The write-ups are so flattering."

"Which reminds me," said the Magician, pushing out his chair to stand. "I would like to propose a toast."

The others at the table seemed unsure as to whether they should stand as well, so shifted their chairs and looked around at each other. The Magician motioned them down and held his glass aloft.

"To my dear wife, I wish her a happy birthday. I would also like to let you into a secret! We will be adding changes to the show. It will be a brand *new* show, in fact. Centered around a new act that I'm sure will be spellbinding. And it will be called," he paused and looked around the room with a flourish, "The Gilded Moth."

Everyone smiled and murmured, and raised their glasses to clink. Only Luna's father remained silent, leaning back with his arms crossed, chin jutting out.

"How exciting! What kind of act is it?" asked Lil, smiling widely, her color high.

"It is a disappearing act, but like none you have ever seen," said the Magician. "No trap doors. No trick tables. None of that stuff."

"And the act is ready now? When will it begin?"

"Well, it has not been announced as of yet. But soon. We begin practicing tomorrow."

Luna felt a clenching in the pit of her stomach. She had held him off on rehearsal for as long as she could. *Could we wait, until my birthday has passed? Please.*

Just one more day to look around a table and see her family's faces. Because if she disappeared, who was to say she would come back?

She closed her eyes, and shuddered, for it had occurred to her for the first time, *What if my soul goes to live in the box of light? And I am trapped there forever?* Her hands trembled because she knew in her bones that it was a real possibility.

But jolted out of her reverie when the maître d' strode in, she listened as he bent down to speak quietly to the Magician.

"Sir? There is a guest downstairs who says he is one of your party."

The Magician, still smiling from speaking of his beloved

new act, looked a bit puzzled. "Who is it?"

"It is a young gentleman, sir."

Luna's eyes went large, and she averted her face from the table. But the Magician had turned toward her to ask, "Darling, are we expecting anyone else? I thought we were all here."

"Um. I don't know." *Please, let it not be Sean.* She had not told him of the dinner. But one of the cousins may have. James, who had declined the invitation. James, who was Sean's best friend.

The Magician turned back to the mâitre d'. "What does he look like? Is he an Irishman?"

"It would appear, sir."

He cocked his head, thinking. Then said," Perhaps you could send him up?"

"There would be a … problem with that, sir."

"What problem?"

"He is not wearing a suit jacket, as is required."

"My wife's family is not cultured, I apologize. Perhaps an allowance can be made?"

The mâitre d', a very tall man with combed-back hair that glistened in the candlelight, leaned closer to the Magician and spoke even more quietly:

"I'm afraid, sir, that the young man is inebriated. He is causing a scene and we cannot allow him to disturb our patrons. I hate to bother you with this, sir, but perhaps …" He paused delicately, motioning to the door with his eyes.

The Magician nodded curtly. "Yes. Yes. Of course. I will come down and see to this matter, right now."

As he strode out of the door, an odd thing happened: Lil took hold of Luna's hand under the table and squeezed. Luna glimpsed her sister's eyes. Lil gave her a faltering smile, fear in her eyes.

"Be strong, Luna," she whispered.

Fifteen

The Magician made his way down the short hallway, flanked by large gilt-framed mirrors that made the place seem larger than it really was. He admired his reflection as he passed, satisfied that he was taller than the mâitre d' and fitter. He smiled at himself in a covert but friendly way.

I have become the man I have always wanted to be.

They made their way downstairs, to the front entrance, where another staff member talked sternly to a young man he recognized. A red-haired young man, one of the brutes who worked at the shipyard. They'd met at the Mulkerrins home. The Magician smiled.

Placing a hand on the waiter's arm, he said, "Excuse me, I'll take care of this now."

The young red-haired man was mid-sentence, "G'wan, tell 'em I'm goin' up directly—" when he saw the Magician. He smiled with cheerful belligerence. "Right mate! How's about ya? Tell 'em I'm family, yeah?"

"I'd say you're not," said the Magician. "What's your name again, son?"

"I am Sean Murphy. Ya know my face, I know ya do."

"I know your face, but that does not concern me. You are not a Mulkerrins. You are a hanger-on. One of those thugs from the waterfront."

"Aye, ya got me in the heart, brother."

"This is a private affair. No one invited you."

"But Luna needs me there."

"How do you figure that?"

"Because I know her. I know her better than ya do."

The Magician frowned at him. He noticed the staff watching warily from afar. "Come with me," he said, taking Sean's arm. "Let's go to the bar. I'll buy you a pint."

"I buy me own drinks, boss," he said, but followed him to the large dark wood bar, which had plush green velvet chairs, and softly glowing bottles lit up from behind.

They had a seat and the Magician looked at Sean's profile. This guy was big, not just in the arms but all around. Neck like a bull. And a white-hot energy emanated from him. It was like being near a live power line. For a moment, confusion and uncertainty washed over him. Even – though he couldn't admit it to himself – fear.

But then he reminded himself that this was just another big dumb mick. And this was *his* party, his dominion. And that was *his* wife waiting upstairs. So he smiled.

"So, Sean. What on earth are you doing here? I would think that you don't feel at home in a place like this."

"Aye. I don't think much of it. Pretentious *wop* restaurant."

The sound of a piano from the main dining room. The smell of cigars from a group of men talking and laughing near the window. The Magician wondered if people watched them, wondered why an elegant man in a tailored suit talked and reasoned with this big brute in work pants held up with braces, his big dumb face reddened by the sun and wind. Obviously a manual laborer. Maybe they were amused by the scene?

"Then why don't you be on your way then, *Sean*? You are disturbing the staff. And making a fool of yourself."

Sean turned his face full toward him and leaned forward slowly, a pint of Guinness squeezed in his big red hand. Again, the Magician was thrown off by the sheer size of the man. It was like standing before a rock face.

"I won't leave until I see me girl on her birthday," he hissed.

"She does not care to see you. She did not invite you."

"I'm here to surprise her."

"You are drunk off your arse, boy."

"Aye. And I'm ready to fight."

The Magician paused and glanced around the room. "Fight *who*?"

"Fight anybody who makes me girl unhappy, and that's *you*, and don't call me *boy*, ya rawny ponce."

"Oh. You think I'm a ponce, just because I'm clean and well dressed?"

"I'll dirty ya up soon, enough. Ya wanna hop on? Hop on, yeah?"

The Magician stilled, his mind churning. He had always been smart. Always been fast. Good with a sucker punch. But his undoing had always been brutes like this. Brutes bigger than him. Like the farmer who used to punch him in the head. *Blood in the milk, boy!*

He would distract him. Disarm him. He used all his willpower to get inside the mind of the big dumb mick. To feel what he was feeling, the same way he could get inside the buzz of a bumblebee, the tender veins in a rose, or the rapid heartbeat and animal panic of his wife. He would feel his way in, *become* him. Then bend him.

"Listen, Sean. Let's don't lose our heads here. I'll give you fare for the trolley. Go home and sleep it off. I know you work hard and play hard, harder than anyone. We will forget this."

"I drove here in me own autocar. And I'm not leaving until I say what I've come to say."

"Which is what?"

"Which is that I love Luna, and I'm going to take her away from ya."

He smiled to think Sean coveted his little fool of a wife. "Well, sorry, gent, but she doesn't love you." The absurdity of the notion made him laugh aloud, shaking his head.

His laughter only inflamed Sean. His big face darkened with blood in a second. "I'm here to tell ya that she does, yeah?"

The Magician battled to get inside the guy He was a fortress. He would have no influence, no power, if he could not get inside. But the sheer force of will of the man overpowered his own: He felt weak and drained. "Come on, Sean. I'm sure you get plenty of women thrown your way. Why would you lose your head over mine? She hasn't got half a brain. No tits to speak of. And there are others far finer."

The brute grabbed a handful of his shirtfront and pulled him forward, so close that all the Magician could see were his pale bloodshot eyes under intimidating brows; he smelled the stink of Sean's alcoholic breath as he hissed, "I will not let ya speak that way of Luna. I'll batter ya right here, fookin' *ponce*."

Flashes of alarm lit up the Magician's neurons like a short circuit, and he couldn't think for a moment. Then he put a hand on the man's meaty shoulder to push him away, but acting as if he were holding firmly to make a point.

"Sean," he said, voice sure and steady, "Why don't we …" his mind raced, "take our drinks and go have a look at the garden they have out back. Come. We'll talk there."

Sean released the handful of shirt and glowered at him furiously. But then with a grunt and a shrug, pushed his way up from the bar.

Out the door, into the balmy night. A relief. "May we have a table to finish our drinks?" the Magician asked as a waiter approached them. "I want to show my friend here the lovely garden. It is my party upstairs, we are only stepping away for a moment."

Sean was already in the middle of the patio, looking around with his hands on his hips. It was a beautiful garden and smelled strongly of magnolia. Most of the white-draped iron tables were filled with happy, laughing people. The faint sound of the piano percolated from inside, alongside the trickling of water from the fountain, on which stone cupids perched all around. A sliver of moon hung high in the sky.

"You see,' said the Magician smoothly, feeling in control again, "It is a European style garden. You will find wisteria, oleander, jasmine, and gardenia. So very fragrant, don't you think?"

And indeed, the fresh evening air, the change in energy, reassured the Magician he had regained his equilibrium. He closed his eyes and inhaled deeply of the rich scents. The perfume of this garden made him swoon for a moment. The beauty of it. Beauty that he, the Magician, had created for himself out of thin air.

To think of where I came from, a baby covered in oily blood left in a basket for the Sisters to find. Sent away from my heavenly home on a train to hell. Beaten by the farmer. Ran away to work in a circus of ill repute. I had nothing. And yet here I am, in this beautiful garden, with music and this tart golden wine in my glass, and it's all for me, me … and I will achieve more. And more. *Because I am the Magician. Because I say I am.*

And for a moment, underneath the sound of the piano and dinner conversation and a trickling fountain, he heard something else. A heavy throbbing pulse, a low, steady current underneath it all, the sound he heard in Cezar's circus wagon, after smoking the opium pipe. *That's the sound of the earth turning, you fool.* He heard it now, though he was not smoking dope. And was no fool. He heard it now, because he was special. Acquainted with the universe and its beauty.

He snapped out of his reverie, to seek out the big brute who had come out here with him. Backlit from the paper lanterns strung up in the greenery, Sean looked less like a man, and more like a bear on its hind legs. He smiled, full of goodwill, wanting to communicate the bounty of his thoughts and feelings with the big dumb mick.

"You see, Sean, you must not accept your life as it is. You don't have to. You can rise *above* your station, you know. I did!"

He saw Sean turn to him, with a slow, incredulous smile spreading across his face. Amazing how focused he was, in spite of being so drunk. Sean laughed, harshly, and said, "Aye. And the higher the monkey climbs the tree, the further up its arse ya see."

"Please, no crude talk, not here. They will make you leave, and I am trying my best to have you *stay*."

"The higher the monkey climbs the *tree*, the further up its arse ya *see* …" Now almost singing it, in a lilting, nursery rhyme style, getting louder. People stopped talking and turned to them. The Magician pulled him away, on the pretense of strolling to see the flowers.

Anger surged through the Magician. The brute was immune to him. He was *mocking* him. He renewed his will, his nerve, to make an impact on Sean's dull reptilian brain.

"You could learn a lot simply by watching and observing, Sean. You could have everything I have."

"And I'm gonna 'ave your wife. Already 'ad her in fact."

All magnanimity running through the Magician's veins transformed into an iciness that invaded his system, and made him very still, the prelude to that blankness that sometimes preceded a surprising act of violence. "Take back your talk about my wife. It is a lie."

"No lie, boss. I know she's got a mole underneath her left breast." Sean smiled again, a slow, sinuous smile.

The Magician grappled with this new information permeating his brain. No. It was not possible. He was no cuckold.

Sixteen

"I do for her what ya don't do at home, ya ponce. Lookin' at ya box a dirty pictures o' man, woman and beast. Some of us prefer a real woman, and know what to do with 'er—"

"Shut your goddamn mouth," the Magician said with deadly calm. But inside, the rage rose up, like bile. The little whore. He pictured that little mole the brute spoke of, underneath her small breast that was no bigger than a girl's. A mole, like a little blot of ink at the end of a sentence. A little blot expanding in his mind now, suffusing it with darkness …

"I'll not be shuttin', it, boss. Because I came here to make a declaration of me love for her, and to make a statement of me intent." He grinned now and lifted his chin.

"Oh, yes, your *intent*?" The Magician's teeth ground in the back, his hands balled into fists.

"My intent to make her me wife."

"Oh, right, as though she'd want to become the wife of a dirty punk criminal, a day laborer with no class, who could never give her a fine apartment, could never give her a party at Barbetta—"

"She is a proper Irish woman who does not like to do with wops. She would be honored. And I will treat her like the queen she is. Not sail her like a kite in the air in some humiliatin' vaudeville show—"

"I am an artist!" Aware he had raised his voice, he made an effort to lower it. "I play before celebrities, royalty. I'm written about in the New York Times."

"They're laughin' at ya. And laughin' at her. Wot are ya gonna do when the moving picture shows take ya out? Vaudeville and magic shows are on their way out, my friend. And ya'll be on the street like a right numpty. And Luna will be with me, and never think of ya again. Except in her nightmares."

The Magician's face drained of color. The audacity of this imbecile. "You … are … *nothing*," he said, lips trembling.

"Ha! Me and me boys are kings of the waterfront. I'm doin' all right, boss. Been takin' ya wife out to see the sights in me new motorcar."

"Liar. You have no motorcar."

"Aye, I do. And ya have not." The thug smiled. The Magician had no effect on him at all. The thug actually thought highly of himself and his rotten life. He was immune, a craggy rock face that he could not scale, could not grip his fingers under.

The Magician's veins popped in his forehead, his neck strained. He wanted to annihilate the stupid mick. "You think you've found a great prize in Luna? I'll tell you, she's nothing. Dumb as a rock. Tits like a schoolgirl. If you have been having a frig with her then you have low standards. You're better off with a ten-cent whore—"

"I'm warnin' ya, boss, shut it right now—"

"Or what? Luna is nothing, except that she is mine. She is my property, for life. Though she is nothing, just like you—"

It happened so quickly: The big brute took the revolver from the pocket of his work pants, one of the new style handguns, so small, almost toy-like. But when Sean drew back and crouched, firing with both hands on the weapon – How could the big drunk man move so quickly, so smoothly? – the bullets that went into the Magician's abdomen were very, very real.

He clutched at himself, doubled over, as though he could stop the flow of blood. He was the Magician. Surely he could see into the nature of himself, and work with it? Because until now, nature had been on his side …

But now it was not. It had betrayed him. The pain was explosive. The pain was *him*. It was all he was. And then even these thoughts blurred and slipped away, careening sideways, losing meaning ... he collapsed to the ground.

After the shots were fired, Sean straightened up again, squinting in concentration. Now he bit his lip and regarded the demise of the Magician with wide, wondering eyes.

The moment stretched, and the Magician's vision narrowed upon all kinds of small, insignificant details. The way the moonlight reflected in the fountain behind him, the cherubs in shadowy, indifferent profile. The way the woman sitting at a table, wearing strands of glistening jet beads and a dark tint on her lips, gaped as though a rapier had passed through her, and screamed, dropping her wine glass which shattered with a bright, distant sound.

I don't … think I can undo this. But I can try. Time is not linear. Time is …

But the moment moved inexorably forward. The big brute did a little hop, a nervous shuffling of his big feet, then turned and ran just as the mâitre d' rushed forward with his hands covering his mouth, eyes scaled wide open to take in the bleeding mess that was the Magician, who looked back at him, blinking mildly. There was nothing else to be done.

He lay on the stone ground under a night-blooming jasmine, and he looked up into the gentle sway of the branches as the chaos unfolded around him, shouts and banging and people touching him. He hated people touching him usually, but now he didn't care. The smell of jasmine was heavy in his nostrils, like incense, and he thought of the little girls in their white smocks at the Foundling chapel, of the kind priest who gave him nuts and oranges for Christmas and told him he was a clever boy. He was *there*, and he was *here* bleeding on the ground, and he was also standing on a stage, not at the Beaumont, not at the Orpheum, but somewhere else, someplace unfamiliar. What was behind the blood-red curtains? He heard a luminous hush as of the whisperings of thousands of unseen souls. He braced himself hopefully, waiting for the curtains to open.

Everything went dark.

Seventeen

The train exited the tunnel and the view that opened up stopped her breath; a mountain vista stretched as far as the eye could see. Below, rivers snaked their way through the scoop of the valley, still wild and green in the full thrust of August. Surrounding all in the background were slate-colored mountain peaks, the sky a fierce, ringing blue, and a single hawk circled.

She had never breathed mountain air before. It was gentler, less dense with oxygen, and felt quick and silvery in her lungs, making her a bit lightheaded. Never in her life had she been above sea level in this way. Never had she seen mountains as bold as these. And yet here she was, with only a pane of glass separating her from the view, her ghostly reflection superimposed on the scene, as though her small pale face was only dreaming these trees, these peaks, this lonely bird with its wide, strong wings, stippled brown and white.

And the room. Her very own room on the train. Luna had not realized when she booked it how dear in price it was. But the privacy it gave her was essential. She could not bear to share space, or talk to anyone, not right now.

Maybe never again.

The room was small, but it had everything she wanted. Two facing seats, both just for her, that at night were cunningly slid together and made into a bed. The green-and-yellow ticking on the seats, rough and nubbly beneath her fingertips. There was also a little closet and her own private bathroom. *Not as fine as the drawing room, should you want that, ma'am, but it should meet your needs.*

Handsome wood paneling on the walls, wallpaper striped like the ticking but in brown and gold, the paper lifting up a little on one edge. And a tassel had unraveled somewhat on one of the window shades. It was amazing how well acquainted one was with each detail of a small room when one spent enough time in it. As if it were an extension of one's own body.

But this space had all she needed. And she had never traveled alone before. Never lived any place alone. And now she was, and it was such a queer and dizzying sensation that she was thankful this little room held her fast in the world, containing her when inside she was spinning out of control.

She had only been there since sunrise, but it felt as though it had been much longer. She may well have had been traveling by rail all her life.

Chicago. That was her destination, the end of the line. But what that future held for her there, she had no idea.

Because she had not been herself when she decided to purchase the train ticket. It was as though some outside force had compelled her to pack her one valise in the dark hours of early morning and make her way to Penn Station, that majestic temple of pink granite from which streams of anonymous people came and went at all hours, even now.

And she had told no one where she was going, not her

father, not her sisters. Though Lil and Mary Catherine had tended to her as best they could in her shock, bringing her meals, not wanting to leave her side, she was finally clear-headed enough to send them away. But once they were gone, she was beset by a crawling panic that drove her to walk the streets, to purchase the newspaper that featured her not in the entertainment reviews section, but on the front page:

MAGICIAN KNOWN AS COSMOS THE INCOMPARABLE MURDERED IN BARBETTA GARDEN, KILLER REPORTEDLY ASSOCIATED WITH NOTORIOUS IRISH GANG

She had mostly stared at the headline, numb, and at the accompanying photograph of her husband lying on the ground, shrouded by a white tablecloth the staff had placed over him, policemen standing around him in their brass-buttoned coats. In the corner were three inset photos, one of the Magician onstage, one softly lit studio portrait of Luna herself, and one of Sean after he had been captured by the police, a sign with a stamped number held under his chin.

The story itself, she could not bring herself to read or comprehend. Just little snatches:

Promising young star of the stage cut down in his prime … No known connection to gang activity … onlookers said the killer declared his love for the magician's wife before the deadly altercation

A *scandal*. Luna was the center of a scandal. Everyone knew it. She could not walk the street without feeling everyone's eyes, everyone's judgment. Her mind would not stop racing. She could not sleep at night. Sometimes she whimpered aloud, because she felt her heart was about to explode in her chest, her head swimming, and she was as sick as on the ship crossing the ocean, except there was no other side to get to …

There were the meetings with the policemen and detectives. The trip to the morgue. Though everyone was polite and attentive to the young widow, she knew what they were saying and thinking. The first nights at home she was convinced she would be arrested, for collusion to murder her husband. For hadn't she sometimes *wished* the Magician dead? In her heart, was she not guilty?

Running up the steps of the train station in the blue light of early dawn, gripping her valise, which she had hastily packed with three lightweight dresses, her underthings, and for reasons she couldn't explain to herself, the Magician's box. Box of light. Box of death.

Memories of her birthday dinner the week before ran in a loop through the circuitry of her brain as she entered the steel-lattice cathedral of Penn Station. She remembered dropping her fork at the sound of the echoing gunshots, the silver tines echoing as her blood rushed into her ears, a sound like steam escaping as she rushed down the stairs to see staff members running out of the door to the garden.

Luna did not remember screaming when she saw her husband gutshot on the terrace stones, blood pooling into the roots of the jasmine tree. She did not remember taking him in her arms and crying out into his slackened face, which had turned an unsettling gray color. Dead, he did not resemble his living self at all. She hardly recognized him. His eyes had looked wide open, astonished, as though he could see something astounding coming up right behind her.

She remembered the policemen, and people shouting, sobbing. She remembered the blood that, on her dark blue dress with the Asian sash, appeared to be black. Wet shadows of black, that dried and clung and stuck to her chemise when she tried to pull it off later.

Men clutched at her arms, lifted her up and carried her away. Questions, questions, questions, that she was unable to answer. And then later, a doctor with his leather bag came to her bed, with drops of ether on a handkerchief, a sickly-sweet smell, and oblivion.

Hysterical, they had called her.

And her mind and nerves had been jangled and confused ever since. Senses switched confusingly. Light hurt her eyes. Shapes had sounds like musical notes. Color intensified, too bright. She feared she was losing her mind.

It had to be this way, that she was in the train station, paying money at the ticket window for the first Pullman sleeper available that morning. She bought the ticket, then paced and wandered the waiting room with its huge Corinthian columns. The amplified sounds echoing against the marble and vaulted glass made her feel faint. In the ladies washroom, she splashed water on her face and stared into her reflection. *Steady now. Steady.*

And then she rested on a wooden bench that looked like a church pew. She thought perhaps she could pray, say some Hail Marys. But no prayers would come to her lips.

It must have been the box. The box of light nestled in her bag at her feet. The power emanating from it frightened her, distracted her. But somehow she knew that she was responsible for it now. No one else could know about it. If she could just keep it hidden.

So soothing, to be on a train, en route to a place that she could not fathom. At last, she felt, if not at peace, at least *still.*

In the warm embrace of the sun, she slept.

Eighteen

By the time the porter had woken her for lunch in the dining car, they had already made a stop at Philadelphia, the day was getting on and she found herself invigorated from her nap, and hungry.

She ate broiled spring chicken with walnut catsup and potatoes, and drank a pot of strong black china tea. She sat alone, not wishing to speak to anyone. It helped that she had dressed in her mourning clothes, a plain black crepe dress with jet buttons up the front and an embroidered collar. Also, pinned to the front was a brooch, a black onyx cameo with a white moth on it, with her husband's name and death date engraved on the back. Mr. Klein from the Beaumont Theatre had given to her. *A homage to your gifted husband and a reference to his great, unseen Gilded Moth act,* the letter had read in slashing strokes of his fountain pen. *I stand in unity with your sorrow, dear lady.*

She wore the brooch. It was better than some other mourning brooches she had seen; the ones that featured photographs of the departed spooked her particularly. But still, she wasn't fond of wearing it. To even remember their plans for The Gilded Moth made her feel ill.

I must be thankful that it at least that is not going to happen.

People were kind and hushed when they spoke to her, the young bereaved, and gave her plenty of space. And so she was free to savor her meal, to close her eyes if she wished, enjoy the speed and momentum of the train and the blurring of the landscape out of the window.

She also enjoyed watching the other passengers, without having to interact. A honeymoon couple touched hands and spoke in whispers. A group of businessmen in suits and watch chains, argued. And children, well-behaved children, wearing their finest clothes and on their best behavior for the train ride. These, she smiled at, even when they goggled at her in her witch-like widow's weeds.

I hope to go like this forever, and never get to Chicago.

She had purchased some magazines at the station, *Saturday Evening Post* and *Vogue*, but they did not draw her in. All she wanted to do was sit in her little room and look out of the window, for once not thinking of this or that or anything. She looked at the passing fields and trees and towns, wondering what it was like to live there. Even ramshackle wooden houses and dirt roads looked different and fresh because they were foreign. Because they were unknown. Somewhere near Harrisburg, she saw a little tow-headed boy in breeches and a Derby, leading a goat tied with a piece of rope. He waved at the train and she waved back. What was it like to be him, walking riverside in his bare feet, under this bright blue sky? She liked this game she had created of changing places with people. It was restful to her mind, and fun. It took her out of her worries.

Perhaps it would be fun to go for as long as she could without uttering a word to anyone. Try not to even think in words, but in only feelings, images. Sensations.

She closed her eyes and the image of the boy returned

to her, in greater detail this time. Sun glinted on the river's surface like diamonds. The boy's bare toes on the cool green moss on the ground. The soft bleating of the goat beside him …

I hope that I may never get where I am going …

At supper time she again ate heartily, her only human interaction that of nodding to another widow, one much older than she, and wearing a veiled hat, her small cragged eyes gazing out at Luna hazily through the dotted mesh.

The day stretched on endlessly, yet passed in an instant. Before she knew it, the porter had arrived to slide her two seats together and arrange the cushions into a bed.

Luna stood by, quietly watching. A black man in a neat white coat, his hair so different from hers, wooly, yet parted and brushed down and to the side.

She had tried not to speak but knew she must. "Sir … do you know how I may send a telegram?"

He stood up from what he was doing, turned to her courteously. "There is an office at the Chicago station, ma'am. We arrive at eight o'clock tomorrow."

She paused. "Thank you, sir. But what I meant was, um … how does one *send* a telegram?"

"Ma'am?"

"You see … well … I have never sent one before. A-and now I *need* to. And I don't know *how* …"

There was a look of kindly concern and then dismay on his face as Luna burst into tears.

She woke with the sun the next morning after a fitful sleep. She had dreamed of the Magician, of following behind him a few paces, through the crowded streets of Broadway. She had kept her eyes trained on him, his tall, erect form, the haughty way he held up his head, the slight bounce in his stride, that jaunty bob of his straw boater. Unmistakable, as always. So easy to spot in a crowd. But in this dream, he did not know she followed him. And she knew he walked to his impending doom. And yet she found herself silent, unable to warn him. Unable to stop what was to happen.

The dream colored her waking hours as she washed and dressed. She keenly felt the absence of the Magician, and it gave her such a hollow, unmoored feeling that it made her stomach ache. Though she had feared him, and sometimes hated him, he had been the driving force in her life; ever since the day he singled her out in the tailor's shop. As though he was her destiny, good or bad. The Magician had been inevitable. His willpower had been her protector in the frightening new world, America. Now she was alone and rudderless.

Am I not special if I am the one he chose? Am I not worthwhile, if he loved me? What does it mean now that he is no longer here?

Her aloneness in the world did not feel riveting on this morning, as she ordered tea and toast brought to her room. Now it felt raw and frightening, and she almost wished she had her husband there, to tell her what to do next.

At least there was the money. They had made a lot of money in a short time; she kept her cash in a muslin pouch, tied around her waist beneath her underthings. Whilst she did not have money to last her whole life, she could be comfortable for a while. Six months perhaps. Until she figured out what to do next.

It was not long until they pulled into Chicago, and she alighted onto the platform, valise in hand, wearing another black dress, ruffled in dotted Swiss, light on her skin. The humidity already oppressive, even though it was just after eight in the morning. She followed the other departing passengers, into the enormous marble-halled building. One station was much like another by now, and she was no longer awed by the size or scope or noise. She arched her neck and scanned the building until she found what she was looking for, a Western Union office tucked away in a corner.

She remembered what the porter had told her, after he had given her a handkerchief, averting his eyes as she cried. From a wooden desk with a box of forms, she took one out, then took up a pen on a chain, and filled out the street address of her family's place in Hell's Kitchen. Then she stared blankly at the section of empty lines, where she would compose her message.

What to say? She certainly had to say *something*. They must have noticed by now that she was missing. It was not fair for them to worry and suffer on her account.

The fountain pen left a large blot of ink where she had pressed the pen down, and she knew she had to start writing.

Dearest Father, Lil, and Mary Catherine.

She bit her lip, face flushed. Too much noise in the place to think.

I am away traveling, by rail. Do not worry about me. I wanted to see some fresh sights, to clear my head. I am quite well and comfortable. I ...

She raised her eyes to the ceiling, to keep tears from spilling out. She couldn't ask what she wanted to ask: is Sean going to stay in prison forever, all because of me? Will they *execute* him? A clerk looked over at her curiously. Must keep composed ...

I am ...

But what was she? Even Luna did not know!

I am endeavoring to exist elsewhere for a time.

Nineteen

Chicago felt not dissimilar from New York. There were some differences; the streets and the alleys were wider and cleaner. Somehow it felt there was more water in Chicago, though she had thought of it as landlocked. The breeze off the lake felt cooling and fresh; she watched a group of ladies in bathing dresses with bloomers as they splashed around on the shore. They looked to be Luna's age. She imagined what fun it would be to join them, but she could only watch, buttoned up in her widow's weeds.

She had been sightseeing all day, not knowing what do with herself after leaving her valise in her hotel room. She was hot from walking the streets, so went into a dark theatre to see a moving picture show. It was one starring Mary Pickford, who she had grown fond of now that she knew who she was. The story was a romantic and tragic one, with Mary Pickford playing a young Spanish woman who ran away with an Indian man she was madly in love with. Luna sat transfixed, hardly able to read the title cards for the tears in her eyes. The sonorous tones of the organ at the front of the theatre vibrated into her very bones.

The Magician had never been fond of her seeing picture

shows. He said that they were killing vaudeville, and killing his profession. So she went to see them secretly, and rarely. But now, she thought, she could indulge herself if she wanted to. This picture made her swoon with the hectic drama, and the sweeping views of what she knew to be California, where all of the picture shows were filmed. Even through the screen, she felt what California must be like, with its rolling hills and blazing blue skies. Endless.

I will go there someday. Maybe I can be an actress – someday.

But after the show, and after a meal of brisket and onions in a dark restaurant, where a skinny man with bad skin played the violin, she had nothing left to do with herself.

She had taken the hotel room for one night only. As the sun set, she returned to the train station so that she could arrange to leave in the morning.

The train station felt safer to her than the open streets. Nothing bad could happen to her in a train station. Even in her hotel room, she did not feel at ease. She heard the people on the other side of the wall, a man and two women. Peculiar noises, thumping and barking type noises, and sometimes long silences, punctuated by the man crying out, "Do a number on it, Susan!"

But here it was calm, there was no line, and a woman worked at the ticket booth. An older woman, with a cushiony bosom and large, kind eyes.

Luna approached her shyly. "Excuse me, ma'am, but I have some questions."

"Yes, miss?"

"I-I would like to purchase a ticket."

"Where to, miss?"

"Well, that's the thing … I'm not sure where it is I want to go." It seemed safe to tell such a thing to this woman, old enough to be Luna's mother, dressed in charcoal gray with a nosegay pinned to her shoulder; the musty smell of the violets somehow comforting to inhale. She went on. "I want to get away from the city."

The woman peered at Luna more closely now, brow furrowed. It worried Luna for a moment that this woman knew who she was. The news item about the murdered magician in New York, the love triangle involved … did they know it in Chicago? Did she know Luna's photograph?

At last, the woman tilted her head and spoke. "You look very young to be a widow."

Startled, Luna thought, She knows! But then remembered she was dressed all in black, wearing a mourning brooch. She exhaled. "I suppose I am. My husband … died in an accident."

The woman considered her, as though trying to place her. "My dear, you, well, are you all right? You look a bit feverish."

"I am well, thank you."

"But are you *really* well?"

"Excuse me?"

"You have a look about you, that you, well, are you on your own?"

"Yes. I am"

"And not from this country, I presume."

"I am from Ireland. I don't know this country well."

"Well, you sound nearly American. Your brogue is subtle."

"I suppose it is." She had been trying to speak as others did around her.

The woman at the counter looked at her for some moments, not saying a word, and then leaned forward.

"I fear," she said quietly, "that you are being pursued by darkness."

Luna thought at first that she must surely have misheard. She gaped at the woman, who upon closer examination seemed older than she at first thought. There were such deep shadows around her eyes. And the violets were so last century. She might have a bustle on, behind that counter.

"Excuse me?" Luna, unnerved, tried to say this lightly, but it came out as a strangled peep.

"Don't mind me, dear. I have your best interests at heart. But it seems to me that you are on the run from oppressive forces. Dark ones. And you are a pure soul."

Luna blushed to her roots. She fingered her velvet pouch and looked down. "Things have not been well at home," she admitted.

"Well, I only mean to help, my dear. Where is it that you would like to go?"

"I want ..." she remembered that first glorious morning of traveling, when all seemed to shine with hope: seeing the mountain peaks outside her train window, the bird of prey circling overhead. "I want to go somewhere with mountains."

"Well, that is not *here*, that's for sure." The woman's skin, on her cheeks and fragile neck, was stained sepia, as though she had seen a lot of sun in her young days. "Do you know, though, of a place called West Virginia?"

"No, ma'am."

"About twelve hours from here, so you would not need a sleeper. There is a place down there my cousin went to when she was ailing. It is called Indigo Springs. She went there to take the cure."

"The cure?"

"The water cure." The woman drew back, as though to gauge Luna's response. "The Indians called it *taking the waters*. Are you familiar?"

"With ...?"

"The benefits of mineral springs."

"I know of them. There is a place that has them in my own country, not far from my village." Lisdoonvarna. There was a saying that it was the place where parish priests pretended to be sober, and bank clerks pretended to be drunk, but she kept this to herself. "I have never been there. But it is popular with clergy and rich folk."

"Well, these springs are different. Indigo colored, truly, like the name. From mineral deposits. They have a genuine healing effect. My cousin was an invalid when she went. Three days in that healing water, and her spleen shrank to *half* its size."

"That sounds remarkable..." She tried to think of more to say, but she knew nothing of mineral baths or spleens. And this interaction was taking the cast of a surreal dream to her. She looked behind her, but no one else queued in line.

"Trust me," said the woman. "If you have no set destination, and you are looking for a lovely, healing place, I can start you on your way there. Do you have no other plans, ideas of what you want?"

"No ..." Luna admitted. The smell of violets and dusting powder intensified; the smell of the past, coal grates and Queen Victoria and candles to bed. She was feeling a bit dizzy.

"Then let me prepare your ticket, my dear. One way?"

"Um, yes. Will I need to make arrangements ahead of time? To tell them of my arrival?" And who was 'them' she wondered?

"No need. They can always accommodate you."

"But … where …"

"When you arrive at the station, let them know to take you to the Manor."

"Is that all I am to say?"

"It is all anyone travels there for. Everyone else is local. Trust me, they'll know why you are there. And they are very accommodating."

The woman bustled about, writing things in a ledger, stamping things, looking at schedules. Luna felt shy about interrupting, but called out, "Ma'am?"

"Yes, dear."

"What if they will not accept me?"

The woman looked at her over the pair of round spectacles that she had put on. A long look of bemused patience.

"My dear. Understand. You *will* be accepted. You leave at seven in the morning." Then, firmly, she laid down the ticket on the counter. "This is your ticket."

Luna took it because she could not refuse. The woman smiled, gratified that she had given into the idea, and told Luna the price.

All that night sleep eluded her, because the earlier exchange at the ticket window played over and over. The oddity of it all mixed with afterimages of the moving picture she had seen that afternoon; the whole scene replayed in her head as though in luminous black and white, the movements herky-jerky and speeded up. The title cards in another language she did not understand. These close-ups of her face showed a pale young woman with darkly fringed eyes grown large, her rouged mouth parted in an "O" of frightful wonder.

In spite of being twelve hours long, the train journey went by quickly. Because she had slept hardly at all in her room in Chicago, the motion of the train lulled her into slumber for many hours, waking only for meals and to look out of the window at the new scenery. Mostly fields, and woods, and scattered small towns with wood frame houses.

I am happiest when I am on the move.

Twenty

It wasn't until early evening that the train reached her destination. The station at Indigo Springs, West Virginia, was very different from the train stations in New York and Chicago. Those had been grand, cathedral-like entities.

The Indigo Springs station was a simple wooden building with an A-frame shingled roof. The town itself was leafy and green, with mountain ridges all around. Though it was six-fifteen, the sun was still in the sky and the sounds of birds high in the trees. She heard the cries of children running and playing on the platform, raggedy, poor-looking children, who stopped to look at her with grave eyes. They followed her as she made her way into the building, but said nothing to her.

Inside the station was one single room, with one counter. A man at the window with a gray mustache stared into space as an electric fan whirred and buzzed beside him. Slowly, reluctantly, his eyes settled upon her.

"Excuse me," Luna said, setting her valise on the rough wood planks of the floor. "Can you help me?"

He raised his eyebrows in answer.

"I need accommodation. I need to get to a place called …

the Manor?"

The man showed little expression but called out a single word. "Crane!"

Luna did not know what to answer to this and then realized there was someone else in the station with them.

A teenaged boy lay on one of the benches, reading a comic book. Grudgingly, he stood up and walked over. Though taller than she was, he had dark blond hair cut in a bowl shape high on his head, and round ears that stuck out, making him look like an outsized little boy.

"Crane, take this lady out to the house."

"She the only one?"

"You see anyone else?"

Without a word, the boy took her valise and led her out of a side door to an old buggy, small, with a battered black bonnet. The horse hitched to the front also black, with a single patch of white on its nose.

The boy went about strapping her bag to the rack, and Luna breathed in the air of this new place: fresher, more pure, than Chicago. It was the gloaming hour, with fireflies in the air. The boy did not help her into the buggy, only indicated with a flick of his head that she should get in.

She sat behind him as he pulled away. He paused and glanced furtively back at the train station as if considering which way to take, before taking a hard left, across an expanse of grass. He had a large Adam's apple and pink skin that looked as though it had not yet sprouted whiskers.

"H'imma take us a different way," he said gruffly. His speech different from any she had heard before in America, his accent sounded almost like a Scotsman's to her ears.

"Oh? What way is this?"

"Up the ole Indian trail."

They entered some woods now. There was indeed a trail, but it looked far too narrow for a buggy.

"Is this … the preferred way to go?" Her voice came out in jumps and starts as they barreled over ruts and rocks; awfully fast, she thought.

"Well. It's quicker. Mister J. don't like it none, thinks I'm ball-hootin' it. But he don't need to know."

A storm threatened. A breeze stirred the tops of the trees. Colors looked different, bright and saturated, charged with electricity against the darkening sky.

"Is Mr. J. the man at the train station?"

"No, ma'am. Mr. J. owns the house. I work for him. You're the last train of the day."

They broke out of the woods onto a gravel road. This they followed around one quick bend, and then before them stood an enormous white hotel, three stories with columns. The lands and hedges meticulously manicured, a large, circular flower bed in the center of a roundabout made of red petunias, which blazed weirdly in the blue stormlight.

Crane pulled up at the front double doors and retrieved her valise. As he opened the door for her, he whispered in her ear, "Don't tell about the Indian trail. Please."

The lobby was enormous, with a floor of echoing black-and-white tile like a giant's chessboard. Across from them a figure behind the reception desk turned away, shuffling some papers; a man with wet-combed dark hair.

Reluctantly, not knowing what would befall her in such a place, Luna willed herself to move forward.

Twenty-One

The storm finally arrived later that night, and rain continued for the entirety of the next day.

Luna sat by the window, watching the rivulets make their way down, soothed by the music of the rain on the tin roof.

The staff called it a "cabin." It was one of several outbuildings on the property, tucked into the woods behind the Manor, though connected to the rest of the estate by a winding gravel path. It was, the desk clerk told her that first evening, "for those who prefer a more private, rustic experience." But it was not rustic in her estimation. Nothing like the little white stone cottage of her girlhood. This cabin, called the Rosebriar Cabin, was small, but shingled, nicely furnished with chintz furniture and eyelet curtains. It was made up of a small living room, two small bedrooms, a miniature kitchen, and a bathroom scarcely big enough to turn around in. Everything about it was neat and dear and lovely, and a fire burned in the fireplace even though it was late summer. Chilled by the rain, it felt good to feel the warmth and enjoy the crackling of the wood.

She could eat in the large formal dining room of the

Manor, or she could have her meals brought to her at the cabin. So far, she had chosen the latter option. Not only because of the rain, but she felt too intimidated by the chandeliers and gilded chairs of the dining room, which brought back unpleasant feelings. It took her some time to realize that the place reminded her of the main dining room of Barbetta.

Luna had not thought of that night in Barbetta since she left New York. Willfully, she blocked all of it out. Those events from scarcely a week ago that had propelled her forward into this strange and unknown future, in which she sat in a posh cabin in a place called West Virginia.

… because if she did think about the night in Barbetta, queer things happened to her. She saw the ever-growing pool of blood on the flagstones, the unspeakable wounds in the Magician's gut which exposed glimpses of his innards, pink and red and glistening in the soft glow of the garden's lanterns. Things that she saw, and could not unsee, until her body shuddered violently, her heart pounding in her chest so loudly she feared she'd lose her mind, with nowhere to run, nowhere to hide from what terrible visions lived inside her …

So she willed herself not to think of it at all. There was no other option if she was to stay sane. That was why she had to leave New York. There were reminders, it seemed, at every street corner, ready to trigger her worst nightmares.

Though glad to be away, she knew she had to tell her family where she was; she planned to stay in this place for at least a week.

The next morning, she did venture to the Manor, if only to the front desk, where she could fill out a telegram form.

Dearest Father and Sisters, I have arrived at a wonderful

resort in West Virginia to which many people from all over the country travel. They say there are healing waters on the property! Of this, I know very little. But I am staying in a lovely little cabin and resting nicely. You may send communication here, as I am eager to know how things are at home.

Luna also sent out her clothes for laundering, and then went out to explore the grounds for the first time.

She walked through a grove of ancient chestnut trees, with enormous trunks that spiraled and twisted, her favorite types of trees. Though the cragged branches scared her a bit and made her think of witch fingers, the chestnuts seemed so dear and enchanted. She longed to climb into the low arching branches, but could not. She touched the rough bark and walked on.

She knew where the bathing area was, in the center of a square of green. It had a copper dome at the top, and there were always people there. She watched from afar, fingering a branch of pink azaleas. Voices of the bathers drifted up to her, laconic murmuring, high and easy laughter; she turned her face away and carried on down a path of straight, majestic pines.

Rain dripped from yesterday's downpour, and the path was rich and dark with damp. It smelled of watery greens, and toadstools. Wet ferns brushed her ankles as she walked, skirts pulled up to keep them dry.

The trail led her along the bank of a great river, its surface strewn with leaves and broken branches. The last night's howling wind had been a powerful one, and the water level had risen, brimming with rainwater.

She walked for a while, opposite to the river's flow, toward the source. Every once in a while she picked up a pebble and tossed it in to watch it carried away by the current.

She heard the sound first, a soft hissing, barely discernable. It got louder. And then, she was standing right in front of it: a waterfall, a tall one, pouring down from the gods. Soft mist obscured the silvery rivulets at the bottom. She *felt* that mist, fresh and clean, on her skin.

And looking down by her feet, she saw a reflection of the sky, the trees, and at the edge, herself. The water looked blackened under its surface, so that the top was a perfect, albeit rippling, mirror. Wondrously beautiful, but it disconcerted her. Luna, for a moment, couldn't tell down from up. A world inverted, with nothing solid or real.

I could dive into that water right now, and come up in another world entirely.

Twenty-Two

It wasn't long before a return telegram was delivered to her door. With shaking hands, she opened it.

Dear Sister, we are all ill with worry over you. It does not seem right for you to be traveling by rail by yourself, and we wish you had given us warning at the very least. You can imagine how we felt to not know where you were that first day! We are all well here, and the news stories of your unfortunate situation are less frequent, although the trial is said to start by next April. Sean remains in Sing Sing where your cousin James has visited as often as he is allowed, and said he is in well enough spirits, in spite of things being what they are. Please come home, love, Lil.

Luna crumpled up the telegram and threw it in a wastepaper basket, then covered her eyes until she could recover herself.

Sean. How could she bear to think of Sean, the most hale and vital man she had ever met, locked up in a cell like a shelter animal? She thought of his body, his muscular arms that held her fast in her skin. His particular smell, a sweetish smell like new-cut hay; his smell hallucinated in her nostrils whenever she thought of him.

The love of her life, she supposed. He might have been

her husband; things might have turned out so differently if she had just left the Magician before. But she had stayed. And now this. Her inaction had set forth an avalanche of repercussion. And it could not be undone.

The cheerful room with the flowered drapes all at once oppressed her, and she felt the old dread return and tighten her chest. She felt the tremors take hold of her nervous system like a hijacking. Instinctively, she leaped up and grabbed the paper-wrapped parcel that sat on the spindled side table, and rushed out of the door.

It was a beautiful sunny day, but Luna saw nothing and heard nothing but the pulse in her body as she made her way down the winding trail, toward the bathing house, rushing away from a monster that wanted to devour her.

In the wrapped package was a bathing costume that she had bought the day before. She had arranged for Crane to take her into town in the black buggy. The "downtown" was very small and quaint, not too different in size from the strip of merchants in her home village of Doolin. A tailor, a cobbler, a corner market. And, thank goodness, a woman's ready-to-wear clothing shop.

The bathing costume itself she was not very fond of: navy blue with white trim, with a sailor collar and bloomers underneath. She had wanted something plainer, more form-fitting, as she had seen in the magazines. But this would have to do, she thought as she unwrapped it from its paper in the shadowy privacy of the women's changing room, a little wood-sided building with stalls. A girl attendant came to hang up her black widow's dress.

Dimly, she saw herself in the full-length mirror opposite her. Yes, she did look foolish. Already a petite woman, she now looked absurdly like a child. But the thought only bothered her so much; it was more important that she was somewhere, doing something distracting, and not sitting in her cottage where an attack of nerves might overcome her, and pull her into darkness.

Out, into the sunlight she emerged, her feet moon-pale and vulnerable on the concrete path as she walked toward the voices lifting to her from the bathhouse.

It was a regal looking thing, like something from ancient Greece. Stone steps led up to it. Luna shaded her eyes for a moment, to look at the weathered copper dome overhead. A statue, of a girl-goddess, poised at the top of the dome, gestured gracefully with her arms as though to extol Luna forward. On one side of the dome was inscribed a word: *Hygeia.*

Another attendant, this one a young boy, took Luna's hand as she ascended the steps.

A group of four, two men and two women occupied the bathing pool. They stopped their conversation to raise a hand and bid her greeting as she cautiously lowered her feet into the water.

Water which, as she had been told, was a rich dark blue, like liquid sapphires! And very warm, like bathwater.

Luna sank in, so the water rose to her chin, saying nothing, but savoring the sensation. Could it be true that these waters were healing? Because she felt better, her mind already quieter, awed by the sheer beauty of the water.

"I wonder," she said aloud, softly, without thinking of what she said, "if this water is truly the color indigo!"

She was surprised when one of the men answered. "No. Indigo is not part of the visual spectrum. It is invisible."

Luna blinked. "Then how do we know it exists?"

The man, who had thinning blondish hair, and an aristocratic face, smiled. "Science tells us. Sir Isaac Newton tells us."

"Please, Edward, don't go on," one of the girls said jokingly. She turned to Luna. "I apologize in advance for his being a bore."

"But it is true!" Edward said. "Seven colors to make up the color white. Think of it. The number *seven*." He looked at Luna significantly, but she had no idea how to answer.

"*Think* of it," Edward went on, moving his hands excitedly, splashing droplets everywhere. "Seven days in a week! Seven notes in a scale! The seven angels, seven trumpets, seven stars. Seventh son of a seventh son, etcetera …"

The other man, who had a mustache and was shorter but more broad chested and sat on the edge with only his feet in, said, "Ma'am, Edward is a man inclined to the spiritual and the obscure."

"That's okay," Luna said, lamely, and she felt a bloom rising from her neck.

The second woman smiled at her kindly. She pulled herself out to sit on the edge as well. Luna noticed that she wore one of the new style bathing costumes that she had coveted, a long knitted one that held its shape to her body, and was sleeveless. Also, this woman's dark curly hair was worn down, streaming long and wild so that she looked like a mermaid. And she had dark kohl around her eyes, smudged a bit from the light steam coming off the water.

The woman said, "Are you Irish?" and it took a moment for Luna to answer, "Yes, I am." She was still unused to human interaction after days of silence.

"Born there?"

"Yes, from County Clare. But I live in New York now."

"Why, that's where we're from!" said Edward, excitedly. There was something sly in his manner, whereby

Luna could not tell if he was having fun with her or not. "How *marvelous!*"

"What street do you live on?" asked the woman who still sat in the water. Her auburn hair pinned back tightly, she wore a scarf around her forehead, tied on one side and draped over one shoulder. It gave her a dashing, gypsy look.

"East 4th Street."

"We live on the Upper East Side," said the small dark man, as he lit up a cigar.

"But we come down to the Village all the time," said the mermaid. "By the way, I'm Agnes. This is my husband Peter, smoking the foul tobacco. And my best girl here is Gertie. And Edward there …"

"I'm Luna."

Inscrutable, Edward peered at her, and Luna could not guess what he was thinking. Then he said, "We've seen you, you know."

She swallowed nervously. "In New York?"

"No. Here. Drifting about the grounds all dressed in black, like an apparition. I called you the maiden widow."

"Eddie, please, don't be unkind. I don't want her to think we gossip." Gertie rose, too, to join the others on the edge. Her simple black sheath of a swimsuit had a narrow belt, and it resembled the suits the men wore. Was it indeed a man's suit? Luna was shocked further to see her take a draw from Peter's cigar.

"But I'm not being unkind. No." Edward had one eye closed. "I am merely interested in knowing who this fascinating creature is. You are very beautiful, you know."

"Th-thank you …"

"Too young and lovely to mourn, I'm sure." He looked at her in an expectant manner, waiting for her to speak.

"I-I lost my husband recently."

The two women murmured their kindnesses to her, and Luna averted her face from Edward.

"Illness?" he asked.

"Accident. Of sorts." Her face, already red, gave her away. "He was, well … shot." She knew she could have made something up. But for some reason, she was compelled to say the word, and then to look shyly up into Edward's face to see the impact.

A look of wonder blurred the aristocratic planes of his face, his eyes grown large. "I *knew* it was you, but I thought I must be mad … you are the infamous Magician's assistant!"

"Edward, you don't need to go on when nothing more needs to be said." Peter pointed the cigar at Edward, as though it were a wand that could magically silence him. "And don't call her infamous. The poor thing."

"But Peter, she doesn't mind! *Do* you mind, dear?"

Luna smiled in a way that she hoped was enigmatic, and not just dumbstruck.

"See? See there? I think Luna just needs someone to talk to. And I am a good listener."

"Well, I'm sure you've been through great hardship." Agnes smiled at her sympathetically, then lowered herself back into the water and sat next to her, putting a hand on her shoulder.

"Yes. Yes, I have. I just needed to get away from the city. The papers …" she shuddered.

"And you are alone?"

"Yes."

"Well, not anymore. You have *us* to look out for you."

Peter was the quietest one, the one who watched the most, his dark eyes penetrating. "You are in show business, then. So are these two ladies."

Agnes simpered drolly. "Well, Gertie sings in a music hall. She is quite good. I am no longer on the stage myself."

Gertie winked at her. "Pay Agnes no mind. She used to be a Ziegfeld girl. Not everyone can say that. She can keep her nose in the air forever."

Agnes stuck her tongue out at Gertie. "I don't miss it." She turned to Luna. "I left when I married Peter. I got tired of the hustling."

"That's, well, wonderful!" Luna was stunned. "I never went to the Follies, though."

"And none of us ever got round to seeing you," Peter said to Luna, tapping the cigar into a small silver dish. "Which is unfortunate."

"Yes," said Agnes. "We tried once, but your show was sold out. It is all such a pity. Your husband was an overnight success. I'm sure he would have become a national star."

"Well, he certainly had ambitions," Luna said, wanting to change the subject but not knowing how.

Edward, who had goggled at her the whole time, asked, "Was it really your lover who shot him?"

"*Don't* answer that," said Agnes, low in her ear. Luna turned to look at her, and saw a smile playing around her lips; then both women burst into nervous laughter.

It must have been the heat from the springs or the smell of cigar smoke, but all at once it was as though again, as at the ticket counter, Luna's day had taken a detour into a dreamscape. The warm, deep blue water, the echoing of their voices against the copper dome above them, gave everything they said a sense of being doubled. Luna had never met people like this. She had seen them from afar, sometimes, the people who came to her shows. But she had never had any as friends. In fact, had she ever truly had friends, besides her sisters? Her lover hardly counted.

"Do … do you come here often? You all … seem at home here?" Her head swimming, Luna strove to reground herself into normal talk.

"Edward came here on business once, last year, and said we simply had to come as a group." Gertie retied her hair wrap; Luna had not realized at first how striking she was. Even makeup-free, she was far from plain. "He's a lawyer, if you can believe that."

"Yep, yep. For JP Morgan himself. We were down here for a strategy session once, and I could scarcely believe it. Out here in the sticks? West *Virginia*? And yet here it is! They have high tea. They have falconry, though I'm not one for that. So it's all very decadent, and yet they give you your space. They leave you alone!"

"A lot of New York people come here," Agnes yawned. "I think mostly businessmen and such. But I adore it. Which is your room, Luna?"

"I am staying in one of the cottages."

"How quaint! Will you be here much longer?"

"Just the remainder of the week." She knew she couldn't afford much more. The whole trip was a reckless waste of her resources. She had an idea that these were quite wealthy people. It was possible that they mistook her for one, too.

"Come up to our place tonight!" said Agnes, suddenly gripping her by the arm. "We have two adjoining suites, on the third floor."

"Well, maybe, I …"

"Oh, please," said Edward. "We will have a lot of fun, I promise you. We aren't stuffy like a lot of other folks staying here. We like to have a gay time. Do you dance?"

"Edward, darling, she's still in mourning ..."

"Shush, now, Gertie." He smiled at Luna. "Do you like ragtime?"

Luna, who knew nothing of ragtime, answered, "Somewhat."

"It's settled then. Meet us for dinner at six. Main dining room." Then Edward winked at her, and said, "You won't regret it."

They dined first on a platter of oysters, and Luna drank what they told her was a champagne cocktail, which she decided that evening was now her very favorite drink. It made her feel effervescent and giddy.

It no longer bothered her to be in a grand formal dining room; their table was so raucous and friendly, that she did not associate it with *that* night at Barbetta at all.

She wore her black dotted Swiss, and even wore her mourning brooch; Agnes, who was of similar build, offered her one of her dresses, "In case you are in need of a little color." But Luna wore her widow's weeds. And not just to feel virtuous. The effect was quite the opposite: the dress made her feel mysterious, and a bit scandalous. And she realized, on a level hard to admit to herself, that she did not dislike the feeling.

Certainly, her history had given her a shine in the eyes of this new group. But when asked direct questions, about the murder, the newspaper stories, or the upcoming court case, she only smiled in sorrowful beatitude, though with a certain glimmer in her eye.

Agnes and Gertie had dressed very colorfully. Agnes wore a ruched red dress, and her upswept hair, barely contained, had red feathers pinned in it, her kohl still smeared and dark, her lips painted a deep crimson, dark against her pale powdered face.

Gertie wore a long, sleek frock of bottle-green velvet with a square neckline. It made her auburn hair and porcelain skin gleam; everything about her was so, so luminous, almost alien. Whereas Agnes showed a girlish mischievousness, Gertie was stately and serene, like a Grecian statue, except that her eyes seemed to see *everything*.

It surprised Luna to learn that Gertie and Edward were married. She had not placed them as being a couple, only friends. But they had been married for several years, Edward making a living as a lawyer and Gertie had a small but loyal following as a singer.

"She's very popular," Edward boasted, as he took out a small tin box with a sliding lid. He scooped something out with his pinky, and inhaled it up his nose, blinking several times before he continued. "She has fans, you know. Mostly men. I have to fend them away."

"Oh, don't go on like that, darling. I'm not that important."

"But it's true. She performs in character. *Incredible* transformations. That's how I fell in love with her! From the audience!"

"That's enough about me, darling." Gertie turned to Luna, focusing her clear, serene gaze straight onto her face. "Luna, tell us what your plans are."

"Yes! You should spend them with us, though. We're planning to go to Tangier next spring."

"Shhh! What did I just say?"

Luna, the champagne taking effect, was more forthright than usual. "I don't exactly know what my plans are. But one thing is for sure, I will need to make some money. I have been spending it all this past week, and I will soon have nothing left. I don't want to move back in with my family."

"Have you thought of returning to the stage?" Peter asked, looking at her gravely, considering. Maybe because he worked in stocks, he often had an assessing, calculating look to him when he fastened onto an idea.

"I don't know what I would rightly do! I am a magician's assistant. Before that, I was a seamstress."

"And did you like that?" His eyes so deep and dark, they made her fidget with self-consciousness.

"I liked it well enough, I suppose …"

"But you'd rather remain in show business."

"Well, I …" The words were coming out, just as they occurred to her. "I've considered it, half seriously, of course. But I would not want to do … what I did before. It has crossed my mind that perhaps I would like to be an actress. In the picture shows."

Agnes clapped. "How marvelous! You've such an expressive face. It makes a person take notice of you!"

Luna shrugged with an uncertain smile. The staff took away the oyster shells and brought in plates of lamb with corn fritters and sweet potato. Although it was lovely, she was not hungry at all. "I was thinking, when I was at the pictures recently, how nice it would be to live in California."

"Oh!" At this Agnes made a sour face. "I lived in California. I danced there for a while. I think it is a vile place, full of phony people who would stab you in the back as surely as they'd look at you."

"We should like to keep her in New York, right?" Peter said, holding out his wine glass to be filled. "That's where all the real excitement is."

"Yes! And you live in the Village, of all places. It is so

like the Left Bank!"

Edward gestured his fork at Luna. "Ever been to the Purple Pup?"

"No."

"The Will o' the Wisp?"

"I never really got out much. I was always working evenings."

"Well, we'll remedy that, won't we?"

After their meal, the others led her to the back of the hotel, where a placard stood next to an open door, which read, "The Magnolia Room."

In the shadowy light inside, a man played an upright piano and young people danced.

"This is the one laid-back part of the hotel where we can really dance," said Agnes. "There's one other room with music, but it is very formal."

"We prefer it here, where we can do our animal dances in *peace!*" Peter pinched her arm gently; she perceived he had followed her with his eyes all night, which made her uncomfortable because he gave no hint of what he was thinking.

"Animal dances? What might that be?"

In answer, Edward sprang forward and shouted, "Do the Grizzly Bear!"

As though on cue the pianist launched into a new song with a fast, spinning, tempo. This Luna knew vaguely to be "rag."

Edward led her onto the dance floor. "Do what I do! Go like this!" He held his arms up like wavering paws and lumbered back and forth. Luna, who was quite tipsy by now on champagne and "cocaine huffing" from Edward's tin, was helpless with laughter as she imitated him.

"And like this!"

He showed her how they could interlock their "paws," wrestling around in a clumsy sort of waltz. The others were gathered around them clapping in time and laughing. Every so often they would shout in unison, "It's a bear!"

Luna had never enjoyed such free-spirited fun since she was a small child, before her days were taken up with chores, in the days when her mother was still alive. It felt so good to spin around, and laugh, and to forget herself for once.

There were other animal dances, too. The Turkey Trot and the Bunny Hug. The Bunny Hug was most ridiculously scandalous; even she realized that, but she danced with both Edward and Peter, holding them by their arms and making small, thrusting, humping motions as they circled the room; it was all so silly that she did not feel embarrassed.

They danced for what felt like hours, and then made their way up to their suite of rooms and ordered a bottle of champagne. Peter and Agnes's room had a sofa and two chairs upholstered in apple green, and walls of pale pink stripes. All of this Luna dimly took in. It was late in the evening, and she had already drunk way too much. Her black widow's weeds were damp with sweat; she hadn't realized it at the time, but she had lost her mourning brooch, probably flung off during all of the wild dancing.

"If you want to do that again, come with us to the Purple Pup when we get back," Edward said, offering her the little tin box again. Luna declined; it made her heart race, like a hummingbird vibrating in her chest. The others all had a huff.

But she did drink another glass, a final one, to try to calm herself again after the boisterous evening. Agnes switched off all the lights but for a pair of silk-shaded table lamps with bead fringes. These put out a warm, golden light, and she settled down on the sofa.

"Or she might enjoy the art galleries," said Peter, settling across from her. "I am looking into buying art, myself. As an investment. I'm there a lot these days."

"Oh, you just enjoy watching those bohemian floozies. Those artists' muses," slurred Agnes, who sat beside Luna, close so that their arms were touching. She flicked off her dancing slippers and put her stockinged feet on the coffee table. She did not sound angry with Peter, only amused and indulgent.

"I don't know art, but I would like to learn," Luna said, stirring the beaded tassels of the lamp, making them click softly.

"You know who's *really* talented? You know who knocks me flat?" asked Edward. "Marcel Duchamp. You know Cubism? You should see this one painting I saw in France. *The Chess Players*. It as though ... as though he knows how to paint time passing. He shows the players in shifting positions, and it gives you the feeling that time has passed. And you can feel the intensity of the players thinking. He actually captured a *static* moment."

Peter seemed to be not listening at all to what Edward said, but was again gazing at Luna, fondly, lips parted beneath his mustache; Luna looked away, quickly, and said, "Sometimes it feels like time is racing by. Sometimes as though it is standing still. Time is a funny thing. A ... *slippery* thing, isn't it?"

"Oh, darling," said Agnes, taking off her feathered headpiece, and resting her curly head on Luna's shoulder, "You have been through so much, haven't you? Are you still suffering? Are you in very much pain?"

Luna's mind went blank, and she said, "I don't know. I don't know what I feel." And this was the truth.

It was somewhat of a shock when Agnes gently put her fingers under Luna's chin and tipped her face toward hers. Then she kissed her on the lips, not hard, but it was a long, lingering kiss. Agnes looked into her eyes when it was over, as though to see what her reaction would be; flustered, Luna looked down into her lap.

"Please don't be embarrassed, dear," said Peter, looking at her in his dark, avid way as he relit a cigar. "We are all just very open and free with each other. Very close and affectionate."

"I'm not offended … I just have never been kissed on the lips before. By a woman, I mean."

"You may find that you like it," Agnes said and stroked her hand.

Did she like it? It was nice to have human contact, at least. No one had held her or kissed her since that last time she had gone up to Sean's flat, that faraway spring day in Brooklyn when she had rushed up the stairs to his door, unannounced. What joy and fear she had held in her heart, then …

Gertie had put on a phonograph record, a waltz-like thing called "Meet Me Tonight in Dreamland" and swayed back and forth, her cigarette in its long holder trailing smoke. Edward settled back with his feet up, and said suddenly, apropos of nothing, "You know, Luna, there are no roads here."

"How do you mean?"

"No roads. In our world, you need to forge your own path. Do you know what I'm saying?"

She paused. "No."

"One must live in the gospel of the moment, I think is

how the saying goes. There is a lot of sensual beauty in the world, and it is not wrong to meditate on it, let the beauty sweep through you." He looked her straight in the eye. "There are many *lovely vices*."

All at once, Luna felt any resistance drain out of her. Edward's words were hypnotic. Agnes kissed her again, and she tried to give into it. Did it matter that this was a woman? Maybe all that mattered was that she was a friend. All of them, beautiful friends.

Peter moved himself to her other side, stabbing out the cigar in an ashtray. "You must have been feeling very lonely," he said, in a quiet voice. "And frightened. You mustn't feel that way anymore." He had lightly taken her hand. "Would it be okay if I kissed you as well?"

She closed her eyes and didn't move, assent enough. He kissed her lightly, teasingly. Luna turned more toward him, leaning into the kiss. Agnes rubbed her back at the same time, and suddenly a knife blade of desire flashed and flared inside her.

What happened next was later hard for her to recall exactly. What had been tense, relaxed into something fluid, organic. Confident hands unbuttoned the many tiny buttons with loops down the front of her dress. But she wasn't scared. It was as though she were inhabited by another person, a brave, worldly person, unafraid of anything. A person not unlike the others, in this beautiful room with its soft golden light, the whole scene replicated, flickering in the mirror hung on the opposite wall. She saw herself supine, her white body slowly emerging from the black dotted Swiss mourning dress. A lazy smile played about her lips.

Gertie's shadow swung through the periphery of her vision, still lost in her music. Edward, usually so loquacious, watched intently, quiet and very, very still, as though nothing could tear his attention away.

Somehow, this fact fed her bravery, and she turned to kiss Agnes again, such an odd sensation, at the same time as she enjoyed Peter's caresses.

Edward leaned forward, and murmured, like a man talking in his sleep, "What a proper whore you are, what a dirty little whore…"

And somehow, these words shocked Luna back into reality, aware that she was in a strange room, with people that she barely knew, and that she was half undressed.

She sat up with a start and grabbed up the dress that had been slipped down around her hips. Hurriedly, she scrambled to button up the dozens of tiny buttons. Oh, God, what would the church say? What would her father say? Oh, she was going to hell …

"Hey, now, what's the problem, Luna?" Peter asked, brows lowered over his eyes, face florid with blood.

"I … have to go. It's late."

"Edward," snapped Gertie, "Why can't you keep your damned mouth shut? You have embarrassed her."

"I couldn't help it, it wasn't my brain in charge. I was swept away in the moment."

"Luna," said Agnes. "It is okay. What we were doing was a natural, beautiful thing."

"Yes, but …" Dress mostly on, she scanned the room for her small velvet purse. Where was it? She wasn't so drunk as to forget her purse with her room key. Embarrassed, she wanted to bolt as quickly as possible. She snatched it up from the floor and ran.

"Will we see you tomorrow, then?" she heard Edward call just as the door closed behind her.

Down the back stairwell, so no one would see her, she

fumbled with the damned buttons, reeking of booze and smoke. Could barely make it without tripping.

Stupid, stupid. How could I be so stupid?

In the main lobby, she hurried past the desk person, head down. And then she was outside, breathing in the fresh night air in fits and gasps.

The path down to the cottages was narrow and winding but lit by small electric lamps. One, two, three. Third cottage down.

Never was she so relieved to have her own little space to retreat to. The place had been tidied up by the maids. Chintz cushions plumped, everything swept and polished. She would go straight to bed.

But first, she ran to the bathroom, just in time to vomit up a foul deluge. Oh God … she had never drunk that much in her life. The quaint, tidy room lurched and spun. She noticed dimly, behind her, that the maid had hung up her bathing costume on the shower rod on a hanger to dry, and it swung softly back and forth, like a silent reproach, a reminder of how this day of folly had begun.

And a long day it had been.

Finished, she pulled the flush cord and stumbled into her small bedroom that smelled of lavender sachets and fresh-ironed sheets. Not that she deserved such things. She kicked off her shoes, took off her dress, and hung it in the closet. The closet where she kept her valise.

The valise. Inside were her rosary beads – she could pray for God's forgiveness! What would her family think of her? The things they had been doing back in the suite were like the things she saw in the collection of dirty postcards that the Magician owned.

Still just wearing her underthings, corset and chemise and drawers, she pulled the valise out – but could not bring herself to open it.

Because she knew what was inside, though she had tried not to think of it this entire trip. Somehow wishing that if she did not see it, it did not exist anymore. That it would vanish into thin air, go back to the source of darkness from which it came. But it hadn't. It had remained there all this time, radiating a powerful and strange energy that clung to her, no matter what good times she tried to have.

But when she opened the valise, it was still there. The Magician's box. Box of light. Box of magic. Box of pain and everything terrible.

It was only that night that she felt bold enough to look at the box. For one thing, she was drunk. Another, she was so filled with shame, that perhaps, she thought, she deserved to look into the box as punishment.

Because she now had the key. The key they had taken from the breast pocket of her husband's torn blood-soaked shirt, along with the other effects they had given her at the morgue.

The box was the same as she remembered, covered in cracked leather with brass studs hammered around the edges. The size of a large dictionary. And so old. She marveled at the heft and weight of centuries as she held it. How many people had owned the thing? And what had happened to *them*? The Magician had said he had killed a man in the circus and stolen the box. But he might have been telling tales.

The large brass key, with all of its elegant scrolls and filigree, slid easily into the keyhole, and with a heavy *thunk*, the lock sprang open.

The crying of the latches as she lifted the lid: like something alive!

Smell of old newspaper. Lustre of red velvet. And the source itself.

The light didn't hurt to look into, not this time. Less scary now that it was just her, and she wasn't being forced. A strong radiating presence, it almost had an electric buzz and hum to it, not that she heard it, but she *felt* it, in her mind.

This light, this heat, and this hum, all contained multitudes: a life force. A force of restlessness, striving, ambition. Luna stared straight into it, though it was not pleasant, as if looking into a long distance, at the same time as a funnel tightened around her.

As a girl, she had taught herself that it was best not to try too hard to see things in their entirety. She learned to try hard *not* to see, to only look at the edges of things. To unfocus her eyes, and let a different truth reveal itself.

Just as she tried to unsee her mother in her pine coffin, the last time she saw her, before she was loaded onto the wagon and taken to the churchyard. Just like the Magician, her mother had looked so different dead. A stranger. Someone who did not know Luna or her grief. Lying in the box, wearing her best pink-sprigged dress with a cameo at the throat. But her lips so blue, her eyes very slightly opened to show the tiniest sliver of white, that horrified and repelled Luna.

Always, since then, she had not looked at things as they really were, a service to her soul.

But now, looking into the box of light, she knew deep inside that would change from this moment on. If she could look at this, the thing that frightened her most, she could look at anything.

She had taken the box with her on the train because deep down, she knew it belonged to her now.

Letting the strange secret light bathe her, seep into her, she knew something else to be true.

I am the Magician, now.

Twenty-Three

"Daddy wouldn't buy me a bow-wow. Bow-wow!"

A smoky haze hung over the crowd. The Sixpenny was a dinner theatre, though a darkish one, made up to look like a dive-ish "saloon" From their table near the stage, Luna had a perfect view of Gertie, mesmerized by her: her auburn hair slicked back into a bun low on her neck, she wore a man's white tie and tails, even a top hat which she took on and off and waved as a prop. Luna had never seen such a thing before in her life. Gertie did indeed resemble a lean and compact young man, though she still sang in a woman's voice, and went by the stage name of Miss Lady Gertrude.

"I've got a little cat, and I'm very fond of that, but I'd rather have a bow-wow-wow!"

Everyone sang along raucously with the bow-wows, and for this number, Gertie held and stroked a little black kitten with large green eyes. She sang in an arch, mincing way, with an ironic smile on her lips. Her face powdered very pale, her eyebrows penciled thin and lips rouged dark, she looked neither completely male nor female. She looked not of this world at all, but a being from another plane. But she was terribly fetching and attractive, and the crowd adored her.

She dressed as different male characters for her variety act and sang sly Victorian style songs. One character was a boy street urchin named Poor Lil' Petie, who in a cockney accent sang a song called "Dustbin Days." Another, a minister in robes who sang of going to London and getting lost and having his clothes stolen, which everyone laughed at. She also appeared a sailor who sang of his adventures chasing women on shore leave.

Luna sat with Agnes, Peter and Edward. She had stayed in touch with them despite that disastrous end to the evening in West Virginia. It was the first time they had all gone out together since they had returned to New York. Luna at first was too embarrassed to see them.

But once a little time had passed, and summer edged into fall, loneliness crept in. She lived alone, in a little walk-up on Cornelia Street. Not nearly as nice as her old apartment, no tree-lined streets or private entrance. The Sixth Avenue elevated train rattled where she lived now and laundry flapped from clotheslines. But she had access to the rooftop, where she could sit and let her hair dry after she washed it, and watch the vibrant September sunsets.

Gertie's set finished, she joined them at their table, dressed in her elegant evening jacket and tails. Peter lit her cigar, and she took languid puffs as she spoke; so many people came over to meet her, to tell her how talented she was.

Luna watched carefully, noting how at ease Gertie was in her own body. So complete was her confidence in her talent, and her place in the world. She smiled with benign radiance at each person who spoke to her. On the stage, she had been alternately serious, mincing, clownish. A chameleon. But now she was her soft-spoken, serene self.

She blew a kiss at Luna, once she had settled down to her drink. Luna, aware she'd been staring, grew flustered. But then she reminded herself that she was no longer the type anymore to *get* flustered.

At least, she did not want to be.

So she cleared her throat and said, "My God, Gertie. You were marvelous. Does it take a lot out of you? To be so many people up there?"

Gertie looked into her glass of neat whiskey, thinking. "No," she said at last. "I would say the audience gives *me* energy. Not the other way around."

"But do you ever … doubt yourself?"

She shrugged. "Maybe. When I was young and just starting out. But after a while, if you try to emulate something enough, you *become* that something." She gave Luna a smile of special significance.

Edward kissed Gertie on the cheek. "A lovely sentiment, darling." Leaning together, they looked like two dapper young men out on the town. It shocked Luna all over again to imagine that they were man and wife.

Luna did not go out anywhere else with them afterward but walked back to her apartment. She smiled mysteriously when they asked where she was going next.

"The Magician's Widow never tells," said Peter, waggling his eyebrows.

They walked her part of the way, and then parted in the street in a flurry of kisses. She liked her new friends, more than ever. She just did not want to end up in bed with any of them, as seemed to be the way with their crowd.

Sometimes the words *gilded moth* popped into her head out of nowhere. Words that used to hold a particular claustrophobic terror for her. But now they connoted something different. As though she had wrapped herself in a cocoon of golden silk, and when ready, she would unfurl, and metamorphose as another thing entirely, wings blazing like a church window.

Twenty-Four

… but whenever her father looked into her eyes, she retracted all over again, shrank into something small and inert.

Judgment in his eyes, his silence, the way he held his chin jutted out. They were all in the apartment in Hell's Kitchen, after church. Lil and Mary Catherine had made a stew, and it was the first time they had sat all together this way since Luna returned from her impromptu train trip.

Church … she had worn her mourning dress and kept her head down. But still, everyone had gazed at her, their eyes boring into her; she heard the whispers. "That's the one, the one from the papers!" a young girl had said quietly to another as they walked down the church steps to the sidewalk below.

Her face burned red, and her heart pounded as it sometimes did when she had an attack of fear. *This is what I left to get away from … but it was waiting for me the whole time.*

Luna's father, quiet under the best of circumstances, but now there was no mistaking the way he studied Luna as they sat around the table with family. She knew he was unhappy that she ran away without telling anyone, and wasted the last of her money on hotels and train fare. But when the people stared at her in church, she saw the shame in her father's eyes.

"I-I'm sorry to have worried you," she said to him when the others were busy talking, and the two of them silent; no one else was listening. "I just had to clear my head from my troubles."

"Ah. But ya can't run from yer troubles," he said, stonily. "Ya must atone for 'em."

"Atone … for what?" she asked, dreading the answer.

He pursed his lips and gave her a *look*. He thinks I'm a whore, a floozy, just like the rest of them.

"Pa? Pa."

But it was too late. Shaking his head, he stood up and walked down the hall, from which came the sound of his bedroom door slamming.

She felt a hand on her arm. Mary Catherine. "Don't mind him, Luna. He is only worried about you."

"But I sent a telegram as soon as I could, I—"

"It's not only that. He doesn't like that you're living on your own."

"But it's so crowded here, I didn't want to trouble—"

"T'isn't trouble."

"But I just …" Luna put her face in her hands. "I feel like I don't belong here anymore. Pa hates me."

"He doesn't. "

"He does. I see the shame in his eyes. And I saw the people looking at me at church."

"It's probably because of the news," Lil said, coming to join them. "It was in the paper this week that Sean was arraigned."

"Oh." Luna was not sure what that meant, and not sure she wanted to talk about it further.

But it was too late. At the mention of Sean's name, Cousin Patrick livened up and wedged his chair in next to Luna.

"Ol' James here?" he indicated his older brother, a raven-haired young man with dark, heavy brows and a knife scar across his cheek, "He went to visit Sean at Sing Sing. Ma said I wasn't of age, so I couldn't go, she won't let me do *anything*."

"Well. Isn't that a thing," Luna said nonchalantly.

"An' you know what he said? Tell Luna what Sean said, James."

Cousin James, always quiet and yet hot-headed at the same time, rolled his eyes to her without turning his head. "Sean says to pass along that he loves ya, and will always love ya, and is not one bit sorry to be in prison for the sake o' ya."

Luna did not know what to say. She realized her right hand clutched her left arm hard enough to make it go numb; she let go and said, "Well, that is something I cannot help."

James, surprisingly, smiled. "Aye. I've known 'im for years. Very intelligent when sober. A madman when he's langered. He used to get in fistfights, one time he was mad about something and he ripped the gas pipe from a pub wall and set it aflame, a huge fireball, holy *mother* …"

Patrick talked over James, eyes shining. "They have him in there, an' they know he's mixed up with the White Hand Gang, la. He could get off right now if he gave 'em the info they wanted. But Sean will *not* talk."

James nodded soberly, lighting a corncob pipe. "Sean is a man who is much respected. For his loyalty. And his talent. He is one very talented gangster. At the end, he was working with Dinny Meehan *himself*, under Manhattan

Bridge."

Luna sprang up to clear dishes, though not everyone had finished. "I don't want to be privy to any more information, thank you!" she said. Though a frightened little thrill ran up her spine at the word *gangster*. It was something she had always known, yet wouldn't admit to herself.

"But ya should be proud o' your boy!" cried Patrick indignantly. "The stuff he did was stout-hearted! One time there was this ship captain, didn't pay tribute? Sean set his boat on fire and cut its ties to the pier. We watched it burn as it drifted across the East River! And *laughed*, I tell ya! I was there! He let me help!"

James laughed as well, said, "Aye! And one time a longshoreman paid money to have this guy offed for not payin' his union dues. Sean shot the guy between the eyes, dumped 'em in the river, then went and 'ad his steak and kidney pie and a pint! Was nothin' to 'em!" he shook his head, then looked at Luna, serious, and pointed his pipe at her. "Ya know what? I was with 'em, that night of ya birthday dinner."

"Oh?" She peeped, keeping her head turned away.

"Aye. He'd been drinkin', and ya know what I said, about his temper. He was gettin' himself all worked up. He couldn't take it, that ya married a wop."

"He wasn't Italian! I've told people time and *time* again, he was a foundling. Probably Arab if anything."

"Well, in Sean's mind he was a wop, and treated ya terrible, and he hated 'em. But I think that dinner was the last straw."

"'Cause the restaurant was Italian, like!"

"*Quiet*, Patrick. Yes. It *was* a wop restaurant, and a fancy one at that, and he thought the Magician was takin' the piss outta our family by goin' there, and Sean was gettin' mad and actin' the maggot, and I tried to stop 'em, but ..." He shrugged, philosophically.

Throughout all of this, Mary Catherine listened, eyes large. But Lil came over and slapped her hand on the table. "I don't want you fellas talkin' anymore about this subject. You're upsetting Luna. And Mary Catherine is still in school, for heaven's sake."

Though Luna couldn't say herself whether she truly was upset; merely stunned. Remembering her lover, and the way he held her so tenderly, almost weeping with love for her. Such a kind, gentle man ... a killer dropping bodies into the East River? True, he never spoke to her of what he did with his "boys" but it was hard to reconcile that he could do such things.

She looked down and said nothing.

"Aw, Lil, Patrick and I mean no harm."

"T'is true. We just want Luna to know he loves her, la?"

"Well you do not *know* that he was any sweetheart of hers, do ya?"

"Yeah ... but ... but?" Patrick's eyes goggled, and his mouth moved, not saying anything more.

"That's all I have to say on the matter, so gladly drop it!"

"But Sean is a hero, la. A *hero*. He will *never* rat!" He looked at Luna, a rhapsodic expression on his young face. "And everyone in the gang knows ya are his girl. The gang will protect ya, too! Do anything for ya!"

"She is not his girl. She's a grieving widow who misses her husband."

But Luna had to cover her face to hide the smile that played about her lips at Patrick's foolishly earnest words. To imagine such things ...

"Sean could kill a man and be at the table for steak and kidney pie! Wont nothing to him to shoot the man who treats his girl bad! He is king of the gangsters. He—"

"ENOUGH!" Lil took away the bowl of stew in front of each young man and slammed them onto the counter. "I warned ya! Now there will be no more stew for either o' ya. Now out with ya!"

Twenty-Five

Luna got back her old job at the tailor's, even after so long. Everything about the place seemed the same. The same long room lined with bolts of cloth, the same creaking floors, the same grimy windows, even the same Russian women working at the tables beside her.

Everything was the same, and yet she had changed so much from the girl who had once sat at this desk and been beguiled by the young Magician and his gift of a white rose; harder now, her experiences had caused her to grow a protective shell over herself. Whether that was good or bad, she could not say.

These New York streets no longer cowed her: She had walked these city streets, and others, and knew her way. She walked with her head held high and knew to avoid eye contact.

And though she felt braver, she missed her previous girlish innocence sometimes. No longer did she have a child's faith in God's love and protection. And sometimes this gave her a most hollow feeling, that she was all alone now.

A good worker, though, she sewed even faster than she

had before. And if she finished a stack of work, she used that time to practice her magic surreptitiously at her work table.

The Magician had told her once that he had begun with small things, and built up strength and tolerance and skill little by little. So she chose for the first time to practice on her seam ripper.

It always sat in easy reach, just a small thing made of brass with engraved vines on the sides, quite tarnished from use. During quiet interludes, she would stare intently at it. At first, she thought she could impel the thing to move through force of will. By simply *wanting* to move it.

This proved to be ineffective, so after a while, she changed tack. Instead of forcing herself on the poor thing, she tried to be one with it. She concentrated on the essence of the seam ripper. The smudged brass of its casing, and the metallic tang it left behind on her fingers. Someone had told her brass was a mix of different metals. She imagined these metals running deep through the earth in their secret veins. *Focus, focus.* She looked at the small object and felt its connection to the enormity of the earth beneath her feet, and all of its mystery.

And that was when she felt the thing twinge, just a bit; although the movement was barely discernable, it made her heart leap for joy; she clapped her hand over her smile, but when she looked around the room, all she saw was an old woman in a plumed hat, comparing different shirtwaist patterns at the front counter. Two teenaged girls, whispered and admired a roll of lovely aqua crepe de chine; dust motes floated in a wide beam of light from the window.

The next day it rained, so foot business was slower, giving Luna more opportunities to commune with the seam ripper.

This time, instead of just trying to get inside it, she intertwined the essence of the object with the essence of *herself*; she thought of what looking into the box of light had awakened in her. A deep sense of longing, an impatience for life to move faster. A hunger in her bones to find her place in the world and be noticed. The dull ache of ambition awakened in her would not be silent.

I want … I want … I want … more.

Even though she was doing this thing, she couldn't exactly name what it was. Intuition led her. And it worked. This time the seam ripper not only twitched three times but lifted into the air. Not much, but just enough that it broke contact with the surface of the sewing table.

This time Luna did not just smile in surprised delight. This time, a deep, rich wonder flowed within her, a profound feeling. Those millimeters of space, between the small piece of brass and the scarred dark wood surface of the table, were the most beautiful things she thought she ever had seen. More beautiful than the cliffs of her homeland. More beautiful than seeing the Statue of Liberty as it beckoned across the blue waves at the end of her voyage. More beautiful than the freckles on her lover's muscular back.

As the rain pelted and lashed the windows outside, and motorcar tires hissed through large silver puddles, and ladies' voices murmured in Russian, she sat in the small circle of light from her lamp and felt something new in her young life: power. And it felt better to her than anything she had ever experienced.

As though in sympathy with these feelings, the seam ripper lifted up ever so slightly higher, and joy bloomed in Luna's chest like a blossoming rose. She laughed just one breathless, high note. And the instrument gently dropped back to the surface.

Twenty-Six

30 September 1911

My Darling Luna,

Would it amuse you very much to know that I am a shoemaker now? I have gone from building ships to building women's shoes, and aye, I am quite good at it! I have a good eye and a steady hand, and I can cut out the leathers, stitch them, attach the top-pieces to the heel, scrape them, sand them, tack them, put all them drobes together so nice, like that the guards all say, "Damn boy, you are a regular industrial machine." And they give me tobacco in gratitude, so it all works out nice, you see.

I must have made hundreds of pairs by now, but one style in particular made me think of you. It was a pair I made in ivory leather. It had the low pointy heel, pointy toes, and two straps that crisscrossed across the instep and buttoned. The first time I made one of those, it was in a small size like you wear, my darling. When I finished it, I held it in my hand and imagined slipping it onto your little foot. I do love your feet, I never realized it until that moment. I held that shoe and it was like to make me, a grown man, start to weep. But I did not. I wanted to keep that shoe all to myself, to feel connected to you. But I can't take a shoe like that to my cell. That tiny, stacked wooden heel could dig real nice into a man's eye! I would be flogged if I was found to have such a thing.

So I remember you in my mind instead. I don't need nothing but that. You've never seen such a place as this. My cell is seven feet deep, and with a width of thirty-nine inches. As for height, I'll say I can just stand up. If I stand on me tiptoes, me head brushes the ceiling.

But don't feel sorry for me, darling Luna. A man gets by, he does. You should see me, I wear striped pajama-type things, with a matching striped cap. We all do. The men here are all shapes and sizes and come from all different places. But the thing they have in common is every man has scars. Some on their faces. Some on their bodies. But all scarred, somewhere. The guard checks us every morning for fresh scars, fresh blood, and if you got them, you get flogged, or worse.

Do you know where the name Sing Sing comes from? It is from Indian words. Words that mean "stone upon stone." Can you believe that! It like to made me laugh out loud when I heard that! This place is built on a big rocky slope. But it also describes how a man gets to thinking about his life, and getting through, day by day, hour by hour, second by second. Stone by stone.

I am not sad, Luna. They give each man a Bible when he comes here, but that ain't what gets me through. What gets me through is believing the things I did were right and true. I take strength in the feeling of loyalty and brotherhood I feel for me fellow Irishmen. I will never let them down, no matter what they do to me. And me love for you, even more, makes me feel strong and alive and ready to face whatever the day brings me. I dream of you constantly. You loom larger in my life than God did when I was a little boy and went to church. God scared me then. God doesn't scare me anymore.

I have always been a man of strong emotions. At times it seems I have felt more passion than the average bloke, and it is hard to control. I am sorry if my actions have caused you pain, or infamy. That was never my intention. It was just my love for you was overpowering, and drove me to do what I had to do to protect your honor. I am the youngest of six, all sisters I had. Me mam is an angel from heaven. Me father is a brute. I was aye but thirteen the first time I busted him in the face for hurting me mam. The fear in his eyes at that moment gave me life. And from then on I vowed always to protect the women I love.

So you see, I am unrepentant, and I am willing to pay my debts. It is not so bad here. I work in the factory and I do it well. They make all kinds of things here. Cabinets. Cane seating. Saddles. I make shoes. I smoke when I can. They let us run out in the yard a little bit. They say it used to be worse around here, each man vowed to silence. God help him if he made a sound, he could be strung up like a hog or subject to what they call "the bath" which I won't get into.

I have found here and there a good Irishman to befriend, both guards and prisoners. They know me name and show me kindness. That is why I am able to write you this letter, they gave me the pencil and paper because they know I must speak to you. James will deliver me letters to you. James is a good bloke but don't believe everything he tells you about me, he likes to tell tales, he's a right divil!

I hope that this letter finds you happy, dear Luna, and that you know that I love you above all others. Please wait for me, I know I will get out of here one day, or else die with your name on my lips. I hope you are not frightened at the way your life has changed. You must not be afraid. We are both immigrants. It takes a certain kind of bravery to cross an ocean, not knowing what lies on the other side. Will they hate you? Will they turn you away? Or will they accept you as one of them?

I remember the time you told me that part of you died on that voyage and that you were reborn a stranger as you entered New York Harbor. Remember, we can always be reborn, again and again! I am twenty-two years old and I intend to live many lifetimes, one of them will be with you! I will give you the life you deserve, my queen, and you will banish from your mind any memory of that brute who will not be named.

Until then, you have the protection of your family, both of

blood and those loyal men of the White Hand, who are everywhere and watch over you benevolently. Do not cry, my love, be strong! I will see you in the courtroom, at the very least. Please send your photograph with James. Until then,

Yours in eternal devotion,
Sean

Luna held the pages in her hand, onionskin paper, crinkly to the touch. The words had been written in smudged pencil, hurriedly, she guessed, as the penmanship was sloppy and the lines tended to slant at an angle. And the words themselves got bigger as the letter went on, until the word *devotion* was written double-sized, and darker, the pencil lead gouged in as though stabbed into the paper.

She had accepted the letter from James as they were leaving church, and she had been careful to show no expression on her face either way. But she had eagerly pulled it out as soon as she was alone at home. Now that she had read it, she wasn't sure what to think. It seemed almost as though Sean had been writing to a stranger; she didn't feel a connection. With a pang of guilt, she admitted to herself that she did not spend a lot of time thinking of Sean these days. Not nearly as much time as he evidently thought of her.

She folded the letter back into quarters with trembling fingers; she wavered, not knowing what to do with it. The tightly folded paper felt full of energy, like contents under pressure that might detonate. She didn't feel right throwing it in the bin. Neither did she feel that she could keep it in her rooms. She held it between her fingers, frozen and staring into space.

At last, she decided to keep the letter, but in a place where it would be hidden from view. From a shelf she took down a book, one Gertie had given her, written by a French woman named Colette, which Luna had not yet had time to read. She tucked the letter deep into the center of the book, and put it back on the shelf, breathing a sigh of relief.

But when she tried to sleep at night, bits and fragments of the letter reverberated through her head. *I cut out the leathers, stitch them ... stone upon stone ... the White Hand, who are everywhere, and watch over you benevolently ...*

Not one day after reading Sean's letter, another letter came for her in the mail, this a short one on elegant cream stationery emblazoned with the initials A.M.G. at the top:

Dearest Luna,

Won't you come out with us the evening of October tenth? I have a wonderful surprise for you. Peter and I know a lady, a very remarkable lady named Aimée Crocker. She has just returned to New York after traveling in the Far East, and she is giving a party. I have told her all about you and she would like you to come.

Her parties are not very formal, but they are legendary! She is an heiress, but a very enlightened one, and she loves to be convivial and have a swell time. She once gave a treetop party in Paris. Here in New York, she hosted a Salome dinner, and at a café, she threw a "snake ball!"

That was before we were lucky enough to know her, though. This one will be a smaller affair, given in her home uptown. Oh, please do come, darling! Peter and I will pick you up at seven if you say yes!

Love,
Agnes

Twenty-Seven

And she did say yes, with some trepidation. Lately, she had been keeping to herself, practicing her magic compulsively, and trying to build up her strength. But the magic took a lot of energy out of her. She wasn't sure about going to someone's grand home. She had never met an heiress and did not know what a "snake ball" was. But she did not want to disappoint her new friends, so she wrote back a short note saying yes, and on the evening of the tenth, Peter and Agnes came to pick her up in their dark green touring car.

The building was five stories high, of blinding-white limestone. French windows, stone balconies, carved panels of fruit, ribbons, and cherubs in the spaces between floors; it was certainly the most impressive mansion on West 56th.

What am I doing here?

Now, looking up at this grand building, Luna felt somewhat out of sorts, dressed in a way that was new to her. A long loose skirt, a white peasant blouse, and a fringed and embroidered shawl she had bought at Chinatown. She also wore strings of glass beads around her neck, and though she was not brave enough to wear her hair down, she wore it in a braid that coiled softly around the sides of her face, most of her curls escaping.

Agnes was not afraid to wear her hair down and wild, and she wore a long purple crushed velvet tunic and pointed gold silk slippers. Around her neck was a large pendant of faceted amethyst. "You look fantastic, Luna! No more widows' weeds for you!"

"I don't think anyone cares about mourning anymore, honestly."

"You look like a gypsy princess!"

Luna blushed, but with pleasure. She had studied the way women dressed in the salons and clubs and coffeehouses, hungry to emulate them. They looked so bright and enchanted. Maybe if she looked the part, she would feel it, too.

As they rang the bell, Peter put a hand on her waist. "We met Aimée when she and Jack used to go slumming in the Village with Chuck Connors. Aimée always says 'Chuck silently rules the underworld.' Isn't she the most?" He laughed, but Luna did not know what to say. "Don't be nervous, dear, they will love you."

A Japanese man, his hair pulled back in a low ponytail, answered the door. He wore a smart uniform of black with gold braid. He made a small bow, and with elegant gestures of his hands, ushered them into the front foyer.

All sounds of activity emanated from one of the front rooms, where they were led. A large room, with a heavy blood-red carpet, velvet sofas with fringes, it had a bewildering array of curiosities. Large metal bird statues of cranes flanked the fireplace. Rainbow-hued Moroccan lanterns, stone Buddhas, a gilt-palace birdcage. Indian chests of drawers brightly shellacked and set with patterns of inlaid bone. And everywhere, depictions of snakes.

Paintings, statues, coiled snake snuff boxes. A stone boa constrictor leered at Luna with a knowing look in its eye …

Lost in contemplation of the room, Luna stared into the birdcage at a set of tiny parakeets, when the servant who had shown her in came around with a tray of drinks. "Sake," he said quietly.

"Try it, it's Japanese. Rather like white wine," Agnes said, appearing at her side.

Luna sipped it. It was strong and clear and cold and tasted of apples.

"There, now. Come along and let's meet Aimée."

Agnes led her through a throng of people, among whom a pair of grinning bulldogs wandered. This was a varied group of people, not all of them wealthy looking either. Some dressed elegantly, as were Peter and Agnes. Others looked downright shabby, with worn shoes and crumpled clothes. One man had a long gray beard, a velvet waistcoat, and a hungry, wolfish expression on his face; he looked at Luna with frank curiosity, and she hurried to look away and follow Agnes.

"Aimée?"

A woman standing at the center of a conversing cluster turned around.

She looked to be in her mid-forties, a woman Luna would describe as "handsome," but not inordinately beautiful. She was somewhat broad, with a wide jaw. At first glance, she looked about like any other well-to-do lady of middle age and privilege.

But close up, there was much more to see. Draped with strings of pearls, which clicked and glistened in the warm lamplight, she also had pearls strung in her dark up-do. Though her silk dress was somewhat conservative, the sleeves were three-quarter, displaying the tattoos on her lower arms.

Most striking of all, though, was her demeanor. She radiated keen intelligence and had a way of looking straight at things, as though she could see right into them, seeking forth riches. She gazed boldly into Luna's face, saying nothing. And yet it did not seem rude. She had a child's openness and lack of self-consciousness.

"Aimée, this is my friend Luna who I have told you so much about."

"Yes. I know who she is." Shockingly, Aimée held up her hand for Luna to kiss it; Luna did so, noting the multitude of diamonds glittering on her fingers.

Aimée continued to look at her, mutely, and then said, "I have seen you, you know. On the stage."

"Oh?"

"Yes." She smiled sadly. "I saw you, in that filmy white dress likes a bride, hanging in midair above the stage. It made me feel bad for you. You looked as though you were caught in a spider's web."

Luna said nothing, her face suddenly slack.

"Don't take it that way, dear. You look different now. More alive. Has the press bothered you terribly?"

"No. I, um, avoid the papers. I traveled for a bit, after … what happened."

Aimée blinked, head held regally. "I am a recent widow too, did you know that?"

"No."

"My husband, Jack, died in this very house. Blood poisoning, officially. He was in the music business."

"Oh?"

"Ragtime. You may know his songs, silly things, but they seem to bring people such joy. Do you know 'Waldorf Hyphen Astoria'?"

"I am not sure."

"'He's My Soft Shell Crab on Toast'?"

Speechless again, Luna did not know if this woman was having fun with her.

But Aimée shrugged it off. "No matter. We had our fun together, Jack and I. When he died, I traveled, as you did. A trip to the Far East. Not a terribly long trip, though. I have just got back. Travel is *healing*, don't you find?"

"It can be very … educational." She did not want to share that she had just ridden blindly on a train with no destination. She could not let Aimée Crocker, world traveler and socialite, see how uncosmopolitan Luna was. She hurried to change the subject. "When you saw my show, did you enjoy it?"

Aimée pursed her lips, lost in thought for a few moments. "I was intrigued. I knew what I was seeing was *real*."

"Yes. It was real."

"But your husband, I thought, was enthralled to a demon."

"E-ex*cuse* me?"

Aimée shook her head. "Don't mistake me. The show was mesmerizing. It was the talk of New York. I saw a woman faint dead away when he plunged a knife into you. People whispered that your husband was a genius, he would usurp Houdini himself. But I suppose I took a different tack. I was amazed but disconcerted. So much so, that when we went home, I burned incense, and set out a food offering by my door, to keep the evil spirits at bay."

Luna looked at her, again not sure if it was all a joke. But Aimée looked deadly serious. She pulled up one of her sleeves and held out her arm for Luna to see.

There were many things inked on Aimée's arms. A

Japanese beetle. Two snakes intertwined around the initials "JG." But it was one in particular that she pointed to, on her upper arm. The head of a terrifying creature, with gnashing teeth and a hungry, coiling tongue, like a serpent. It had three eyes, wide open with flames licking out of them.

"My goodness," said Luna, hesitantly. "It's … um …"

Aimée laughed merrily. "It's okay, Luna. Say what you think!"

"Why, it's quite terrifying. What is it?"

Aimée rolled her sleeve back down. "That, my dear, is Mara. Mara is a demon written about in Buddhist texts."

"I did not know that Orientals believe in demons."

"Well, scholars wonder if he was meant literally or figuratively. Mara was the demon who attacked Buddha under the Bodhi tree, to try to prevent him from becoming enlightened." She looked into Luna's eyes now, her face very close, her eyes heavy-lidded, but burning with a deep fire. "Mara is the ruler of desire and death. Once a human is in his possession, Mara will destroy them. With violence. Sensory beauty, pleasure. Mockery."

"And you think my husband was in bondage to this … Mara?"

Aimée raised an eyebrow. "It is my inclination to think so. That rapt expression on his face. Those heavenly powers in his fingertips. And you, poor child, felt the brunt of all of it. Helpless."

Luna blushed and looked away, almost swooning from shame. She tried to focus her gaze on something, anything else. Full of people, fascinating people dressed in velvets, dressed in rags, all of them scintillating and alive, they moved through this large elegant room full of rare and beautiful, but dead, objects.

She no longer saw it all as it was; everything in this remarkable room had shrunk, contracted. Only shadows moved about them. She and Aimée seemed to be the only ones in the room.

Aimée smiled kindly and put a hand on hers. "I know these must be painful memories for you."

"Oh, I'm all right. I'm just—"

"You're young. Very young. And that part of your life is over now. We all make mistakes. To learn from them." She threw back the chinchilla stole she wore as casually as a bed jacket; she had an inward-looking smile on her face. "I have had three husbands. My first divorce was *all* over the press. Humiliating at the time. But now?" She shrugged sanguinely.

Transfixed again Luna said, "Did you love your husbands?"

Aimée smiled as if reminiscing. "I only loved Jack, truly. But the other two gave me a wealth of experience. I wouldn't begrudge them that. They were both seafaring men. That's how I became inclined to tattoo myself. Like a sailor."

Aimée smirked at her mischievously, and Luna flickered a smile in return before she fell into a despairing mood again. "Well, I don't know if I can survive my mistakes as elegantly as you have, Mrs. Crocker. For one, I haven't money ..."

"Yes, but you have spirit. I can see auras, you know. Yours is powerful. Electric blue and soft gold. I think anything you want to achieve, you can."

"Well, I—" Luna stopped herself for a moment, but unable to hold back. "I haven't told anyone this. But I want to become a magician myself."

"Oh?" Aimée cocked a dark penciled eyebrow.

"Yes! I can do it, too. I'm learning, that is. First, I levitated a seam ripper. Then I kept practicing. Now I can change a glass of water into ice. You see, the trick is—"

"Darling!" Aimée hissed, unexpectedly fierce, gripping her arm. "Listen to me." She looked her straight in the eye. "I want you to be very careful."

"Why?"

"Because ..." She glanced around, and then took her into a secluded corner of the room, near a large potted palm in a blue-and-white Chinese vase. "You are working with some strong forces. It is important to stay balanced. *Grounded.* Do you know what I am saying to you?"

Luna gaped at her, at a loss.

"Think of it! Think of what happened to your husband. I saw him. He was a conduit to large and mysterious *forces.* He was not careful and became a slave to it. Slave to adulation. Power." She abruptly raised her sleeve and pointed to her tattoo again. "Do you know, dear, why I have the face of Mara inked on my skin?"

"No ... why?"

"As a daily reminder. To stay vigilant. Or the ruler of desire and death will *destroy* you." She drew back, looking Luna up and down appraisingly. "You must be strong, spiritually, if you are to practice magic. Your husband was a weak man. And that is why death and violence found him."

The two women looked at each other for a few beats; Luna thought of the box of light that waited for her at home, burning its secret fire only for her. More and more the box was like her very own heart and soul, giving her strength. Could Aimée even guess about such a thing?

Luna drew upon that strength and sustenance now, and raised her head and said, "I *am* strong, Mrs. Crocker."

"Aimée. I am your friend, Aimée."

"*Aimée.*" She tried to smile bravely. "I intend to be a great magician, and I will not be felled by any demons, I promise. Mother Mary protects me always."

"Well, Godspeed, darling. I do wish you well. Mother Mary is a loving goddess. I do so *adore* Catholicism. The saints and the candles and beads. Ceremony is essential to the *soul.*"

"I go to church every Sunday with my family."

"Well. Be prepared if your church is not exactly accepting of your intended occupation."

"My family will never abandon me." Though she remembered the shame in her father's pale eyes and the way he turned away from her. The memory ran through her heart like one of the Magician's silver knives. Except this time she felt the pain.

Aimée took a cigarette from a silver case on a side table, put it onto an ivory holder and struck a match. With satisfaction, she looked up into the plume of smoke, as though she were perfuming the room with wafts of enlightenment.

Then she turned back to Luna and said, "I understand the call of the stage, myself. I'm rehearsing for the Follies Bergère Theatre. I am to be in a vaudeville piece. A bit of satire entitled "Hell," with music by Irving Berlin. You *must* come to opening night."

"Yes." Luna was overwhelmed by the sheer amount of dissonant information imparted to her this evening.

Aimée, as if she sensed this, gave her a little pat. "Anyhow, welcome to my home, dear girl. I would invite you again and again, but I think I shall be moving to Paris in the near future. I miss Jack so much it is hard to be here in this house."

"I understand."

"If you will excuse me …" Across the room, the two bulldogs were growling at each other over a dropped canapé. Aimée clapped her hands. "Dicbutau! Boola Boy! Stop that!"

Luna took the opportunity to go back into the party at large. Agnes stood in one corner of the room, talking to the wolfish-looking man in the velvet waistcoat.

"Luna, dear, come over! This is Abraham. He's a most talented poet."

The man eyed her again, almost leering. After shaking his hand, Luna said, "I think I shall fetch myself a drink."

"Please, allow me," said the wolf man with a flourish and a bow. As he disappeared into the crowd, Agnes grabbed her arm and pulled her close:

"I was watching you two! Everyone was. You and Aimée looked to be in the *deepest* conversation."

"She is very nice. And extremely, well … interesting."

"Yes. That. To say the least. She certainly took an interest in you." Agnes looked at her coquettishly. "So what did you speak about?"

"Oh. Nothing too much. Widowhood. Dealing with the press. We have that much in common."

"I just knew you two would get along. And she knows *everybody*." She leaned closer, her eyes somewhat unfocused from drinking too much sake. "She can help you get another husband. A rich one."

"I'm not sure I'm up to that right now."

"But you will be. You will marry someone rich and elegant, and then you can travel the world just like Aimée does."

Even hearing these words, Luna had a queasy recollection of Sean and his avid jailhouse letter: Those loyal men of the White Hand, who are everywhere, and watch over you benevolently.

The wolf man came back with the drinks, not sake this time, but something called a gin fizz, and they continued exchanging pleasantries until there was the sound of someone stirring the keys of a piano in another room, and the general movement of people toward the sound.

This room had enormous candelabra, whose dangling prisms fired rainbow sparks in the lamplight across small groupings of chairs and sofas, and in one corner a gleaming baby grand piano.

"Everyone. Everyone!" Aimée called through cupped hands. "Enrico is going to sing for us now!"

Enrico! Enrico! The name tumbled through the room, said with delight and wonder.

Peter whispered into her hear, "Enrico Caruso. He is very famous, a great tenor. He sings at the Met. Aimée's good friend ..." His breath tickled her ear, his hand again clutched at her waist. "We are all very lucky to see him, believe me."

Aimée bent down to kiss the cheek of a large man in an elegant suit at the piano bench. He had dark, shadowy eyes and bold, dark eyebrows that met in the center. But his expression was warm and humorous.

"Everybody!" Aimée scanned the room with a brilliant smile. "Please welcome Enrico."

Silence followed scattered clapping, and then the pianist struck the opening chords. A somewhat melancholic sound: a slow melody, quiet and understated, then Enrico started to sing:

> *"Una furtiza lagrima*
> *Negli occhi suoi spunto*
> *Quelle festose giovani*

Invidiar sembro
Che piu cercando io vo?
Che piu cercando io vo?"

He sang quietly at first. But then his voice gained wind like a full sail. It was like velvet, rich and intense, manly yet full of feeling and empathy. Though Luna did not know what words he sang, the emotion coursed through her.

"Che piu cercando io vio?"

The power of it infiltrated her very bones. Without Luna realizing it, tears trailed down her cheeks. The song went on, and time stopped, and the emotion of the song built and built unbearably, until at last he reached the crescendo of the last line:

"Si puo morir, si puo morir d'amour!"

Thunderous applause at the end; Enrico stood and made a few small bows, held up his hands. So strange, he looked like someone's funny uncle, not someone who produced such heavenly sounds. People gathered around him, blocking him from sight.

She still held her drink, forgotten, in her hand. Peter went over to join the throng around Enrico; Agnes turned to her, beaming.

"Wasn't he so amazing? If you hear him through the gramophone, it's not the same. The hiss and the little scratches. It's a whole different experience, live!" Something about Luna's face gave her pause, her brow furrowed. "Are you quite all right, dear?"

"Yes, I'm fine. Why do you ask?"

"You just look a little overwhelmed. And you are crying?"

Luna tried to smile through her tears. "Oh, it's nothing. Just a bit swept away by the evening."

Agnes kept looking at her. "What *else* did you talk to

Aimée about? Did she try to sweep you up into her Eastern philosophies?"

"No. Well, maybe a little."

"She means well. She's very intelligent."

"It was all fine. *This* was all fine. I just need to be going now, I think."

"But we've hardly been here!"

"That's okay. I go in to my job tomorrow morning."

"Oh, bother that job!"

Luna pulled her fringed shawl tighter around herself. "Please thank Aimée for me. She's busy right now."

"At least come to tell Peter goodbye?"

"Tell him for me. I don't want to cause a fuss."

"Very well." Agnes kissed her on the cheek, and Luna smelled her perfume, like incense and spices. "Will you get a cab?"

"I think I may walk a while. I'm a bit overheated."

And at last, she broke free and slipped through the front foyer and onto the street. It wasn't very late yet, and there were still many people walking the streets, but Luna, alone in her own world, felt free to savor all that she had seen and heard at the party.

It had rained since she arrived, and the lamplight reflected in quivering puddles in the streets and off the glistening asphalt. Luna was still filled with Enrico's song. There was such sadness in it, and such longing, but the final line had been uplifting, as though he were full of hope and thanks.

Si puo morir, si puo morir d'amour!

Life looked bigger and brighter now, and so full of beauty that her vitality returned to her, and she wanted to skip and race through the streets, twirling her skirts and jumping luminous puddles.

Even in her elation, though, every so often she had an unbidden flash in her mind's eye, back to that terrible demon with the bulging eyes and gnashing teeth. Mara. Though just a creature of ink on a wealthy woman's skin, the image had penetrated her mind, and she could not unsee it. Devourer of souls, ruler of desire and death. The thing that would now lurk in her nightmares, the thing she could not help turning away from.

Twenty-Eight

No matter how much Luna tried to clean it, the reflection in the dark, spotted mirror was dim and hazy. Full-length, with an ornate gold frame, it had no doubt once hung in an elegant home. But the silver had crumbled away in large spots, leaving patches of opacity.

She had bought it, cheap, from a cluttered junk shop around the corner. It now stood propped against a wall in her small living room.

Looking into it, she saw the foggy impressions of the sad little room, which had come furnished with a worn mohair sofa that smelled of damp, a scarred dark wood table, and a rickety, crooked brass lamp. Farther back were the blurred images of the wooden icebox and tiny gas stove range that made up her kitchen.

And in the foreground, herself, rendered ghostly and featureless. Oh well, she thought, it wasn't a perfect mirror, but it would serve its purpose.

She brought the brass lamp a bit closer, brightening things as best she could. Then took a deep breath.

Luna flattened herself against the front door, then practiced how she would walk onto a stage. Head held high, back straight. But where she used to smile broadly, when joining her husband on stage, she went for a different effect now, keeping her face still and implacable. Serene.

No, not like that. It made her look too still, too withheld. Even fearful.

She thought back to watching Gertie on the stage, singing her cabaret. Had *she* smiled? Yes, she had. And it did not look false, neither did it look ingratiating. Her face had been aglow with a beatitude that could not be faked. Gertie had that ease and grace in her bearing that was genuine, and the audience had responded to it. *Luna* had responded to it.

I must try again.

Back again against the front door. This time she took a deep breath in, and centered herself. Imagined that she was sure of herself, and her talents, and her ability to make the audience fall in love with her.

But I'm weak. I'm a ragged little immigrant, in a land where I don't belong. Everyone will see through me, for the fraud that I am.

These voices played through her head in a loop, tiring her, enervating her. Binding her in ropes of despair.

Looking up at the wretched, stained and patched ceiling, though, quiet music came into her head. The sound of a piano and the swell of Enrico's voice. She found it helped if she remembered how it felt, witnessing art and pure beauty in its rawest, living form.

This way, she lost herself for long enough to walk across the small room, like a woman about to sing an aria.

The woman in the mirror followed her instruction, and stood front and center, spread her arms wide as though she had all the love and bounty in the world to share with the invisible audience; a smile on her face as though she knew all the secrets of the universe, and eager to share them.

After turning upstage and down, she pulled forward a wooden chest, pretending a stage assistant had done so. Slowly, she opened the chest, full of fabric pieces, bolt ends and remnants that they had let her take home from work. Many were of silk, in solid colors and floral and dot prints. Some were organza or tulle. All of them light and airy. She had spent the night before trimming them and hemming the edges.

Luna stood over the open trunk and paused, seeking the center of herself. Because she *had* to reach deep down into her center, or the magic wouldn't work. It made her wonder if she were quite ready yet, to show her act to the world, aware of some hesitation between thought and effect, like the space between heartbeats or the pause between breaths.

She called forth upon the nerves in her hand, the synapses in her brain, her very life force, the life deep within her that made her Luna.

Simultaneously, she had to become one with the fabric. She concentrated on a sky blue piece of raw silk, always the one she started with. She imagined the silk fibers, and the delicate strands produced by a living, breathing thing: a moth. She knew that there were ladies in Chinatown who had trays of moths they kept warm and healthy and fed. They snacked on mulberry leaves, she learned. Because only a happy, healthy moth would produce good quality silk threads, strong and durable.

Focus: the plump, healthy moth, thrumming with life in its tray. The silken threads, strong but light as air. The blueness of the dye, saturated, bright and essential. Blue as the sky on a blazing autumn day, when anything could happen.

Focus. If she concentrated hard enough she could hone her focus to a bright burning shaft of light, strong enough to pierce the reality of the object she looked at, and then, slowly, the magic poured forth, like the soft rainbows thrown off by a prism: the most wonderful feeling of all. The birthing of a miracle. No man could ever make her feel the way she did when magic filled the room like invisible music. It made joy fill her to the brim so that she could hardly stand it, like a beautiful dream from which she did not have to wake.

The bit of blue silk stirred and unwound itself from the other colors in the trunk. Up, up, at first hanging down like something pinned to a clothesline. Her mind flashed to a clear spring day in Ireland and her mother pegging up the sheets and petticoats, turning around to hear something Luna said, hand shading her eyes from the dazzling sun, laughing in response, her cheeks pink and hair wild in the wind.

Higher the silk lifted. The one good thing about the apartment was its high ceilings, the more space to practice in!

The silk undulated, like a flag flapping at the top of a pole. Then slowly it spiraled around and turned in on itself, creating different shapes.

One by one, the other fabric pieces rose up to join it, at first each doing its own unhurried thing, before coordinating like a high wire act full of acrobats. Luna stood very still, her eyes fixed, rapt, forgetting herself entirely. This was always the point when the magic was fully born.

The energy increased, until all of the fabrics, sky blue, forest green, tiger orange, tulip purple, spun into a multicolored kaleidoscopic blur, dizzying to look at. Once they reached a crescendo, she slowed them down inchmeal, and then bid them be still. Then each lowered, one by one, back into the trunk.

She closed the latch, then remembered her imaginary audience. She looked into the dark and fogged mirror, smiled beatifically, and then gave a short, modest bow.

She stood straight and closed her eyes. The magic rushed through her now, like a train barreling down a tunnel, around twists and turns and bends, unstoppable. Luna gave in to it, joyfully. Raising her arms, she lifted herself little by little into the air. Energy swirled and churned in her solar plexus, where she kept it centered, building and building until she moved higher and higher. This was different from when the Magician lifted her up against her wishes. The freedom from gravity felt delicious. She did not lay prone like a corpse this time. She worked with the current, and danced with it.

Never a dancer until now, Luna pirouetted like a ballerina, she leaped and turned with pure happiness, though she remembered the audience and kept her face still and assured. Time, at that moment, wasn't working against her, neither plodding nor racing. It was working *through* her. In the air, time was suspended

Up, up, she rose, until only the very tips of her toes were all that reflected in the mirror. And then, nothing.

She touched the molded ceiling with her fingertips, and connected with many places and many times: a child running across the moors of her homeland, under a sky that stretched to the heavens, or rocking the hens to sleep as her mother sat with her, singing a "My Lagan Love" in a crooning voice. It was possible to be all places at once, the true magic.

Leisurely, she lowered herself carefully back down until

her feet reached the creaking floorboards. The hard part was judging the exact spot to land without looking, she put her arms out to her reflection, gave a wide and genuine smile, and bowed deeply.

Twenty-Nine

She had not been to the Beaumont Theatre in nearly six months, but it felt so much longer. Everything she remembered about it was the same, the grand arches and marble pillars in the front. The same stained-glass windows, and gargoyles guarding the entrance. But something about it had shrunk, somehow. It had been so intimidating, the first time the Magician had brought her there. Back when she was a different girl.

Past the lobby, to a small, unassuming door in the back, that led up a staircase to the offices. She had a flashback of the last time she had been up these stairs. Mr. Klein had shown her the new poster for The Gilded Moth.

Her throat instinctively tightened up as she approached his door, which was ajar. There came a sound of typing, and Mr. Klein singing under his breath, "Let me call you sweetheart …"

She wrapped once, on the doorframe, and peeked her face around shyly. "Excuse me, Mr. Klein?"

Startled, he looked up over his metal spectacles, as though he couldn't place her. His fingers stilled on the typewriter keys. Recognition dawned over his features, and he smiled warmly. "Luna! My dear!"

He came over to her, embraced her. He was in his shirtsleeves, with arm garters. Several stacks of paper blew down from the piles on his desk, the entire room brimming with papers, flyers, and unopened mail. "I meant to call on you but I don't know where you are now! Are you living with your family?"

Instinct told her to answer, "Yes, I am."

He held her at arm's length, to look at her. "Well, I must say you're looking well, in spite of circumstances. I'm still in shock, I tell you. To have lost one of our greatest talents, in such a reckless and senseless way …" He trailed off and looked down, embarrassed. "But … but, uh … life does go on, after all. I hope you got the mourning brooch I sent you?"

She kept her face very still, remembering how she had lost the brooch while doing "animal dances" with Edward. "Yes, I did. I'm sorry I didn't send a thank you note, I was ill-disposed."

He looked her up and down, puzzled. "Glad to see you out and about and looking healthy."

Luna blushed; she should have at least have remembered to wear black to come here.

A silence had befallen them. Mr. Klein sat back down at his desk and motioned her to a chair. He raised his eyebrows expectantly, a friendly smile on his face.

Luna tried to find her voice, remember what she had planned to say, but too many ghosts of bad memories at the Beaumont distracted her. She looked down into her lap, and Mr. Klein cleared his throat and said, "Did you come to ask me for help, Luna?"

Luna heard the slight coolness and stuttered in embarrassment. "N-no, Mr. Klein. Not … I'm not asking for charity—"

"Because I mailed you his final paycheck. Got it in my ledger. I hope you did receive it?"

"Yes. Thank you, sir. That is not what I am here for …" She realized she had wound the strings of her velvet pouch around her fingers and cut off the circulation. She unwound them, took a deep breath, and looked at him levelly. "You see, I wanted to speak with you first. Because I have an act of my own now."

"An act?" He smiled and arched his brows in an ironic way, as though he thought she was joking.

"Yes. I do magic, too. I have been practicing and have become quite good."

"Well, I'm sure you learned a lot from your husband. No doubt. And the crowds always loved you. You must have warm memories of the stage."

She flinched. Memories of the stage at the Beaumont were hardly fond. "Yes, I miss it so. And I know there are some female magicians who do quite well. If I could come back tomorrow, perhaps, and show you my act?"

"What can you do?" He lowered his brows now, in mock seriousness.

"I can move objects. I have an act with silk scarves. I can produce birds from thin air, out of my hands." Well, she had produced one, a skylark. It had been difficult, giving life to the small, feathered thing with its twitching heart. "And I can levitate."

"No strings? Like Jack did?"

"No strings."

Mr. Klein removed his glasses and wiped them on his sleeve "You know, your husband had a rare talent, but he had to convince me at first. He stalked me for the longest time, loitering around my lobby, desperate to set up a meeting. I told him *no* the first time. I thought there was something odd about him. The intense way he had of looking at you. A certain calculating look he had. I thought he was a criminal or a huffer. But then one day I said *yes*," he held his arms out, "and the rest is history. Damndest stuff I'd ever seen. And I've seen everything in this business." He put his glasses back on. "He taught you his secrets?"

"In a way, yes."

He sighed. "Well, God bless you, missy. Those are some trade secrets, for sure. I don't understand how he did the things he did. And he never told me. But I did him good, and he did me one better. We made good money, those months. And that was a load off my mind, with all the moving picture shows sprouting up everywhere you look. People don't realize, though, that it's only a trend, they will tire of it." He searched out Luna's eye, as though appealing to her to agree. "There's no replacement for a live show. Right?"

"Right."

He glanced at the ceiling fan whistling and vibrating above. "I've seen some of those moving pictures. I don't care for 'em. Make me motion sick. Give me magic. Give me vaudeville. Give me the Follies. Something *real*."

Luna nodded. "So, things being as they are, would you allow me to show you my act?" She smiled hopefully.

"No, of course not."

He said it so lightly, so pleasantly, that Luna was thrown off and sat in confusion.

"Oh, come now, don't take it the wrong way, honey." He absent-mindedly flipped through some papers. "It just can not be."

"And why not?"

He dropped the papers and looked up at her from under his lowered brows. "It just can *not be*."

"But you have lady singers and lady actors. Wouldn't a lady magician be something new and bold?"

He compressed his lips and shook his head slowly, back and forth. Then he leaned forward and spoke in a low, confidential voice. "You see, honey, through no fault of your own, I just—" He shut his eyes, thinking. "The incident that happened at Barbetta. You see, it was a scandal, would you not say?"

"I-I don't know what I would rightly call it. I—"

"My dear, your photograph was in the paper, alongside those of your husband and your ... sweetheart."

"But he isn't—"

Mr. Klein held up his hand, to halt her words. "Hearsay or not, everyone knows who you are and knows the story. The trial hasn't even begun yet!"

"No, sir, that is to be in the summer," she said, resigned, spirit sinking.

"So you will be in the news again. I mean, you will take the stand, am I wrong?"

"I fear that I will be called, yes."

"So you see my conundrum?"

Anger, an unusual emotion to Luna, propelled her to boldness. "This is *not* fair! I did not ask for this to happen to me." She drew herself up, narrowed her eyes. "As the shrewd businessman I know you to be, do you not think that my act would be a curiosity to many who read the papers? Think of the publicity."

He looked shocked for a moment, as though she had said something vulgar. After a few beats of silence, he answered, "Yes, but it's the *wrong* publicity." He turned to look at her sidewise, with a tight little smile. "People don't like to see a man cuckolded by his wife."

Luna, feeling as though he had slapped her, said nothing.

"Well, darling, that's just the way it is, fair or not. I don't *know* what really happened. *I'm* not judging you. But *they* might."

"I-I think you are wrong. We will tell them that this is a homage to eternal love … phoenix rising from the ashes. They will be on my side."

He laughed, one harsh note. And again, smiled at her in a way that made her feel small and dirty. Her face reddened from fury. "Don't laugh at me, sir."

"Who's laughing?" he frowned, soulful concern on his face. But the mocking smile flickered back now and then.

"I need to leave now," Luna said, arising from her chair.

"Luna, I'm sorry. This theatre is a place for *family* entertainment. People bring their wives and children here. I can't be tainted by certain associations."

"Tainted?"

"Mobster boyfriend in Sing Sing? Please be realistic. I give you the advice I would give my daughter. I do have a daughter around your age, you know. I would tell her, honey, stay low. Do your penance. In time you can remarry and it will all be over."

"I will surely not do penance when I am not *guilty!*" Tears sprang to her eyes, tears of anger and woundedness. And shame. She wheeled around so he would not see them. "Thank you for your time, sir. I am leaving."

"Darling, it's just business!" he called as she exited the room and rushed down the stairs.

Thirty

October 31, 1911

Dearest One,

How are you, my Luna? This letter finds you well, I hope. You did not answer my last one. I hope that you are not afraid to write to me because of my being in prison. James will make sure that I alone get it. You do not have to write about anything to do with us, or the trial, or any of that mess! I just want to know what you do day-to-day, who you see, what you do for pleasure, what you eat, what you dream of. All of the things that one wants to know of their beloved. Things that to most would seem inconsequential, but to me means everything. Everything!

I am not making shoes anymore. Those bastards in the union shut us down. For the moment, at least. The factory is not making anything. No shoes, no baseball gloves, no cabinets. Nothing! I did not realize how attached I was to the factory. The work took up the largest part of my day. And I was the best man on the floor because I'm a shipbuilder, attuned to detail. Meticulous. That's what the foreman said. Now I don't have a way to occupy my hands. And it's hard to get enough tobacco anymore.

So in my idleness, I sit and dream. It is All Hallows Eve, my love, and here I am locked in this slot of a room. Hallowe'en makes me think of being a wee boy. It makes me think of my homeland. Our homeland. Ireland is such a green and wild place. Nature is a greater force there. There, the stars feel closer at night. Do you know what I am saying? The smell of the bonfires. All Hallows Eve! We took our livestock in on that night. Sprinkled holy water on them. We understand the forces that be, in Ireland.

Did the children in Clare play Shaving the Friar? Where you made the pile of ash with a piece of wood sticking out nice right, and each kid digs a bit more o' the ash, until the stick falls? And we all called out:

Shave the poor Friar to make him a liar;
Cut off his beard to make him afeard;
If the Friar will fall, my poor back pays for all!

Funny, that! The things that come back to me. The things the mind does when you're an idle man. I get to thinking about the veil between two worlds. And how it is thinnest at Hallowe'en. Can the dead really walk among us? Would a great rising of the murdered folk come upon Sing Sing to have their satisfaction with their killers? Not everyone here is a murderer. There are swindlers, cocaine sellers, blackmailers, robbers. And in their old lives they have done all kinds of ordinary work. Paper hangers, cooks, sailors, policemen, moving picture operator. Even a newspaper boy. No one is immune from bad fortune. It can find anyone.

Not all murderers go to the chair, either. Many of them are here for life. And some get out.

I have no fear of the dead. If your husband were to walk these halls to have a reckoning with me, I would send him straight back to hell. And that is a promise.

The food here varies. There is a clam chowder that they serve that is the best I ever had. But then again, there is a hash that is not fit for human consumption. A lot of men will take bread and water before the hash.

We run in the yard for exercise. To keep my strength, I lift rocks in the air while I look out at the Hudson River, which is always a different color, sometimes gray, sometimes a deep and thrilling blue that could pierce your heart. I am a model prisoner, they say. I keep my head and I never get flogged.

The newspaper boy I spoke of earlier has not been so disciplined. He has a raving look in his eye and is prone to fits, poor bugger. His back is all striped from his punishment, but it is the only thing that subdues him. He mauled an old granny, you know, because she said a cross word to him about the price of his newspaper. She did not know that the boy is mad.

Enough about me, I'm tired of me. So tired.

James said that you want to do magic shows, on the stage. Why would you want to do that? I find it puzzling. Though not wrong. If that is what you mean to do, then I hope you are able. You are certainly beautiful and enchanting and I picture you in all sorts of cunning stage outfits. Would you wear a cape, my love? Perhaps a dress with a lace-up bodice, exotic style? I wish you could wear those pointy-heeled shoes I made for you. I see it in my mind. I have made some drawings of what I think you would look like, they are enclosed.

James said you do have an act, and that you have a talent for it. But that you have approached many different establishments, and no theatre will take you on. It hurts my heart to think that the trouble you had with me is ruining your reputation. But it appears that is what happened. James said that you are very down about it all. Do not feel that way!

I have many brothers out there, brothers of the Hand, who are willing to vouch for you and help you in any way they can. Do you need help at all? My brothers can help persuade these theatre men that you are absolutely wonderful, and deserve to be on their stage. They would be privileged! They just do not realize it yet. Let my brothers do the talking, they are very convincing, and they will find you a venue in no time at all!

You will become the most famous woman in New York, and I will tell everyone here that you are my girl. Though they already know that, as I speak of you all the time. They even tease me about the girl I love so much that I was willing to go to the chair!

That is just a joke, though "old sparky" does exist, it is behind a green door at the end of the hallway. I am sure I will never go there, though. And even if I did, they would never kill my love for you. I will help you in what ways I am able for you to be a success, but please promise me that you will not even look at another man. For I would not be able to bear it, and I must keep up my spirits in this place. It is easy to fall into despair living in such a hovel. You don't want me having a fit and getting lashed like Poor Paperboy, do you?

If the veils were thin enough between the worlds, I would walk through these prison walls and find you my love and sweep you in my arms and kiss you. But as it is, these walls hold. I understand that you are unable to visit me here, but I will see you, I am told, in the courtroom this summer. Be prepared, because I will make love to you with my eyes. Until then, be strong.

Your best boy,
Sean

The drawings included with the letter were done in the same smudged and dull pencil. There were two. One appeared to show Luna dressed in a low-cut gown, her cleavage enhanced greatly, hands held up in a dramatic gesture with star sparkles coming from her fingertips. The face did not look like hers, the lips fuller and parted in a most lurid fashion. The eyes were spaced too far apart, the forehead too high. Underneath were written the words, *Luna the Magnificent!* in large, slanting black letters.

The other drawing showed her full-length, wearing what appeared to be a burlesque costume, a short-fringed corset and a matching short skirt that showed her legs, wearing what must have been the "pointy-heeled shoes" he referred to, because an drawn arrow pointed at them, along with an exclamation mark. He'd portrayed her holding a wand in the air and smiling widely.

God damn that James! she thought to herself, as she quickly threw the pages into the bin. She would never share anything with him or Patrick again. It made a panicked feeling flutter her heart to know that Sean knew what was happening in her life. She did not even want to know any more about the "brothers of the Hand," and certainly did not want them to "help" her.

From then on, as she went about her day-to-day existence, working at the tailor shop, going to market, coming home again, she felt watched. To be the object of another's obsession had once thrilled her when they were lovers, but now, as she gripped her string bag on the trolley, swayed in the press of bodies, she felt afraid. Tainted. Sean's frenzied thoughts of her covered her like an oily sheen that she could not clean off.

As the trolley swayed around a corner and came to a stop, she pushed up from the wicker seat, for once in her life fatigued. If only there were a way to undo things done and said; to be free.

That heaviness persisted as she made her way up the street to her building. November had come in dark and stormy, and orange leaves blew up the street along with bits of newspaper and fish wrappers and other things that brought her mood down.

And then she saw Cousin Patrick waiting for her on the front stoop. He rubbed his hands together in the cold, hopped from foot to foot, looked in the wrong direction; for just that moment Luna stood still and considered walking in the opposite direction. She was not in the mood for the boy's exuberance and his hero worship of Sean.

But quick as a sparrow, as if the boy sensed her presence, he turned his head her way, broke out in a grin and waved as though she couldn't see him otherwise.

"Hello, cousin!" he called and rushed to take her bag from her. "About time ya got home."

"Been waiting here long, have you?"

He rolled his eyes upward in thought, then said, "Naw, I

been here about fifteen minutes only. Ya landlady said usually ya are back by this time. She's a bit of a huffy ol' maid, ain't she? Not friendly, la."

Luna compressed her lips; again she had the sense that eyes were on her, all the time. It was enough to make her want to hop on a train again. If she had money. Without a word she went up the narrow stairs, Patrick close behind.

Once in, he said, "Aw, blessed radiator steam! Me ears are about frozen off." Indeed, they blazed bright pink, as did his cheeks.

"Well, what are you doing here, Patrick? Doesn't your mam set the table around this time?"

"Aye, but I told her I had an errand."

Luna unpacked her things onto the counter. It had not been a spectacular haul. Parsnips. A packet of oats. A bit of ham, that as she unwrapped from the butcher's paper, she saw had gone a little dry. Trying not to show testiness, she said, "So, are you staying to supper with me then?"

"No, cousin! I'm just here to deliver a message to ya!"

Luna set a jar of tomatoes on the counter with a loud *thunk*. "See here, Patrick, I already got a letter from Sean this week. I have a problem with you and James—"

"It ain't from Sean. James hasn't been to the prison this week. See, they do odd/even weeks, and Sean's number is—"

"Well, who is it from, then?" She hadn't meant to snap at the boy. It was only that she was so tired and dispirited.

He did not notice her irritation, however, too focused upon the bit of paper he pulled from his coat pocket. With a flourish, he handed it to her.

It wasn't a letter. It had the name Grover Bates, with an address on Eldridge Street, and "Monday, round two."

"What is this?"

Patrick grinned. "Ya know of the Fox Theatre? Down the

Bowery?"

Luna sighed. "Yes. Crummy looking place with a ripped awning that flaps in the wind." She went there some weeks ago. She had spoken to a short man in a checked suit about her act. He told her he knew who she was, and he could not have a Jezebel performing on his stage. Her cheeks flushed at the memory. "I thought it a very no-count establishment."

"Oh, cousin, don't be mad he didn't take ya on! He had a change of heart."

Luna leaned on the counter heavily and fixed the boy with a keen look. "What do you mean, he's changed his mind?"

"I'm sayin' I know ya had been down there, ya been everywhere. We had some people go down and talk to him about ya."

"What *people*?"

"Ya know, James and some of 'em, la." He still looked pleased with himself, but now he shuffled a little, sheepish, under Luna's withering look.

"Are you telling me it was men from the White Hand?"

"That's right!" He beamed at the very name.

She shut her eyes, took some deep breaths. A plethora of emotions washed through her, all conflicting. Fear. Exasperation. Confusion. But also, underneath it all, exhilaration. Exhilaration started slow at the gate, and overtook the others.

Still, she looked at Patrick sternly. "I don't see what the White Hand Gang has to do with theatres or magic shows."

Patrick looked at her in disbelief, as though she had gone dense. "Luna! I thought ya understood! You are Sean's girl. It means you're like ... I don't know ... royalty or something." A smile of delight at his brilliance spread across his face. "You are the queen bee!"

"Really?"

"Yes. And we … that is … *they* are the ones who protect ya. Sean knew ya wanted to get a show. So Sean put the word out and … *la*. Ain't it great?"

Her heart raced. Her own show. Could it be true? Her magic was an obsession, driving her thoughts, always. Also, the idea of sharing the magic, of feeling the warm embrace of an audience again, consumed her. She guessed the box of light made her so. Her ambition burned more hotly than any shame at her ill-gotten gains.

"So Patrick, dare I ask … how did they … persuade this man?"

"Oh, it was a brilliant proposition. He would have a meeting with you and seriously consider you for his act. In exchange for the Hand's protection."

"Protection?"

"Yes! Protection from … vandals and whatnot. Ya know the Bowery can be one rough area. Full of hooligans, like. He wouldn't want anyone to burn down his theatre, say, or smash things up, or mug his patrons—"

"Patrick, this sounds very suspect." But she could not hide the faint trembling of a smile at the edges of her lips.

"Aye, ya are happy, cousin! I can tell it pleases ya! Sean will be so glad to hear it—"

"Please! Would you boys stop talking to Sean about me? I won't have it! Tell him nothing from now on. Promise me. Or I will be very upset."

Patrick smiled mischievously, and then surprised her with a kiss on the cheek. "It's all so brilliant, ain't it? He's going to fix it all up nice for ya, posters and everything. They'll know ya all over town. I'm gonna go home and tell—"

"No." Luna sobered up all at once. "Keep it to yourself." She looked away. "Especially don't tell my father."

Thirty-One

… holding, *holding*, willing her cells to vibrate so fast that she hardly felt human anymore. She lifted up one arm and stretched in a gesture of triumph, an angel pointing to the heavens for the crowd below to behold. She trembled from the effort, but drew her powers from the ether, and remained still for some moments, to be seen, admired. Like some wondrous creature trapped in amber. Making the moment last and last. Until it was time to reverse the current and lower herself down again. With a great letting go. A great sigh. That was the hard part.

Gently, down she came until the soles of her feet made contact with the floor of the stage. As so often happened when she performed magic, time yielded to conform to her will. She raised both arms to a hush, an intake of breath, not just a beat, the moment suspended, infinite.

The prolonged moment gave her time to look around her, to notice the splinters and worn spots on the floorboards, the poor quality of the floodlights making the shadows pitched and uneven. The pieces of plaster broken off the ballasts of the walls. No, it was not the most elegant theatre in town, but in her triumph, she did not mind. The blood rushing through her veins made her magnanimous, forgiving of any flaws.

She wore no shoes. She had considered high-lacing sandals, but when she stood before the clouded mirror for the first time in the costume she had made for this performance, the voluminous harem pants that hung low on her hips, the tight gold bodice top, the jeweled headband that covered her forehead – she had decided going barefoot added to the exotic allure she sought. And the decision had been a good one. Bare soles helped her feel more grounded back on the stage as she at last looked back at the many faces aimed her way.

The moment held, and then ended in a great release and exhale, as the applause thundered forth. There were men, women and children, not a full house, perhaps half filled, but the people who had come to see her looked upon her with joy and astonishment. She mirrored it back at them. It was the first time she had shared her secret with the public. Her connection was to them only. The energy thrummed in the room like a live, hot wire, and it felt like the sweet sickness of first love.

She bowed three times, deeply, with a flourish. Only dimly, at the edge of her consciousness did she take in the fact that four members of the White Hand were in the back of the house, young men in slouchy suit pants and matching boaters worn back at an insouciant angle, arms folded, leaning in to talk to each other from the sides of their mouths.

But as promised, Mr. Bates had done her proud. The poster on a stand out front showed a sleek, shining version of Luna, dressed in a mish-mash of flowing Middle Eastern garb. An Irish girl dressed as an Egyptian queen, but who hadn't seen more absurd things in a lifetime? The woman on the poster looked intently straight out at the viewer, rays of stylized light shooting from around her. The image, allegorical, was almost like a tarot card just flipped over, an omen of the future. And at the top was born the legend:

BLYTHE
OF THE GATES OF SEVEN WONDERS

"I just had the papers drawn up this morning. I've barely had time to look them over. Let me know if you have any questions."

Luna sat on the other side of the desk, reading the contract that would make Arthur Haywood her manager.

She dipped the pen into the bottle of ink and signed her name, and the date, February 17, 1912. Then she blew on it and passed it back, with a smile.

Arthur was a small, delicate man perhaps in his early thirties, though already losing his blond hair at the top. But his gaze was direct, his lips always quirked in a twinge of amused cynicism. He had a world-weariness about him for such a young man.

"Luna Mulkerrins, huh? Didn't know you were a Paddy lass. No accent."

"Not anymore, God willing. I've been working on it. I only lapse when I'm angry."

He laughed, and then held out his hand. "Pleasure to take you on. You are certainly talented. Kicking up a fuss wherever you go. Fox Theatre to the—"

"The Knickerbocker."

"Yeeeessss …" He contemplated her closely, as though she were a mysterious painting he wanted to divine. "So how did you come upon your stage name? Blythe?"

She shrugged, smiled lightly. She strove for lightness a lot these days. It got her far. "I just like the sound. I got it from a poem I liked as a girl. A poem about a skylark. A bird that was a blithe spirit. I just spelled it with a *y*."

"Indeed, indeed. I like it. Elegant. Beguiling. It works, you know? Blythe is an English name, I believe. Anyway, *sounds* English. It contrasts nicely with your Middle East garb. That stuff is the trend now, you know. Exoticism. You're on point."

"I have friends who have worked in show business. I watch and learn. They have influenced me, I suppose."

"For the better, I'd say." He tilted his head away from her a bit, regarding her with one eye, and pointing. "I like how you've handled the, you know. The old business. The scandal."

"Honestly, it kept me from getting work in the beginning. They thought it would be bad publicity."

"Well, they're idiots. Obviously. I would say it adds to your ... allure."

"Well, there's no hiding it, is there?" In fact, her poster at the Knickerbocker had been altered to add **WEEPING WIDOW RETURNS TO THE SPOTLIGHT!** "I gave one interview to the paper, but I only speak of my past in the most refined, or, well ... *oblique* terms."

"Yes, I have the clipping, I read it. Where you said, what, that you, uh ..."

"That I was paying homage to my dear departed husband and carrying on his tradition. That he had taught me the ways and secrets."

"And as far as the other fella in the slammer, I forgot—"

"I said only that I pray for his soul, nightly."

"Nice, that. Vague. Makes them wonder."

Luna laughed, then motioned to a glass box of cigarettes on the desk. "May I?"

"Please do."

Smoking was another new habit of hers, one that she liked very much. He leaned forward and lit it for her with a silver lighter. "These are nice, you'll find. They have the cork tips."

"Thank you, Mr. Haywood."

"Artie, please."

She leaned back in her chair, contented, and breathed out a plume of smoke. Artie leaned back, too, with a quizzical smile.

"Shall I call you Luna or Blythe?"

She thought for some moments, before she said, "I guess Luna. I'm still feeling my way to Blythe."

He chuckled, and then grew serious looking for a moment. "Do you want to tell me anything? About the newspaper incident? Confidentially, of course. Very sad thing. It must be hard to talk about."

Luna sighed. "I don't know that there is much to say. It makes me feel a bit embarrassed speaking to you of it. It all must seem very sordid to you. Working in entertainment, I'm sure you never have to encounter tales of bloody crime scenes." She laughed faintly, though her face had tensed; she fidgeted with one glass earring and looked down.

But Artie merely waved his hand dismissively. "Hey, I wasn't in this business *all* my life. I used to be in the service. A veteran of the Spanish American War here." He shook his head. "You want to talk about sordid. That march into Santiago. Sleeping in mud, mud in my mouth, mud in my eyes. When we got there, it was all over already, but I saw people starving to death, dropping dead. The ship that took us home had just carried a cargo of mules. I had to sleep on a poncho spread over manure ..." He stared into space for some moments, and then came to again. "I don't mean to speak of crass things. What I mean is, I've seen a lot. Nothing about your story can shock me. So don't worry."

Luna was lost for words; Artie looked at her kindly.

"I'm sure you must still miss him very much. Your *husband*, I mean," he was quick to add, holding his hands up defensively.

She thought about this. It had been six months. Six months that felt like a lifetime. Sometimes it seemed she could not quite remember what the Magician even looked like anymore. Sometimes, if she heard a loud noise from the neighbor's apartment, it gave her a start and she thought he was back, in ill-humor about something, ready to break or punch things, ready to let her have it.

But then she realized it wasn't him, and never would be again. Still, she would have to calm herself …

"Yes, I do still notice his absence and it is a shock all over again." But mostly he evinced as an abstraction now, his memory like a phonograph recording. Scratchy, wavery, through a metal tube.

"Well, you are certainly doing him a great justice, going into the business. A homage to his memory. I'm sure he would be proud."

He would most likely be contemptuous, she thought, but Luna smiled, eyes downcast as in sad resignation.

"Now." Artie folded his hands on the table; without thinking, Luna did the same thing, and leaned forward, like looking into a mirror. "For the future, where do you see the business taking *you*, Luna?"

"I want to travel. I want to take my show on the road. I … I would be perfectly *suited* to travel. I have no children—"

"I'm sorry for that," said Artie quietly; Luna sat stunned and confused for a moment, slow to take his meaning, but then went on, "I do not have set pieces, or equipment, so I imagine that expenses would be spared?"

"I've seen you perform. The minimalism is an asset. It keeps the focus on you, and you only."

"At the Knickerbocker, I have had an organ player accompany me."

"We can easily play recorded music for the interludes."

"Yes. Something unusual, dramatic, I don't know what yet."

"And why do you want to travel?"

She tapped her ash a bit nervously into the mother-of-pearl ashtray. She wanted to travel because at all of her performances, the White Hand Gang loitered ominously in the shadows, the back rows, or flanked the exit doors. Always the young men in tipped-back boater hats, properly dressed, but with the quiet aura of menace about them. Tattoos peeked out on their arms. Guns and batons in their pockets.

Protection, Patrick had said. He joined them more often than not recently. But though they treated her with chivalrous courtesy, they frightened her. She detested being watched everywhere she went. All movements reported back to Sean! She had to get away, she had decided. To get bookings on a tour, she needed management. Frightened desperation had led her to this office.

She thought of what Artie said about being in the war. Would he understand, about the White Hand Gang? Would he take it in even stride?

Best not to risk it. She could not be a liability. Better not to tell him.

"Well, I suppose I want to see the country. Expand my horizons a bit."

"You came here off the boat? Ellis Island and all that?"

"Yes. It's been maybe two years."

"And you've only lived here? In New York?"

"Yes."

"Well, then." He opened up a leather-bound ledger on his desk. "Guess you're ready to see the sights. We could send you to the Midwest … or you could play the east coast circuit."

"I-I have been to Chicago once. And I spent some time in West Virginia."

"Hmm. I can't say I'd send you to West Virginia. I could see you in Atlanta. Maybe New Orleans." He toyed with a pen, drummed on his knee, as he thought. "We need to send out some press releases. Reviews. Publicity. Maybe add a bit more to the show …" He studied her now. She wore a loose-fitting brocade dress, with strings of beads and heavy silver rings on her fingers. "I like your look. Bohemian princess. You thought of wearing your hair down onstage?"

Thirty-Two

Puffs of steam drifted through as the inward train pulled into the station, and the noise disturbed a flock of pigeons, flapping and cooing up into the rafters. Artie had made the arrangements, and sooner than she expected. It was all happening. It was time to begin her journey.

Luna stood up, and reached for the handle of her valise tucked under her bench; but Jacob quickly stooped to take it himself, and then motioned for her to enter the train before him.

Jacob, her assigned assistant. Jacob, a boy of nineteen, with dark curly hair that he had attempted to slick down flat to his head for the train trip. Nineteen was not so much younger than her own age, but something about him made her thoughts turn maternal. He was tall, but gangly, as though he had not quite grown into his body yet. Hands large and knuckled that clutched about awkwardly. Eyes that were very large and very dark and very grave. An expression of child-like solemnity on his face.

And he did not talk very much. Perhaps it was because of the small stutter.

My goodness, she thought. What have I signed myself

on for? I would have done better traveling alone.

They had met only once before, when Artie had arranged an afternoon at a practice space. He had not discussed Jacob with her before, and so she was surprised when the boy had loomed there, shuffling his large feet, smiling, but not quite meeting her eye.

"This," said Artie, slapping him on the back, "is Jacob. He is to introduce you on stage, assist with music and set changes, and generally be Blythe's eternally faithful servant!"

And indeed, the boy was to dress the part for the stage, all in white, a linen tunic and matching loose pants, with a gold-colored sash and some Moroccan type of slippers on his feet. Dressed in the stage costume, he was foreign, enchanted, like a young man from a fairy story.

He was also to help her from station to station, transport her tagged luggage and deal with the tickets. And now they were settled and pulling away in another great puff of steam, Luna relaxed into the plush velvet seat, at her best when traveling, between points, neither one place nor another. The feeling of motion vibrated blissfully within her.

But after that interlude of quiet contemplation, which she so savored, but compelled to talk to the boy, with mild resentment she opened her eyes and said, "So tell me, Jacob. How did you come to work for Artie?"

His eyes darted to hers for an instant; rattled, he blushed and looked away. "I came to him to help me f-f-find acting jobs. I work on the stage, no big parts yet, though. B-b-but I was in the *Tempest*. I was the Boatswain. A-a-and I was in *Sherlock Holmes*, at the Empire. But I had no lines, I was a pedestrian."

She smiled. "Pardon me for saying, but I would not

have guessed you an actor. I guess I assume actors are, well, ego driven? And you seem so modest!"

His eyelids fluttered as he struggled to form the words. "I-I-I-I used to do practices to help me with my s-s-stutter. I found that if I acted a role and read a memorized script, I did not stutter. And the practice stayed with me. I am most comfortable when on the stage, playing a character."

"How remarkable, Jacob! I'm sure you play your parts quite well."

"Thank you, Lady Blythe."

It threw her off balance when he called her that. Had Artie told the boy to do so, in jest? But if she corrected him, would Jacob be embarrassed all the more?

She decided to say nothing about the matter. "How long, did you say, to Philadelphia?"

"W-w-we should be there around ten-thirty."

"Oh. That's not long at all." She had the urge to check again, to make sure that her valise was in the upper compartment. She knew it was there, Jacob had just put it there for her. But her mind kept darting anxiously back to it. Because the valise contained the box of light. She feared ever becoming parted from it. It was a part of her now. She wanted to feel its otherworldly quiet radiance at all times.

Funny, how she had feared the thing so when it belonged to her husband. Now, she hardly remembered not being its owner. The cracks in the leather, the peculiar musty smell when opened on its ancient hinges, the worn red velvet lining … it was as though the thing contained her very heart. Her very soul.

"Would you mind, terribly, if I …" She stood from her seat a moment, slid open the compartment, and touched the valise with her fingertips. "I'm sorry," she said, settling down again. "I get a bit compulsive at times."

Because if she lost the box, she'd lose her power. The thing that made her different from everyone else on the train. Everyone else in the world. And then what would she have?

She closed her eyes again to ward off the small throb of a headache. She had drunk some wine the night before when Agnes, Gertie, Peter and Edward had thrown her a going-away, good-luck party. They had all been impressed about the tour, though sorry to see her go for some months. Gertie had sung, Agnes had cried, Edward had made great use of his snuff tin, and Peter had tried to nibble her earlobe in the kitchen because he already missed her so terribly …

They are my friends, they wish me well, and I adore them. And yet sometimes in the midst of their good times, she felt at a distance from them. She saw that they drank too much and huffed too much, and were sometimes overly self-congratulatory.

But I owe them so much, for saving me. And yet, she no longer liked to get drunk and wild with them, always too focused on keeping her head together for her next show.

Because more and more, it was her shows that gave her life.

They arrived at the station, and Luna all at once felt grateful for Jacob after all, as he dealt with the luggage and arranged their cab.

He helped her into it. It was late March, the sky overcast, and slushy snow had just started to fall, melting as it lay on the fur collar of her coat, dampening the peacock plumes of her hat.

As the horses' hooves trotted up ahead, she looked up and around at this new city.

"Philadelphia seems a bit … older than New York, don't you think, Jacob? Something different about it that I can't put my finger on."

His black Derby had accumulated a small ridge of snowflakes along its brim, melting away even as her eyes lay on it. "Well, to me it seems like parts of Queens. One city can be very much like another when you've seen enough of 'em."

After lunch in the hotel restaurant, Jacob made a stiff little bow as they each went to their separate rooms to rest up for the evening's show. Alone at last, she drew the curtains and looked outside. Not as clean as Chicago, not as high energy as New York. But this was the city of the founding fathers, was it not? Brick walkways, church spire in the distance. This place had a weight of history about it.

Perhaps this country is becoming mine now.

She closed her eyes to remember the Ireland of her girlhood, but it was hard to see it anymore. But with a little effort, she summoned it into existence. Sunshine through wind-whipped clouds at a particular time of day, when her chickens clucked and strutted, preening their mottled black-and-white feathers, when she swore she could feel the earth's vibrations through her bare feet in the grass.

Maybe someday it would slip away from her entirely.

"Ladies and gentlemen, boys and girls, your attention, please! Here on this stage, I present a most remarkable wonder, the likes of which you will not see anywhere else. A remarkable lady, gifted with uncanny powers, previously the bride of the great Cosmos, the Incomparable. Cosmos made his great mark in the world of magic, only to be assassinated by a crazed fan. His widow wept tears of sadness and loss and hid from the world and the press. But now, this talented lady has taken it upon herself to share these great gifts with the world. The gift of magic, born unto her through tragedy." Jacob paused dramatically and looked around the room, holding the eye, one by one, of each front row audience member he looked at.

"She has been bequeathed the gift, to bypass the gates of perception, the laws of nature. Her husband bore magic in his blood, through his noble Arabian heritage stretching back generations. He shared his teachings only with the woman he loved. And now, in honor of a great fallen man, a brave woman heeds on!

"From the great New York City, ladies and gentlemen, I bring you Blythe of the Seven Gates!"

Jacob looked so very different on the stage, under the hot lights. So unprepossessing in daily life, he stood bathed in a glow of power, a different person entirely. Watching from the wings, Luna wondered how she had not seen it before. He had the command of a matinee idol, in his white tunic and sash, his rajah's slippers. He turned to where she stood and held out his arms, her cue to step out onto the stage.

The phonograph played a song from a record called *Songs of Araby*. It was a Tin Pan Alley record, with a beautiful smiling girl in a turban on the cover. It did not truly sound Arabian, to Luna it sounded a strange hybrid of Indian and ragtime, but Artie had chosen it.

Luna came out and smiled radiantly, took her bows, then slowly undulated her hips like a belly dancer. Another thing Artie had recommended, in fact, pantomimed it himself, and described how he had seen it performed in a short at the Nickelodeon once. It was, he said, to "showcase her feminine wiles." Silly enough, but it went along with her husband's so-called "Arabian heritage." And it was fun to do, so she did not mind so much.

She knew her act by heart at this point, so hardly had to think about anything. It used to be she had trouble creating a bird out of thin air; it took all her concentration to birth the small feathered thing in the cups of her palms. Now she could produce a bird easily, at will, whatever color she wanted. That night she wanted a cardinal. She saw the blazing red feathers in her mind, the jaunty quill on its head, the *tick tick tick* of its tiny heart. She opened her palms and a whole fleet of them poured forth. Disoriented by the applause from the crowd, they flew haphazardly up into the rafters.

Midway through was the one new part of the act, where Jacob laid out an embroidered cushion for her to sit on, then bowed and offered her a hookah pipe. Luna took one long, languid draw from it and then blew out a plume of smoke, while holding the thought in her mind of what she intended. The plume drifted center stage, grew larger and more defined until it became a humanoid figure, sexless, featureless, but able to undulate its arms and legs in a graceful dance. The audience gasped.

She blew two more plumes, which joined the first in formation, dancing together; Luna got up to join them, dancing in the forefront, their moves perfectly synchronized. Luna clapped her hands sharply then folded her arms, and the three smoke beings dissipated into vagueness and drifted to the ceiling.

The applause was such that Luna forgot herself entirely for a time. It felt as though the stage were her true home now, and the rest of her life no longer real.

Thirty-Three

The telegram reached her when they got to the hotel in Baltimore.

Luna, I hope you are well, and I am grateful that you gave me your itinerary. Pa knows nothing which is for the best. Sean had his pre-trial hearing, and his lawyer will plea that his was a crime of passion which may lessen his sentence greatly, maybe even set him free. You will be called to the stand. The trial has been officially set to begin July 20 and I pray you know that you have to be back in time. Much love, your sister, Lil.

Luna groaned and threw the telegram away. She had known about the pre-trial, Artie had sent her the clipping from the paper, along with copies of the local press releases for her shows. There had been a pen-and-ink drawing of Sean on the courtroom, handcuffed next to his appointed lawyer. The courtroom artist perfectly captured Sean's close-lipped smile, his chin defiantly in the air.

Even from the illustration, before she read the story, it was evident that Sean had no remorse for his actions, though others wished he would appear otherwise. She suspected he didn't truly understand that he might go to the electric chair if things did not play out well.

And once again Luna reminded herself that she was not responsible for the fate of another, no matter how much she'd once loved him.

She composed her telegram back to Lil, saying, My dear sister, I intend to be back in New York with time to spare. Please don't worry about anything. All is well on the road. Please give Pa, Mary Catherine, and all the rest my love, and I will see you before you know it. PS Show tonight sold out!

Trains, hotels, restaurants. She found it so freeing to live anonymously, no family, no ties to bind her to her old life. Jacob, by her side proved a silent and attentive companion. She had resented being made to travel with him, in the beginning. But now she found him good company, thrown together on the road so often, sharing meals, navigating train trips. Jacob said very little, she knew nothing of what he was thinking, but Luna found the fact restive rather than disturbing.

Deep in her heart, Luna knew she could go on this way forever, and never miss home.

Washington, DC. Richmond, Virginia. The shows sold out quickly, both due to positive reviews, and people nationwide following the courtroom story in the paper. In response to the new attention focused upon her, Luna endeavored to stay cool and aloof. Artie had asked her to do so. "I want you to go for stately, regal. Don't ever say too much. You are Lady Blythe. Act English."

"But I'm not English. I'm Irish."

"You're in America now, honey, where you invent yourself as you go along."

Now, there were even photographers who lay in wait for her when she exited her venues, cameras set on tripods on the street, expandable cartridges thrust in front of her.

The flash lamps that they held up popped and blazed like fireworks, and smelled like gunpowder.

Jacob guided her by the arm, looming tall and stern and calling out, "No pictures!" And Luna would look at the ground, and to their shouted queries of "Was he your lover?" "Was he really driven temporarily mad?" "What would you do if he went to the chair?" she simply answered quietly, "No comment."

Eyes dazzled by the flaring light, she allowed herself to be led to a waiting car, where she thought, *Artie is right. If I was not an American before, I surely am now.*

Thirty-Four

Luna spent a solitary afternoon in downtown Raleigh, North Carolina, seeing the sights and shopping. The weather had turned mild and lovely, with blooming forsythia and cherry blossoms against a dazzling blue sky. She ordered some new summer dresses in mint-green and blush pink, in a simple style, softly draped and almost Grecian in design. For the warm weather, she thought. Her bohemian princess outfits that she wore back in New York were rather too layered and heavy. Then she chose one other, a dress to be made up from an airy fabric printed with medallions of blue and green Chinois flowers. She arranged to have the dresses posted to her hotel in Charleston, South Carolina, where they were headed next and where they would stay for a solid week.

In another store, she chose a pair of t-strap sandals with a stacked heel, which showed her toes prettily. But even as the shop girl helped her on with them, she had a memory of Sean's letter, the first one about making shoes, making shoes in a prison workhouse and thinking of her feet.

The memory made her panicky for just a moment, but the feeling soon abated and dissolved in the loveliness of this long afternoon. She rested in a teahouse with her bags and sipped a cup of fragrant jasmine, and lost herself looking out of the window at the passersby, all right again, for the first time in a long time.

I am Blythe now. I can do what I want, and not what is expected of me.

Charleston was a city unlike any she had ever experienced. She had never seen a real palm tree before, and here they lined the streets. There were also enormous live oaks. Spanish moss hung in great curtains from the trees. Something from a picture book or a magic lantern show.

The carriage-house inn, their hotel for a week, sat behind a large, spiked iron gate. A neoclassical brick house with wide porches, the ocean breeze billowed filmy curtains in the windows, in and out. As their cab drove up the brick carriageway, she admired a garden with box hedges and azaleas, waxy white magnolias, and a small fountain with an old iron statue of a girl, dipping her toes in the water, arms crossed behind her back, her face worn featureless.

She and Jacob had adjoining rooms with views of the ocean harbor. As soon as Luna got to hers, she opened the French doors and smelled deeply of the salt breeze.

Funny, how it was the same ocean everywhere she went, but it looked and smelled so different, whether she was in New York, Ireland, or here, where she saw the water glitter brightly, like the spangles on her stage costumes. And the smell more sharp and briny than she ever remembered the ocean being.

Four-poster bed. French provincial furnishings. She lay down on the white-flocked counterpane, watching the ceiling fan turn for a while, getting her bearings. The travel had been warmer than she was used to, and had tired her. She would have a bath in the big claw foot tub and put on a silk robe.

But first, she took up her valise, opened it. On top as always, were her pink glass rosary beads that she traveled with, always, though she rarely said her prayers anymore.

And then, under her nightgowns, nestled the box, the box of light. Box of her heart. She took it into the bed with her, laid her cheek on its cracked leather, and fingered the hammered brass studs.

Aw, we have been through so much together, my friend.

Even with the lid closed, the almost electrical thrum of energy from inside made her tingle. She rocked back and forth, breathing in its ancient smells. The smell of time and history and yearnings for greatness.

You – you have been my greatest heartbreak. But also my savior. I hate it, but at the same time, I love you more than anything in my life. I need nothing else, not anymore. I've never known another like you before

… except, the next day, she did.

It was the first time she had ever seen a moving picture camera.

It was *also* a hinged box, made of wood, propped up on its end upon the tripod. And it was the same size as the box of light. Although not covered in leather, it did have brass studs and brass fixtures on its corner edges.

The camera operator showed her how it worked. He opened one side to show her where he kept the reels of film. He showed her how to look into the pop-out viewing tube in the back. He even let her turn the hand-crank on the side, which is what made the camera work.

"How *remarkable*," she said in a reverent whisper. She

instantly felt a kind of second-hand love for this one object that so much resembled *another* object that was so dear to her heart. She touched the camera and even felt a similar energy signature. *This* wooden box had power, too. A power of light and heat and dreams.

Luna was in her costume, a new one. Still the harem pants, though these were red with gold spangles, and the top to this one cropped, gold beaded, almost like a breastplate of some warrior goddess.

Her makeup had been done for her this time. They told her it needed to be dark, to show up properly on the black-and-white film. Her eyebrows were plucked and penciled, her eyes kohl dark, and her face powdered very white.

Most different of all were her lips. Though she always kept her lips rouged for performances, this time a woman had painted them a very dark, deep, purplish-red color. It looked nearly black in some lights. It gave her face in the mirror a queer look, someone she did not recognize.

"I look like a she-devil," she laughed.

Her hair had been braided the night before, and now she wore it down her back, wavy and wild looking, with a gold headband across her forehead, a large, red paste jewel in the center.

It had been arranged through Artie that moving picture footage would be made into a movie short. The cameraman arranged to meet them on two mornings, take the footage, and then splice it together later, "So that it flows. So that it tells a story."

"But what is the story?"

"The story of *you*, of course!"

The camera set up in place, directions given, Luna stood dramatically posed with her arms akimbo, facing away from the camera. On the count of three, she turned and smiled, and danced exotically toward the camera. Then Jacob wheeled in the trunk of silk pieces, and bowed.

Luna always began her shows this way, but everything felt different now. There was no audience, for one thing. The empty theatre echoed. There was only the sound of the camera whirring and clicking, and the cameraman saying, "Good. Good. Good."

How could she perform without the energy of the people washing warmly over her?

But then the cameraman said, "Stop!"

She stopped in her tracks, startled. "Is something the matter?"

"There's nothing wrong, honey. Just to do it again. You're a little stiff."

"I am?"

"Well, you know …" His watchman's cap hung low on his forehead, his sleeves were rolled up, and his suspenders draped loosely below his belt. It was so warm in there; everyone looked wilted. "I seen you perform before. Usually, you look a little more relaxed."

"Well, I'm surely not afraid of *you*." She raised her head high; Lady Blythe was a star, cool and imperious. So too must Luna be, from now on.

"No, you don't look afraid. You just look a little awkward, maybe you're just not used to the camera?"

"Well, it's awfully *loud*, I suppose. I'm used to performing for people, not a protruding lens."

"Take five, maybe, and we'll start again?"

Luna strode into the wings and lit a cigarette from the packet she always kept nearby now. She sat on a folding chair. Jacob approached her, leaning down.

"D-d-don't let it get you down, Lady Blythe."

"I'm not I just … oh, I don't know."

His eyes were so large and earnest, a deep brown. Looking to meet hers, and then looking away again. He seemed to drift into deep thought. Then he said, "There are some tricks to it, you know, working the camera."

"I thought you were only a stage performer."

He shrugged and smiled wryly. "True. Primarily. B-b-but I was an extra, once, in a silly short film about a bank robber."

She laughed. "Don't tell me you robbed the bank! Did you wear a mustache and shift your eyes around?" She drew deeply on the cigarette and exhaled in nervous sputters of laughter, feeling too brittle to even genuinely laugh.

Jacob shook his head. "No. I was just a person standing in the background. But! I got to listen in on the director speaking to the actors."

"And?"

"And he told them, to translate well on the screen, they had to project."

"What? Like a singer?"

"Yes and no. A singer uses his voice. A moving picture actor projects their being."

"And how to do that?"

He looked to the side a moment, and said, "J-j-just imagine that you are not encumbered just by your physical body. Imagine that you are huge. Imagine that your being is immense enough to fill the whole theatre, that the camera is not making a small object of you. You are beaming right into that lens, and straight through the enormous screen, filling up a moving picture theatre."

"But Artie said the film will only be in Nickelodeons. I'll be tiny."

"No! Well, maybe. But I think they're getting bigger

screening rooms now. Anyway. Think full screen, city after city. You filling up space on those screens, and in people's minds and imaginations."

"That's a tall order. I'm only a five-foot-three girl from Doolin!"

At that, Jacob looked at her incredulously. "No. That's not all you are. You are Lady Blythe of the Gates. D-d-don't you know that you are full of such life and talent and beauty and … a-a-and …?" This last part seemed to have escaped without him thinking. He blushed.

Luna smiled at that; he was such a boy. Had she ever known anyone so good and innocent? "Jacob, darling, I will try it out."

"I know you will do great."

"We will do great. Together. Now let's go out there, they're paying the man by the hour, Artie said."

Thirty-Five

"I toast this celebration. To *us*," she said, raising her glass of tart white wine. "To a wonderful performance this morning. And a well deserved evening off."

A breeze through open French doors in the stately dining room energized Luna. She wore her new medallion print dress and the sun bathed the wainscoted walls and oil paintings in gilded frames.

She touched her glass to Jacob's. "Many happy returns," he murmured, but he looked distracted, and he had hardly touched his food. They had both ordered the specialty, seared flounder with grits and shrimp on the side.

Luna was famished, though. "I have never had grits before. I am guessing this is a sort of, what, a corn porridge?"

"I suppose it is."

"And this is regional?"

"Southern cuisine. Can't get it like this in New York."

She had a long sip of wine. "I can do without going back to New York. I wish we could keep on, and never return."

"But you will tire of the road eventually, I would

imagine. You'll be homesick."

"You'd be surprised! Trains and inns and hotels. I like the anonymity. It feels more welcoming than home. It feels … like a mother to me."

Jacob looked at her searchingly. Luna shrugged. "Just the way I am, I guess."

"Is your mother … your *real* mother back in Ireland?"

"No. She died some years back. Diphtheria."

"I-I-I'm sorry for that."

"Yes, well. Not much could have been done for her. And she was so unwell in the end, I suppose we all thought it was a mercy." Radiant with fever, swollen neck and an odd, barking cough. Blue-tinged skin. Luna was ashamed to remember being afraid of her mother in bed at the end, looking so unlike herself.

"Please, don't think of such things now, Lady Blythe. I don't want for you to be s-s-sad." The boy certainly did look somewhat distressed.

"Oh, Jacob. I am not sad." Though she was fighting off the wave of shame engulfing her. "I have vivid memories sometimes, that's all. Another time, another place and it … I don't know. It seems I was a whole other person, then."

He shook his head. "If memories of that time only make you unhappy, you c-c-can always just let them go."

Luna put down her fork and looked into her lap. She tried to imagine just letting it go. Even though she had been no more than a girl, it was the most shameful memory of her life. Her reluctance to go into her mother's sick room. The helplessness of those long afternoons tending the chickens, hauling the eggs to town, hanging out the laundry. Anything she could do to avoid her sick mother. And they had been her *last* hours!

Not even brave enough to visit the gravesite, for shame,

for shame …

But to just let it go? Simply, easily, like dropping a leaf into a stream, letting it be carried away? Was it possible?

She tried to imagine just that. Letting her old life slip away. Letting her home country die away in her heart. An old life burned to ashes for a new life to finally emerge.

I am Blythe of the Gates. Anything is possible, because I will it so.

Making an effort to be light again, she said, "Jacob, I don't know anything at all about your life. You are always so quiet."

He shrugged. "Not much to tell."

"But where are you from?"

"Connecticut. Out in the country. M-m-my parents own a hardware store."

She smiled. "And you are not there, selling hammers and bolts and saws?"

He blushed. "It wasn't f-f-for me."

"And so you wanted to be an actor? Why? For the fame? The girls?" She smiled coquettishly.

He looked horrified for a moment, his Adam's apple moving up and down in his throat. "N-n-n-no." He took a moment to recover. She guessed he was rehearsing lines in his mind, making a script, to correct his stutter.

At last, he turned to her. "I act because it's just what I'm inclined to do. I like to mirror other people. I empty myself out and *become* another person. B-but I don't expect anything remarkable to happen to me. I'm not that kind. The kind of person that fortune gazes upon."

"Really?" she tried to joke. "I think you are very good. Your stage presence is remarkable! You saved me today!"

His gaze fixed again, briefly. "It is not my destiny, to be one of the great ones." He fidgeted with his water glass. "I hope at least to be an instrument to you. You are the one with a special destiny."

Luna laughed, flustered. "You shouldn't flatter me so."

"But I mean it."

"Well, I …" She was taken aback to see him look at her with the same quiet intensity he often had. But this time something akin to anguish in his expression alarmed her. "I don't know what to say."

His face blazed now. "I-I-I will always protect you. And do right by you. B-b-because I love you, Lady Blythe."

"I … surely you …"

But his eyes pierced hers now, avidly, almost reproachfully. "It is true, as true as anything can be. I love you, and it is okay if you don't love me back. So you don't have to say anything at all. I-i-if you don't want to."

She looked into his eyes, stunned. He had never maintained eye contact with her for more than a few seconds at a time. Now he would not look away, though his eyes trembled, back and forth, in their sockets. He was willing himself not to look away.

She knew that he spoke the truth. "But, Jacob … how long have you known this? And kept it secret?"

"I've known since the first time we performed together."

"Since before we got on the train?" She laughed in a gentle way, but he was not smiling.

"Y-y-yes. From nearly the moment I met you. I thought you were so dear and so talented and so terribly brave, to be carrying on as you are despite the shooting, and the press, and all those things I would protect you from if you were ever to say the word, darling—"

"I surely appreciate that, I do, but I …"

"You do not have to love me back. It is a gift merely to

h-h-hold you in my sight."

She looked down, blushing. Her husband had thought her stupid, had held her in contempt. Sean had said he loved her, but she had always had the impression that he merely loved the idea of her. Like those ludicrous pencil drawings he had done of her in the showgirl corsets. An image she did not recognize.

But Jacob was in agony. He reached for his wineglass and drained the thing quickly. Jacob, who was not a drinker.

Luna was quiet for a long while, taking it all in. The boy was so pure. He would never lie to her. It was so rare to meet an honorable soul.

The room, with all of its sounds of tinkling cutlery and conversation; the pianist had started playing the opening chords of "My Melancholy Baby," the notes hesitant and questioning … all of it felt oppressive, pressing in on them from all sides.

"Jacob, would you like to go now?"

"You haven't finished your meal."

"All at once I am not so hungry. I'm a bit dizzy."

Jacob signaled for the check. They collected his straw fedora at the hatcheck, and in short order were in an open carriage on their way back to the hotel.

The colors of the setting sun looked saturated and electric. The palm trees, the brick walls. So many people still walked the streets, visited the shops. A man sold shaved ice from a cart, children gathered around him watching him take a blade to the great block of translucent blue ice. Their voices high, keening, delighted, with a slight echo.

"I will always remember this," said Luna. "It already feels like a memory, it is so lovely."

Jacob said nothing at first, but watched her intently, sitting very close to her.

"Are you feeling better now, Lady Blythe?"

"I believe so."

"T-t-the ocean air is good for you."

"I suppose it is." But she hadn't been sick in the first place. She'd just needed to get out of there. Her thoughts tumbled in her head, too confusing to make sense of.

They passed by a small storefront of a fortuneteller, with a sign out front with an outline of a hand. Luna leaned against Jacob a bit, and pointed and said, "I went to one of those places once."

"Oh? What did they tell you?"

"The usual. I would meet a mysterious stranger, go on a trip. Enormous changes."

"Did you believe her?"

She thought about it. "Not really. I think it was only that I wanted some lyricism in my life. I was an unhappy girl, then ..." She trailed off. Allowed the thought to vanish, dissipate, like the mist that cloaked the curtains of Spanish moss in the morning when she walked through the park.

But as the horse's hooves clip-clopped down the road, she felt clear-headed once more. Everything came together, and had a sense of rightness again.

Because she knew that her life had truly changed when she became Lady Blythe. She had let her shame slip like a heavy coat from her shoulders. *All of this beauty is here because I wished it to me. And I want more. And more. And more.*

At the spiked iron gate of the carriage house, Jacob took her arm to steady her. It was rather difficult to walk up the brick path in her heeled sandals.

The garden was dark and full of late birdsong, the waxy white magnolias threw out an intoxicatingly heavy scent. Luna held the words deep within herself for some moments before she said them. "Jacob, would you come to my room? I have something I wanted to run by you. For the show."

Jacob did not answer, but like a man in a trance, nodded his assent.

The room smelled of fresh linens, the bed neatly made, the counterpane turned down just so. Her brushes and bottles lined up on the bureau. The windows open to the dark garden air.

And in a corner, stacked with her other luggage, was the box of light. Her old friend. Its presence filled the room like something tangible. A humming, electric energy, connected to her very solar plexus. She pushed it into a closet and shut the door. No one must ever discover it.

She motioned for him to have a seat on a tufted chair; she sat on the bed.

"Well, Jacob, I was thinking of ways I wanted to vary the act. There are some things I want to try that perhaps we can perform for the camera tomorrow."

"Of course." Sweat glistened on his upper lip. Though he shaved every morning, the dark shadow of tomorrow's bristles hinted already.

"And, well, it's something I have not done before. I was thinking levitation."

"But … you already levitate, Lady Blythe."

"Well, what I meant was, this time I could levitate *you*."

Tension filled the silence, until Luna said, "Only if you would be comfortable with the idea, of course."

"I don't r-r-rightly know what to say." Funny, how he sounded younger, more like the country boy he had so recently been.

"Well, I've never elevated another living body before. I would have to practice. I have only ever lifted myself. The process is a little different, working person to person."

"How might it be d-d-d-different?"

Luna thought for some moments. "It's hard to explain. It's very visceral. You work from your gut, your intuition. When I lift myself, I communicate deeply within myself. To lift you, the communication would be a bit different. It is rather an intimate act."

He looked at her, his eyes large, shifting his straw hat around and around in his large-knuckled hands.

She held her tongue between her lips. "Well. It is … my atoms would have to communicate with your atoms. I would concentrate and find my way deep into the center of you. The part where you are densest. And I sort of communicate spaciousness."

He said nothing.

She laughed nervously. "That sounds strange, I know. It is not dangerous. There is just a difference between doing it to yourself, and having it done to you. By another."

"And you have had it d-d-done to you, Lady Blythe?" As soon as he asked the question, he looked away blushing, as though the question presumed too much.

She was quiet. But then said, "Yes. Yes, I have." *And I hated it*. But she could not say that! "It is not so bad. There is a tickling, a fluttering inside you. And it moves you. It holds you up." *And binds you fast. And you cannot escape …*

He set his hat on the bureau beside him and stared thoughtfully into space. Then he stood up.

"Well, then. You can do that to m-m-me."

"Are you sure?" He had the look about him, with his head down, of a man condemned.

"Yes. I want you to do it."

Luna stood now, too. At first she could not do anything, her thoughts whirling again. Was it good? Was it right?

The room grew dark, but she did not feel compelled to turn on the lamp.

She stood back from him and looked him up and down. Dressed in a slightly rumpled seersucker suit, Oxfords of pale woven leather on his feet, his curly dark hair was parted and held back with heavy pomade. He looked down like a supplicant.

Concentrating, she worked to find her way into this young man's pure heart, until she could just detect it. A strong, young, healthy heart, beating wildly in his chest like a trapped bird. She imagined what it would be like to hold it in her hand, to soothe it into relaxation.

She tried to imagine who he had been, and who he was now. A good boy, an honorable boy. A boy who did not know himself. A boy who looked for himself in others. As an actor on the stage, he opened himself up like a portal, letting other personas in. But what did he lose?

His soul, she felt, was a spacious, wide-open place, and he had invited her in. She began to inhabit that, until she seeped into his very being, and merged.

Up, up, up.

Little by little, Jacob's woven Oxfords, worn without socks, rose from the floor.

The last of the day's sunlight glowing through the window was just enough to highlight the thin stripes of his suit, his white collar, and the paleness of his face. And his eyes, perceptibly larger.

"It's happening," he murmured, as though to himself, like a prayer. "It's happening."

Just a little higher he rose until he was about six inches

off the ground. "I have had dreams of this. Dreams of flight. This feels like a dream."

She laughed gently. "Well, it's not." It felt as though in the whole world, only the two of them existed, and the sound of night birds rising from the dark garden. "Do you like it?"

He looked down at her, with that look of exquisite anguish. "Yes, I like it," he whispered.

Luna felt a thrill of power surge through her veins, lifting him an inch more. His face. He breathed hard now and a smile trembled about his lips.

"Let me know if you want me to let you down."

But as she knew he would, he whispered, begging, "No, no, no. It's extraordinary."

"Really?"

"The first time I have ever felt … *extraordinary*. I love it. I adore it."

He said these words in a sort of chant, a mantra. Was he praying to her? The feeling she had was intoxicating. Holding a man aloft in thin air. Holding this man who was in love with her, who would do anything for her. For the first time in her life, she was the one in control.

Higher he rose, his arms out like Christ on the cross. Smiling with the pleasure of it, she spun him in a lazy circle.

Thirty-Six

The wooden seats were hard and uncomfortable, the air close and stagnant in spite of the large electric fans whirring away to the sides. Nickelodeons are the scourge of the earth, Luna reflected, before scolding herself for the uncharitable thought.

But she had been invited to the première of her short moving picture, *Lady Blythe, the Miracle Magician,* so she *had* to be there, crowded into the room among little children with their scabbed knees and high black shoes, working men wearing flat caps, and most of all, women, girls who reminded her of herself, their dresses plain and careworn, but eyes that yearned for *more*, for romance, for some wonderful eventuality to come into their lives, like the stories on the screen.

Also, there were men there to take pictures of her for the newspaper, so she wore a dress of peach and mint-green stripes and a matching mint-green woven hat with small silk flowers on it. Artie wanted her to always dress like a proper lady when not on stage, "It adds to the allure."

A dreadful place it was, though, it had to be admitted.

Gaudy posters on the outside (the most prominent one showing her image, lips rouged and eyes twinkling, dressed like a swami.) But inside, bare walls, lines of machines with people peering into them, transfixed, looking like tethered animals … *to think I used to frequent these places. In the bad days. The desperate days …*

Her picture was being projected in the new theatre room, which wasn't as bad as the parlor room. But the heat still made her feel sick. She had to will herself to smile for the cameras as they clicked away around her.

How do you feel, Lady Blythe?

I feel so happy to be back in New York.

Are you proud of your sudden fame?

I am proud of my work, and proud I entertain people.

Are you prepared for your trial testimony later this month?

Lady Blythe, are you…

A relief when finally they turned down the lights, the piano player tickled the ivories with some tune she did not recognize, something jaunty with Egyptian-style rhythms. And then the title card rolled:

Secrets sifting through the Araby sand, as old as time, known to few …

The gift of magic the heritage of Cosmos the Incomparable, great magician of his era … His life cut short by the bullet of a madman.

And his dying wish that his beloved wife carry on his legacy
And she is: Lady Blythe, of the Gates of Seven Wonders!

The screen filled with the image of Luna, her back to the camera. The piano keys trilled in suspense as she turned around, smiling, arms stretched out.

Although Luna had prepared herself beforehand, nothing could avert the shock of it. Still pictures of herself she had seen before, but to watch herself in motion was so surreal, her mind couldn't take it in. The darkly shaded eyes, the lips that looked smeared black. That *look* in her eye, alight with power and mystery …

The effects of the film were a bit quick and jerky, speedier than real life, but even so Luna appreciated the fluid grace of her movements. Was that truly her, moving that way?

I wished for this so badly that I made it come true. I'm on the screen like Mary Pickford. I am a whole different person now.

The audience politely applauded each trick she did. Scarf trick, the bird trick. But they gasped most of all for the finale, when Luna rose in the air, and then straining with the effort, lifted her assistant to join her. The camera angle shifted crazily for a minute as the cameraman struggled to capture them as they floated toward the ceiling, hands clasped, dancing a kind of airborne minuet, eyes locked in one another's in a terrible, fearsome wonder.

Thirty-Seven

"Luna, I hardly know you anymore!"

Mary Catherine gazed at her with shining eyes, sitting by her side at the family table when the others had gathered outside on the stoop to try to catch any cool breeze they could on that stifling Sunday.

"You were gone for so long this time. Longer than the other trip. Sometimes I was afraid you would never come back."

"Whatever are you saying?" Luna laid a hand on her cheek. "How could I stay away from a dear little sister like you?"

But could she? Luna had the guilty notion that her family weighed her down, even young sweet Mary Catherine. The sights, noises and smells of the Hell's Kitchen walk-up encased her like a giant fist. She felt wild, desperate to break free even as she sat there.

"Tell! Tell me about the places you visited!"

"Of, I don't know, Mary. Towns tend to look the same and blend into each other after a while. Although I did like Charleston very much. It had lovely big houses, and the sea, and palm trees, and big creepy trees with hanging moss that looked like spooks."

"Wow! That sounds about as different from Doolin as you could imagine!"

Luna laughed at the girl's endearing innocence and gave her a little kiss on the cheek. But at the same time, sadness enveloped her. She had spent so much time traveling, watching things speed by in a blur through windows, it was hard to sit still and really be with Mary Catherine this moment. What might this girl's life be? Working a job at the flag factory, marrying a man from the shipyard? Or worse yet, marrying a man from the White Hand Gang, and getting bound up into *that* world.

"Well, it's true. There are a lot of places in this world that are completely unlike Doolin. Or Hell's Kitchen, for that matter."

"Oh, Luna, I want to go with you someday. I want to go on a train and stay in a hotel in some fine city with palm trees."

"Well, maybe you can. We'll see. But I think your studies are the most important thing now. Be sure to do well in school, and maybe then we will take a trip."

"Oh, thank you, Luna! I would love it so!"

Lil came in to shut the windows. "It's starting to rain out there a bit, thank goodness. It is so humid I thought I had been swimming all through the church service." She sat next to Luna and said quietly, "Are things any better between you and Pa?"

Luna sighed. "I don't know what to say about *that*. He doesn't say anything to me, or even look at me. We just circle each other warily, like growling animals."

"Why, what a thing to say! Pa would never bite you."

"Well, that might be better than ignoring me completely."

"Don't worry, sister. He will come around. It's just his way."

"Well, I've had about enough of his way. If he doesn't want to talk to me, well then, so be it."

"Why, Luna Fiona! How can you say that!"

Lil looked shocked; she still had such great reverence for their father, for elders in general, that Luna felt that she lived on another planet, with a different air and gravity. And using her middle name, their mother's name, added to the intended wound.

"No disrespect to Pa, Lil. But he is a grown man and can make his own decisions. As will I. I will not kill myself to court his favor."

"Well, I think it is a terrible shame, I do."

Luna fanned herself with her hands, and then rose. "The heat. This heat will be the death of me. I think I will be going. I need to wash my hair tonight."

"Please don't be upset, sister. Pa will be proud of your profession one day. It's the courtroom stories, he thinks they're lurid ... but when it all dies down—"

"Aye, there, Miss Luna, don't run out the door just yet!" Cousin Patrick had just come in, hair damp, shirt flecked with rain.

"I need to leave now, Patrick."

"But I got something to give ya first! James gave 'em to me as he can't be here today."

"Whatever it is, I'm sure I—"

But he handed them to her anyway. Little folded-up pages of smudged onionskin paper. Five of them this time. She held them at a distance, distastefully.

"Patrick, I don't want them," she whispered, annoyed that he was so open in front of Lil and Mary Catherine.

"But ya got to take 'em. James'll be cross with me!"

"Fine!" she hissed and shoved them in her bag. If she had to stay one minute longer in this place, she feared she would lose her mind. She kissed each sister on the cheek and cuffed Patrick on the side of his shaggy head.

"I saw ya in the picture show!" Patrick called down the stairway after her. "Big as life ya were! Looked like the bride o' the mummy, like!"

"For Christ's sake!" she vented when she was home at last. Because of the rain, the streetcar had been crowded and noisy, just when she badly wanted to be alone.

She kicked off her heeled shoes and lay on her bed, eyes closed. *If this day doesn't end soon, it will be the death of me …*

The letters in her bag … what to do with them? It would be best to throw them in the bin, she thought. But she was having a hard time actually doing it. The letters had a sort of pull on her, and before long she had taken them out, opening each tightly folded little square, and spread them on her bed.

She chose one to open at random.

June 21, 1912

Dearest Luna,

I would love so much to have a letter from you one day. James can deliver it, no problem. No danger to you. I dream that you will send me a letter saying that you love me, and that you will perfume it with violet water. I long to smell the essence of a woman. There are no women here. Well, there are women here, but they keep them separate from the men, as it should be. But you are the only woman I crave.

I believe it is my longing for you that drove me to at last get into trouble the other day. I was out in the quarry with the paperboy I had mentioned before. Remember him? The one who is very young, but very mad? We were out working with our hammers, and he has a habit of muttering under his breath, always very peculiar things that make no sense. Anyhow, that day he kept muttering, "T'aint the kibble, t'aint the bone. T'is something in between."

Usually I leave him to it, pay him no mind. But it was one of those days I was in a dark mood. I get them sometimes, ever since I was a boy, and I am sometimes likely to do a wild thing, like smash something or set something aflame. It was always getting me in trouble.

Anyhow, the paperboy kept muttering this nonsense, over and over, and so quiet-like that I could barely hear it. You know how sometimes something is so quiet, you're wondering if it's actually just in your mind the whole time and it's like to drive you crazy?

So I said, "Shut up, boy, no one wants to hear your gibberish." He just turned to me and gave me this empty-eyed look, and bared his teeth. Jagged and sharp, like fangs. But he is a little chap, no more than a hundred and twenty pounds soaking wet. So even his queerness did not scare me.

It seemed to scatter his train of thought, though, and he was quiet for a bit. But then he started up again. T'aint the the kibble t'aint the bone t'is something in between t'aint the kibble t'aint the bone but something in between.

Then I got so mad! I just lost my temper and grabbed him by the back of his shirt and threw him down into the rocks, I said "Shut it, boy, or next time I will stab you with my shank!"

You see, it had been building up. Missing you, knowing that you were on the stage with men looking at you in towns I've never even been to. My days all being so much the same. Did I mention the size of my cell? It was immaterial to me in the beginning. I welcomed their punishment, then. But it has been doing my head in, I will tell you.

I did not throw him far. We were shackled together at the ankles for God's sake.

Anyhow, the boy made a ruckus, a terrible screeching as he came at me and bit me on the face. Just the same as he did to that poor old woman, back when he was selling newspapers.

Well, it didn't even hurt so much as it made me angry, and this time I started to knock him about the head pretty good. That is when the guard came.

There are guards who like me, guards who are fellow Irishmen and look out for me. This was not one of those guards. This was a big fat wop with pig-like eyes that glisten when he looks at me. He had it in for me, of course. He called another guard over and they unshackled me and carried me off.

They took me to the shower bath.

As you are a lady, a lovely and pure lady, I am sure that you have never heard of such brutality as the shower bath. I can tell you, any sane man would prefer to be lashed by the cat. To take my stripes would be far preferable to the bath.

You see, my darling, it is a device where they put you onto a wooden chair and strap your arms down onto blocks on either side so you can't get away. And then, from there, it all depends on how ornery and cruel the guards are feeling. They can use regular water, or they can put ice into the barrels. They can sit you under the stream regular, or they can attach the bowl around your neck, it's like a dog collar with a stand-up rim.

That piggy spiteful wop attached the bowl.

The bowl collects the water and it drains real slow, so you have to keep your head angled up, nose just out enough for you to breathe.

And they just keep pouring the water over you, from a great height. Just tremendous amounts of water. They say they do it for ten minutes. This I cannot say. Time becomes warped. It could have been ten minutes. It could have been ten hours for all I could tell. The suffocation and the terror and the panic made me feel not human anymore, but an animal.

I had never experienced anything like that before. I like to think I am a brave man. I have seen and done many things that would truly chill you, my dear. But the cruelty inflicted on me blinkers my mind.

I thought I could live here. I thought prison was not so bad, I was making my way, truly I was. For a while. But I think that while has come to an end.

This is not to say I would take back anything I did. I live and die for the sake of my love, you, and the brotherhood of the Hand. But Mother Mary, to try to breathe through a deluge of water, rising, rising, no escape, choking, dying ...

Luna dropped the letter in horror. She could read no more. Face ashen, with a grasping need for breath herself, she snatched up *all* of the letters and threw them down the trash chute.

Since Jacob had become her lover, things had changed for her in ways she hadn't expected.

It was her first time with a man in which she did most of the talking. Jacob would watch from her bed as she moved about her apartment, going about her day. The look on his face was always solemn, and a bit in awe.

"Why do you look at me like that?"

"Like what, Lady Blythe?"

"Like I'm an angel in a church window."

"Well. I cannot say why that is. Does it bother you?"

It did not bother her, quite the opposite. It made her feel anchored to sanity in her increasingly chaotic life. Jacob's quiet and steady presence made her feel capable of even more feats of magic; somehow, having him for an audience made her able to do anything.

Once, sitting at her window on a quiet, sunny afternoon, she cupped a shaft of light in her hand and turned it into a rainbow, as though she herself were a prism.

"Jacob, come see before it stops!"

The sun shifted behind a cloud by the time he came to her, but he was pleased for her nonetheless, and kissed her on the forehead, and called her a wonder.

Lately, it felt as though her heart itself had become the prism, something she could breathe radiance into.

The only problem was the fact that she had to keep Jacob a secret. From *everyone.*

"But why must we always hide?" he had pleaded, "Gladly, I would marry you, if you would have me."

"We have to hide because I'm watched. The White Hand would put a bullet in you and toss you in the river, Jacob. You must do what I say, and stay quiet."

"But we can't go on like this forever! Can't you call the police? Have them stop following you?"

"It doesn't work like that."

"Then how does it work?" He gave her a long, searching look, until she tried to reassure him. They could go away, they could leave New York for good …

"But your family, Luna! You would miss them!"

"Oh, bother my family. I'm through with them."

But in having said this, it seemed Luna conjured up a visit from a family member the very next day. James showed up unexpectedly, ringing to be let in. It was fortunate that Luna was alone at the time.

"How are things, James? Doing well, I hope. I will miss church on Sunday I'm afraid. You can pass along my regrets to—"

"I ain't here about church."

She took a deep breath. "Well, what brings you my way, then?"

"Why have ya never written him back?"

She kept her face still. "Written … who back?"

"Ya know who I'm speakin' of."

"*James …*"

"He's not doin' well. His mind is full of torment in that place."

She sighed heavily and threw her hands up. "Why should I be responsible for Sean's well being? I owe him nothing."

"He went to prison for ya, ya know."

Luna crossed her arms, bent her head down, but looked up at him from beneath her furrowed brow. "That is not a fair thing to say."

"But he did."

"James, the things Sean does, he does without thinking. I truly believe shooting my husband was simply another impulsive decision, nothing more than that. Just the way he's gone about everything in his life! Brawling, ripping that gas lamp off the pub wall … He probably did what he did in Barbetta that night because he had a sudden whim. And now he's paying for it in a way he's never paid for anything. But I did not ask him to do what he did! He makes his own decisions and it has nothing to do with me."

James cocked his head to the side, with a wry smile. "Be that as it may, ya gotta admit, ya are a long ways better off then ya were."

"What do you mean?"

"Ya are happier now."

"How do you know that?"

"Ya are doin' what you want to do now. Ya used to be so … drawn. Ya looked strained and unhappy."

"Yeah? Well, I had my reasons."

"But that's just what I'm sayin'. Ya see?"

Luna sighed and sank down into the sofa. The musty mohair sofa had come with the furnished apartment. Someday, she would get around to buying her own things, getting a new place. And not give her family the address. "James, I am not writing to him."

He nodded, eyebrows raised ironically. "Very well

then. But ya are gonna testify in the courtroom for 'em, aye?"

"Yes, but it's not for him. I have to testify whether I like it or not. I'm a witness."

"A star witness."

"Oh, I'm some such I suppose."

"But what you tell 'em may have great sway on the outcome."

She looked at him and said nothing.

James went on. "If they convince the jury that this was a crime of passion, he could get a lesser sentence. And even get out down the line."

Luna stared into space for some moments. "Out, you say?"

"Well, not tomorrow or anything. But who knows, he could get two years for manslaughter. With good behavior, who knows what could happen."

She had no reply to this. Her mind had gone blank. This was not a possibility she had ever seriously heeded. Sean, free?

James came and sat down beside her. "Listen to me. Ya are the one with the power here. If the case goes badly for him, he could get the chair. He could die, Luna."

"It is not for me to say what Sean's fate is."

"Ya once loved him, Luna."

She flushed red. "That was … I was young then."

"It was only last year, for cryin' out loud!"

"Yes, well. I was immature. Naïve. I didn't know him well. Didn't know a lot of the things he had done with the White Hand, terrible things. I just fancied him."

"Well, he loves ya."

"He doesn't know me."

"He thinks of ya all the time."

"I wish he wouldn't! Because it doesn't make me happy. It makes me feel weighed down and … and … and smothered."

"Ah, come on, ya are a good-hearted girl, have some compassion—"

"Don't you dare try to make me feel guilty, James!"

"Whoa now." He held his hands up, as though to ward off blows.

Luna composed herself again. "I just think Sean has nothing to do right now, so he's making ideas about me in his head, making me into this larger-than-life thing that has no resemblance to *me* anymore. We had our moment. We were young and we had our fun. Now we have to grow up. I have outgrown him."

"Okay, okay. I see that. I understand that. But please, Luna, I'm asking ya. Have some mercy."

"And what does that mean?"

James leveled his gaze at her, his eyes shrewd, assessing, beneath his straight dark brows. A scar ran alongside the right side of his mouth, the legacy of a knife fight a number of years ago. It was the face of a thug, a hoodlum. And held such kindly intelligence, too. Her cousin was a walking contradiction. And she could not bear to look at him.

"Luna, ya can't always just walk away when ya want to."

She looked down.

"Listen, my cousin, my good girl. I'm family, right?"

"Of course," she admitted with a resigned sigh.

"Then ya will be hearin' what I'm sayin'. Sometimes our … roots, our destinies get mixed up with other people's. Even when ya don't want 'em to."

"Yes, and I really, *really* don't want them to. I'm sick and tired—"

"And yet, here ya are. You and Sean had ya moment."

"And it's over."

"But is it? Ya moment may be over, but it keeps, sort of, vibrating, don't it? Like a bell."

"I am losing your point, James."

"My point is, for better or worse, ya *are* involved with Sean, still. He's in a bad fix right now."

"Of his own making."

"But ya still caused this bend in his life's road. Oh, come on, Luna. Help set things right again."

"And how may I do that?"

He turned his head to the side a bit, smiled grimly, and looked at her askance with his eyes lowered. "Ya tell that judge and jury exactly what it was Sean saved ya from."

"What … do you mean?" But coldness snaked up her spine. She knew his meaning.

"Tell 'em what ya suffered under ya husband. Tell 'em that ya were trapped, tell 'em ya were helpless, tell 'em what that mean bastard—"

"James, please don't go on anymore. I wasn't helpless. I was just stupid and made a foolish choice and I deserved what I got."

He nodded curtly. "Well. All right then. So basically, ya tell 'em the truth. And tell 'em Sean behaved honorably when he shot the mealy wop bastard."

"Sean *behaved* like his brain was a buzzing bumblebee knocking around in his head, as always!"

"Or maybe he couldn't stand to see ya mistreated in such a way by ya husband. We all knew what he did and—"

"No one knows anything! You don't know went on in my marriage!"

"Luna. It's okay. No one was judgin' ya for it. Least of all me. Ya were young, you were green, ya had just gotten off the boat in a strange new land …"

Tears of anger welled, and Luna willed them back. "That was the past. And I'm through with the past."

"But the past is still alive, and now a young man in the prime of his life, is livin' in a three by five cell and gettin' drowned in the shower bath, fa Christ's sake!"

"James, you need to leave now."

"But first, ya have to—"

"GET OUT NOW!"

He calmly stood up and walked out of the door, shutting it gently. She took deep ragged breaths, her face in her hands, red flashes before her eyes, her heart galloping, until she heard his steps down the stairwell, and then she burst into tears.

The only thing that calmed her and made her feel better was to take out the box of light, unlock it, and open it up, the creak of its ancient hinges, comforting and familiar to her ears. The smell of old newspapers as welcoming as an old friend. The pulsing and buzzing, the heat and light of the thing, soothed her soul like a balm, making her whole again.

Everything will be all right, as long as I still have you.

Thirty-Eight

I am Blythe of the Gates now. I am Blythe of the Gates.

She repeated the phrase in her head like a mantra as she hurried down Fourth Street to meet Agnes, Gertie, Edward and Peter. They promised it would be "a most raucous party," in an art gallery that was just opening up in an old storefront. "Everyone will be there," Agnes had said excitedly. "And Aimée Crocker, your new best friend?" She waggled her eyebrows. "*She* might even be stopping in as well."

Since James's visit, Luna had been restless with pent-up energy. A great wildness dwelled deep within her, and it needed a release. The party was just the thing, at just the time, and she readily said "yes".

At the address, she opened the door. The gallery was already packed with reveling partygoers.

"Darling!" Gertie was the first to spot her, and swept forward, wearing a Japanese kimono in a vibrant tangerine print, her hair combed straight back like a man's. Despite her pale face, devoid of rouge or lip paint, she still managed to be the most striking figure in the room. "Let me look at you!"

She held Luna at arm's length and looked her up and down; Luna had worn one of her Grecian gowns, her hair down, long and loose. She wore a necklace made of long strands of crystal and onyx.

"My dear Lady Blythe! You look the *goddess* tonight. We haven't seen you in forever!"

"Sorry I haven't been in touch."

"Well, that's understandable, darling! You are the talk of the town! You are the brightest new star. We are all thrilled for you."

"Oh, it's not as exciting as all that. It's just that I got back in town not so long ago and I'm just getting my bearings again."

"I know the feeling. We got back from the Riviera last month and I still don't know if I'm coming or going." She and Edward had gone once again with Agnes and Peter. "I carried a parasol the whole time because I don't take the sun, but I still got a bit of a tan, and my shoulders are peeling. Anyway, it was fabulous. You must come with us next time we go. We are going to have a magic lantern party soon and show slides."

The rest came over and kissed her, European style. Edward took both her hands excitedly. "And we made a stop in Paris. A Duchamp showing. Know what I saw?"

"What?"

"I saw *Nude Descending a Staircase*." He looked at her significantly, his face solemn with reverence.

"I am not familiar."

"You *will* be. It is the future. It *is* futurism. It was full of motion, you should have seen the movement, like stop-motion photography. It was going ..." He gestured, screwing up his face extravagantly, "Counterclockwise. I nearly fell into a trance."

"You had been smoking so much dope though, Eddie Boy. You got so close to the painting and your expression was so alarming that the guards were practically drawing weapons. They nearly threw us out," Gertie said.

"Perhaps. But it was life-changing nonetheless." Edward stared into space, lost in the memory as if to form his thoughts about it. Then he abruptly spun to Luna, eyes wide, and said, very fast, "Time is speeding up, do you feel it? Like an overwound watch in a giant's breast pocket."

"Excuse me? I don't follow." She laughed nervously.

In answer, he dug out his snuff tin and held it out to her.

"Luna doesn't huff anymore," said Agnes gently.

But Luna laughed. "Oh, I don't know. I may tonight. Why not?"

"That's my girl," said Edward. He slid the tin open and scooped out a bit with the long fingernail on his right pinky, then held it under her nostril.

She did each side, and immediately felt a cold, clear sparkle in her synapses; all at once, she knew that everything really *would* be okay, that she was in control of her destiny, that she held the world in the palm of her hand.

Peter led her around to look at the art. Much of it comprised portraits, strange-looking portraits in which the subjects had odd, segmented faces with eyes noses and mouths arranged in scrambled ways. They gave the illusion of being flat and leaping out at you at the same time. There were sculptures, too. Mostly of human bodies made up of plain geometric forms, squares and cylinders and circles.

"What do you think," Peter said low into her ear. "Is it the future, or is it a grand fraud? I'm not as enamored as dear Edward."

"I would not know what to say. I don't know art. I'm just a country girl from Doolin, you know."

"Oh, you are much more than *that*, my dear, so best get used to it! Say, you might want to know more about art so you can invest someday. I do. I buy what Eddie tells me. I bought a Picasso, but the thing is so odd and distorted-looking that I hang it in the study where I cannot see it, it jangles my nerves so. But, supposedly, it's going to bring in the cash one day, a sure thing."

"I see what you're saying. I may just need to get myself educated. Become a modern woman." She had taken a flute of champagne that went by on a tray; she looked around the room. Yes, it was another one of those regular Village crowds, a mix of wealthy and downtrodden bohemian. You would think they wouldn't get on together, but she had a sense that each always watched the other, preening, performing, enjoying the mutual show.

Unlike the old days, though, people knew Luna. Or knew *of* her, in any case. She had very few moments on her own, to just observe. People wanted to ask her about her show, her travels. But they delicately avoided the subject of the next week's trial. It was all over the papers. She was grateful she did not have to speak of it. Anything, but that

And the champagne kept coming. So busy talking and laughing, she did not pay attention to how much she drank, and it quickly went to her head. That, along with the sparkling cocaine, had put her into a very upbeat and breezy mood, indeed.

"Do a trick for us, Luna, please?" begged one gaggle of party girls from the Upper East Side, until, feeling warm and magnanimous, she relented. She took a cherry from one of their cocktails, put it in her mouth and turned it into a glittering, dome-cut red jewel, and handed it back to the delighted, pink-cheeked girl who held it aloft in wonder for the room to see.

"Another, another!" pleaded a new voice.

"Look, see that woman over there? That's Lady Blythe of the Gates!" said another.

At first, she demurred. Then out of the corner of her eye, she saw Aimée Crocker standing at the other side of the room. Though mostly obscured by the crowd, she was unmistakable with her high-plumed hat, and the distinctive drawl of her voice rising above the others: "I'm going back to Hawaii. I *adore* Hawaii, though the missionaries all *hate* me …"

Something about Aimée's presence set off a fit of daring in Luna. "Okay. I'll do one more trick, if you could all move back a bit, please," she said.

Then, still enjoying the lift of the drug in her bloodstream, she danced as she did on stage, moving her hips in a snake-like manner, as the souls around her whooped and cheered. She took another champagne flute and held it up like a stage prop. Then she took a drink and held it in her mouth until the bubbles disappeared.

Then, lifting her head back and arching her throat, she spat it out; a great plume of flame let forth from her lips, and briefly flared into a ball. Although she aimed it away from the crowd, people cried out nonetheless in surprise and frightened laughter.

"You! Stop!" cried the owner of the gallery as he rushed over. "You can't *do* that here!"

Though the fireball had already gone, the room fell silent and stunned, watching the confrontation as a haze of smoke gathered up at the ceiling.

The gallery owner, a wiry man with a long, looped

mustache, inspected the painting that had hung closest to them, an oddly stylized and smooth-featured nude woman playing a violin.

"You have scorched it!"

"I don't see how that is possible from this far away, I was being careful …"

But upon closer inspection, one corner of the piece was slightly blackened and sooty.

In the quiet of the room, she was aware of Aimée Crocker looking over in a bemused way; she couldn't lose face now.

"Then I will purchase this one myself, sir."

He regarded her with beady little eyes, his lips compressed beneath the ridiculous and showy mustache. "Be that as it may, ma'am, I will not have these high jinx in my gallery. If you do that again, I will escort you out myself."

At one time in her life, Luna would have felt wounded to the core. But this night, it was no longer the case. This foreign urge inside of her wanted her to be the most outrageous person at the party. "It is my painting now to do with as I please. I'll set it on fire if I am so inclined."

"You are quite a nasty woman, with no reverence for art."

"But my money is as good as anyone's, ain't it boss?" This said in an exaggerated Irish brogue.

She turned her back on him imperiously, and took a cigarette holder from a young woman in a feather-trimmed cape, took a triumphant drag before handing it back.

Everyone laughed and cheered. Luna, pleased and so overcome, spontaneously let forth a swarm of yellow butterflies from her cupped palms. The crowd *oohed* and *aahed* like delighted children, smiled and tried to get them to land on their outstretched hands. The gallery owner stared daggers and then tacked a note that said *sold* beneath the painting's placard, that said it was called *Fontaine With Violin, Berlin Evening, 1911.*

Even in the midst of the merriment, Luna scanned the room with a dazed smile on her face, and sensed where Aimée Crocker was, alert to her compelling gaze.

And then Aimée walked straight toward her, the plumes on her enormous hat bobbing, the silk of her long black dress swishing. The dress sleeveless, the better to display her garish tattooed arms.

Luna tried holding her head high, to smirk nonchalantly. But Aimée's eyes were penetrating beneath her straight dark brows. And she was not smiling.

Luna smelled her scent, of spices and sandalwood and something medicinal, something that would emanate from a glass bottle in a doctor's bag. Ether?

She came very close to Luna, indeed, when she said in a deathly calm voice, "Regards, my dear. Regards."

Then lifted her arm and showing her, pointed at the tattoo. The frightening tattoo on her forearm. The tattoo of the terrifying demon face with its bared, insatiable maw of a mouth, its eyes that bore into her soul. The face that haunted her dreams.

Luna said nothing, the smile frozen on her face, though dimly aware that she had stopped breathing.

"Beware, Lady Blythe. *Wake up.* Or it will be too late."

"I … don't know what you mean, Miss Crocker." She hated how her voice came out, faint and stuttering.

"Oh, but I think you do." Aimée nodded at her, sedately, and without a goodbye, circulated back into the party.

A yellow butterfly, as though on cue, landed on Luna's

hand. She looked at it, dumbfounded, forgetting where it had come from.

At the Purple Pup afterward, they danced and laughed, with many retellings of the night's incident. After more drinks, Luna decided she was having a swell time. Therefore she was puzzled when Gertie took her into a corner at one point and asked, "Luna, are things okay? I mean, back at the gallery, and now, even, your eyes look … strained."

Luna assured her that everything was okay, it was just that she hadn't truly let loose in such a long time.

"But, dear, are you worried about the—"

But Luna pretended not to hear her, and went back to the dance floor and danced the Grizzly Bear until drenched in sweat.

She had not been this drunk, well … ever. She knew when she had trouble keeping her balance that she needed to stop.

She sat at one of the wooden tables pushed against the wall and drank a glass of water and watched the room spin around as the player piano tinkled away in the background, and all the people laughed, flinging themselves around the room as they did the Turkey Trot.

A young man with disheveled and sweaty dark hair joined her. He wore summer slacks and a button-down shirt, open at the neck, and stood next to her table.

"This place is raging," he muttered, "I feel like I am in the pit of hell."

She rolled her eyes up to him from her slumped position, said nothing.

"You doing, okay, ma'am?"

"I am fine, yes."

"May I sit?"

She shrugged, and he sat in the other chair.

He gestured to her wrapped package, which was leaning against the wall behind her. "I saw you walk in with that. What is it?"

"Oh. It's a painting."

"A painting?"

"Long story. I'd rather not get into it." Her words slurred because her face was propped up now, hand blocking her mouth.

"You are a lady magician, some folks were telling me."

She did not answer.

"I find your line of work fascinating. Are you a trickster?"

"Please leave me be. I'm not feeling too well." Her actions of the night that felt so bold at the time, now embarrassed her. She longed to go to sleep, to blot out the memories. And yet she had to take home the blasted painting.

"No disrespect. I don't judge tricksters."

"Well, what is *your* line of work?" she asked sarcastically.

He closed his eyes, as though resting them. "Well, let's see. I got kicked out of Harvard last year. That's when I got the idea to go into eugenics. I went to North Dakota to live with the Indians."

"You don't say?" She had a good deal of trouble following his words, and rubbed the space between her eyes that now throbbed.

"Yes. I studied the Mandans. I mean *really* studied them. The culture, the way of life. I even measured their skulls with a tape measure."

He motioned around his skull with his hands. Luna's

own skull, she thought, was about to split open from a migraine. This night needed to end.

"They taught me to ride horses, sing, and dance. Real Indian dancing. It's a hell of a lot better than …" he gestured to the people on the dance floor. "Wanna see?"

"See *what*?"

He didn't answer but stood up and sort of hopped, sort of jogged in place, along with singing a chant in a language she didn't recognize. The people around him drew back, looking at him strangely. He didn't seem to notice.

He came back to their table, panting a bit. "Buffalo dance! Dance of courage and good fortune."

"Oh." He was obviously drunker than she was, so probably be disregarded entirely.

"So, I did *that* for a while. I'm in New York for the moment at least. I was working as a messenger boy."

Luna said nothing but slumped back onto the table with her head in her arms. She wondered if she could even make it home on her feet.

"But that's not my … only endeavor." The young man paused and waited for Luna to ask what the endeavor was. At her lack of response, he said loudly and slowly, "I'm writing an oral history of our time."

"Isn't an oral history spoken, though?" she asked absentmindedly.

"That's the *thing*! People speak to me, and I write it down. People tell me things. I am cataloging what *we* think of as our present time in this great city."

"Well, I can't help you. I have nothing to say."

"Nonsense!" he brought his fist down suddenly on the table, startling her back into wakefulness. "You are part of the history. You are living it. Right now."

"I'm hardly *sentient* right now, I hate to tell you …"

"*Listen*. This moment is more perfect and alive than any other that has precluded it. I quit my messenger job, because there is too much to do. I am wild with life. I sleep on rooftops. I can talk to the alley cats and the pigeons and know what they say. Sea birds, too."

Against her better judgment, she raised her head to look at him. He spoke like a madman, but was he?

His eyes were alight. "I want to be a great historian, the world's greatest chronicler. I've got 70,000 words so far. I write down the murmurings of drunks, random shouts in the streets, jump rope songs sung by children in the alleys, the lamentations of whores—"

"And now you want to record me? For your oral history?"

"If you don't mind." This he said meekly, quietly.

She smiled to herself. She had to admit, the young man's passion was endearing, if annoying. She sighed heavily, and then shrugged. "I'm already in the papers, though. I'm Lady Blythe, you know."

"I don't read the papers. Although I use them as insulation on cold nights."

Luna snorted. "Well, then, it is just as well you don't know me. Yes, I am a magician. The best in town."

"How does the magic feel?" He peered at her with icy gray eyes. Amazing, how he could snap to alertness so quickly.

"It feels like … life itself. It feels like the warmth of the sun. It feels like … I don't know … rich sap rising, like the veins of a tree."

"And you tap into it?" he made a motion with his hands, of hammering in a spike.

She laughed loudly. My God, I am drunk or I would never be talking to this nut. "Yes, *exactly*."

"How wonderful."

"Yes. It is wonderful."

"Then why did you look so forlorn when I saw you across the room?"

"Because of a conundrum I find myself in." She raised one finger, dramatically, and arched her eyebrows.

He mimicked her expression, and they exchanged conspiratorial smiles.

She threw up her hands, rolled her eyes. "I have to go to court this week. I am a lead witness in a murder case."

At this, he grinned. "How fabulous."

"No, it isn't really. Because I don't know what I'm going to do."

The pianist broke into "Maple Leaf Rag." Luna felt a surge of nostalgia. This was the song that had been playing everywhere when she first arrived in America. The stuttering, syncopated movement of it, the bass line and the swirling melodies, all coming together, she would forever associate with setting foot in this strange new land, this city so like a carnival that never ended.

But she halted her reverie, and looked at the young man in front of her, helpless to do anything but state the truth. "I don't know whether to help this other human being or to help myself."

The young man rested his fist under his chin philosophically, though under the table his legs were dancing to the beat. "What is this *human being* to you?"

"Well. He loves me. Or so he claims."

"Do you love him?"

She paused. "I did. Once. But that was then. And his circumstances are his fault."

He nodded. "Is it of any detriment to you to help him?"

"Yes. In a way. It would be in the papers, and it would

ruin the image I have worked so hard to achieve. People would pity me. And I wouldn't be seen as Lady Blythe of the Gates anymore."

"How is that?"

She blushed. Even in her drunkenness, the shame burned through. "They would see me as just another wife who got knocked around by her husband. They would see me as weak. I want them to see me as *strong*." She looked down. "I *am* strong. It's just the way it would all look—"

"Do you really care so much for other people's opinions? I didn't take you for the sort. I mean ..." He gestured at the madness around them in the room, at the people reeling, yelling. Someone throwing up in the bathroom. It must have been one in the morning.

"I don't know," she said in a flat voice. "Maybe I do."

"Did this fellow human being ... how shall I put this? Does he wish you well? Was he a good friend to you?"

"I suppose he was."

"Is he a good and decent person?"

She laughed, thinking of the shocking things he did in the name of the White Hand. How he shot a man in the head and then went out for a steak and kidney pie. But Luna said, "You know? He means well. He means well by me, at least. In his way, he is very moral. And certainly loyal."

"Then why care what others think? Are you a cowardly sheep?"

Anger flashed through her system. "Obviously not!" she said indignantly. "Do you know who I am? Obviously you don't. Who are you, sleeping on rooftops, talking to pigeons, whatever the hell you said ... how can you know who I am?"

"Don't be that way, miss—"

"Sorry. I've had too much to drink. I should have started home an hour ago."

"I'm not insulting you! I just mean … da-d-a-da-da-da-da DA" He had become distracted for a moment, miming with his fingers the piano finish to "Maple Leaf Rag." "There now, sorry, that's such a good one. I just mean … try to remove yourself emotionally and see everything from a state of neutrality."

"Neutrality?"

"Yes! Get into a state of great neutrality. Then work from there. Don't fight against the world. Heal yourself. Work with the world. Then time will be your ally instead of your enemy."

"I have no enemies."

"Your enemy is yourself. You are at war with yourself, *Lady Blythe*. I can see the strain and hurt in your eyes. You got battalions fighting away as we speak. Massive casualties."

The word *casualties* made her flinch. This was too much. "And who are you to think you know me so well?"

At that, the young man shrugged serenely. "I am nobody, I guess."

"Oh, okay, mister nobody then—"

"Or you can call me Joe, if you please."

"Goodnight, Mister Nobody-Joe-what-have-you. It has been pleasant but I must be getting on."

"Well let me walk you home, then."

"No, *thank* you!"

"Hey, now, you are a lady, and quite drunk, and the streetcars are not running any more—"

"I'm not afraid! And I am not in pain."

"Okay then, but just allow me to … here, wait, don't forget your painting!"

She came back and jerked it away from him. "Goodbye!"

She spun around and out of the door, propelled forth by her own self-righteousness, adrenalin speeding the alcohol out of her system, at least.

She walked the many blocks back to Cornelia Street, ranting to herself in her mind. *The things I should have said to him! Doesn't even know me. Called me a cowardly sheep. Said I have militias in my head. Ha! Crazy. He's just a crazy homeless man so I don't know why I'm even upset.*

Such a relief to get to her own building, up the stairwell, stumbling just the smallest bit. Then she opened the door …

… to see Jacob, sitting on the sofa, hat in his hand, looking at her with an expression on his face that was an amalgam of fear and relief and embarrassment. His eyes flicked to the painting under her arm, then back to her face.

"Blythe, darling, I was so worried, I can't even—"

"How did you get in here?" she asked stridently, though she already knew she had given him an extra key so he could fetch costumes or props when she needed them.

His face fell at her tone. "I-I didn't mean to—"

"Didn't mean to what? Break into my apartment?"

"It was just that I didn't know where you were."

"I'm free to come and go as I please. You are not my husband."

His lips moved but no sound came out, his eyes searching hers. She knew this had hurt him. She knew he very much wanted to marry her. She kept hurting him and couldn't stop. It was just too easy.

"But B-B-Blythe. It is nearly two in the morning. You never stay out that late. And you must admit, there are very many scenarios th-that … that … that—"

"What scenarios, praise be?"

"Y-y-you know. I don't trust those people. Those men with the guns and the bats. The White Hand."

"They think they are protecting me."

"Yes, but, what if someone takes a notion to be displeased with you? What if—"

"Malarkey. I don't want to talk about this anymore." Turning, she accidently nudged the lamp. It tumbled over, and the light and shadows on the walls swung and glided crazily until Jacob righted it again. He continued to look at her in a troubled way.

"Why are you goggling like that, Jacob? Do you think I'm drunk?"

"Well, I didn't … well, *yes*."

"So what if I am."

"Let me help you to bed, at least, and I will go."

"I don't need your help."

He stood there, awkwardly, arms at his sides. Once again, Luna felt cruelties perched on her tongue. And once again, she felt powerless to stop herself:

"I'm not who you think I am, Jacob. Maybe you should find someone more like yourself."

"More, like—"

"You know. *Ordinary*."

The stricken look on his face. Oh, the control one could have over someone who truly loved them. That supremacy surged through her body, like a tidal force.

"Oh, don't listen to me, Jacob. I don't mean any of it."

"I-I-I will be going now. Goodnight."

"Goodnight. Oh, I am sorry, Jacob, please—"

But he was already out of the door, and did not turn back to let her see his face.

What am I doing? Who am I anymore?

She ran to the bathroom and vomited, all the drinks she had had that night coming up like acid. The room still spun and lurched. She closed her eyes to make it all go away, and saw flashing lights behind her eyelids, patterns. For a moment she thought she saw a demon's face, the one on Aimée Crocker's arm. Mara. It burned for a moment as though she had just looked at a neon lighted sign. Then it drifted and faded away.

Aw. Oh well. Oh well.

She took a deep breath, pulled the chain, and left the bathroom.

She wanted to collapse into bed, but for some reason felt compelled to unwrap the painting first. She tore away the brown paper, and leaned it against the living room wall. Looked at it. A smooth featureless woman, as though made of metal. She could be anyone. And yes, the whole corner scorched. All that modern glossy surface of the woman, but a big scorched black mark encroached from the side.

Thirty-Nine

The court building faced Broadway at an odd angle; a showy granite building that rose up to a huge domed mansard roof that stood out from the other, taller, modern buildings. It was so lavishly Victorian and old fashioned, hunched there like an old woman wearing ruffles and a nosegay. It didn't belong there, everything about it awkward.

Luna mused these thoughts idly to herself as the autocar drew closer and closer, and then stopped at the curb.

Even though it was a gray and drizzling day, heavy with humidity, there had to have been a dozen men waiting for her, cameras set up on tripods. They even knew which side door she would enter.

"Lady Blythe! Lady Blythe! Do you care to comment before you go in?"

She had barely stepped onto the running board before they closed in on her. Luna rose up to her full height, but kept her eyes trained down, her head tucked in so that her wide-brimmed hat shielded her face from the onslaught.

"Lady Blythe! How will it feel to see your lover for the

first time in a year?"

In momentary shock, she did glance up; this one had been shouted by a cheeky-looking man in an ill-fitting checked suit with no camera, only a pad and pencil. He smirked at her.

Luna waved a gloved hand to dismiss him, to dismiss all of them.

Don't think. Don't think.

She concentrated on the sound of her heeled shoes clicking on the pavement. The feel and texture of her black dotted Swiss mourning dress. (*Dress in black,* the lawyer had told her. *The press will have more sympathy for you.*)

And yet – was that someone with a *moving picture camera,* off to the right? It was, a young boy with floppy hair furiously winding the hand-crank!

It felt more invasive than the shouted questions, the still photographs. Luna drew upon whatever stirring of magic she could summon from deep within to protect herself. Focusing with all her angry might, she opened the latches on the side of the camera, and nudged out the reels of movie film so that they spilled out with a loud clatter onto the sidewalk. The cameraman stooped down, swearing, collecting the ruined reels as she walked coolly by, accompanied by her father, her sisters, and a police escort.

The courtrooms were upstairs. The lower part of the building was the post office. Luna calmed down as they made their ascent. *Just pretend I am the sun, I am the still point. With these planets and unknown satellites swarming around me, as they will.*

Breathe, breathe, breathe.

At last they reached a marble lobby, and then the large open doors of the courtroom itself. This was day three, someone said, of the trial. All this had already been set in motion. The press had already been here. The lawyers, the policemen, the jurors, already known to each other. Luna herself was the main event on this particular day. At the hush as she entered, she felt the charge in the room stir up interest, and prying eyes slide to look at her. A court official escorted her to the front, to sit with her family members until called to testify.

So many people in the room! Her eyes lit on the judge's bench and the vacant chair, the American flag in the back; next to it the table that held the stenographer's funny little typewriter. So many people, so many details to take in.

It took her some moments before she discerned the one person in the room she had been dreading to see for so long.

She didn't even recognize Sean at first glance because he looked so different from how she remembered him. Had it really only been a year? He didn't seem at all the same man. Not the man of her memories, big-as-a-mountain face, merry twinkling eyes full of mischief, always on the verge of a laugh.

For one thing, Sean looked smaller. Shrunken. His face wan beneath his brownish freckles, and dark rings circled his eyes. His cheeks rough and irritated as though someone had shaved him in a rush. His reddish hair with its wild cowlicks was parted in the middle and slicked down. His dark suit large on him, his neck still somewhat bullish, but encased painfully in a stand-up celluloid collar that she could not in a thousand years have pictured him wearing in the old days.

Sean, oh Sean. What has happened to you?

Pangs of pity and remorse ran through her, seeing him this way. He who had once been so full of robust life.

He sat next to his lawyer. She knew he must

intentionally have been looking away from her. And then he looked up.

Their eyes interlocked for some moments. She was used to seeing those eyes squinted in a smile. Even in repose, he had always had a slight smile on his face. A look of joyful belligerence, an invitation to the world to take him on. He had always been so self-assured when she knew him. Now he looked lost. He looked chagrined.

He looked afraid.

So hard to imagine Sean afraid.

It threw her off, it was so unexpected. She gave him a small tight smile, a nod, and looked away as she took her seat.

The ceiling fan barely stirred the stifling air. The set of great windows on one side were open, but with very little breeze. The wooden chairs were hard. People did speak, but only in the most hushed of tones.

Luna had never been in a courtroom in her life. Though it had been explained what would transpire and what to expect, the grand solemnity of the place spooked her. This was the room of great decisions, where it was decided who lived, who died. This room was where judgments changed the trajectories of lives.

She removed her hat, already a film of sweat at the nape of her neck, along her upper lip. The pins that held up her heavy hair pinched and dug into her scalp. Her hands trembled, just slightly.

How am I to survive this?

At long last, everyone stood up as the bailiff came in, and called, "Here ye, here ye, the court is now in session." The judge entered the room, a large, broad-shouldered man with gray hair, made even more enormous by his voluminous black robes. It made her think of the Father speaking at her church. But this man was no clergy. He looked tough and rough-tumble. And he spoke with a honking Brooklyn-inflected voice.

Various things were said, motions gone through. She knew her time was drawing near, and she was so fidgety that she could not listen to what they said, or make sense of anything. The tapping of the typographer's keys sounded louder and louder in her mind. As did the buzzing of a large fly that flew round and round, near Luna's head. Its high whine almost hypnotizing.

"I think, if Your Honor pleases, I may file with Your Honor at this time our affidavits in opposition, so you may have them before you…"

It's my time. It's my time. Can't turn back now…

And it was. She dimly heard her name called out, the buzz of the fly louder to her than anything else, some dead-toned signal from another world. She rose up and on numb feet, approached the bench.

She had to put her hand on a Bible, and swear to tell the truth, the whole truth, nothing but the truth, so help her, God. Idly, she thought of her mother's Bible, packed away in her apartment, along with her rosary beads. She wished she had used them more. But they were somewhere in her cramped closet, pushed back behind the box of light.

I have made some poor choices. Or at least, some poor choices found me.

She sat on a chair facing the room, with a curved wooden railing around her. On display.

She understood it was the prosecuting lawyer asking her questions.

"Where did you live, July of 1911?"

"I lived with my husband at 294 East 4th Street."

"Did you testify at the hearing of the State against Mr.

Sean Murphy in July, 1911?"

All the people, all the things in the room looked so remote and far away, and her voice faltered as she said, "Yes, I did."

"You were a witness for the state?"

"Yes, I was."

"Did you make an affidavit in the offices of the New York World?"

"Yes."

The man had a ruff of silver hair along the edges of his gleaming, bald, pink head, and a penetrating gaze, though his tone was friendly enough; the combination put her on edge. He brought a piece of paper and handed it to her.

"I would like you to read this affidavit and tell me if this is the affidavit you signed in the offices of New York World?"

She took it in her shaking hand. She tried to read the typed words, but the letters blurred together.

"Yes. Yes, it is."

"Did you make an affidavit in the office of Martin Littleton in the Singer Building?"

"Yes."

"Is that the affidavit in front of you? Your signature?"

"Yes. Yes, it is."

"Do you remember where you were on July 28, 1911?"

"Yes. I was at my home. It was the Monday after the … event."

"The murder of your husband, Jack Friday, you mean."

"Y-yes."

"Did you receive a visit from two men?"

"Yes."

"Would you please describe the interview?"

Luna remained silent for some moments. Then

answered, "I was ill-disposed at the time."

"Ill-disposed? Were you sick?"

"Yes, I was sick. I had taken to my bed. My husband had just been killed. I was in a state of shock and had been seeing no one. My sisters had been looking after me …" She trailed off, trying to hold her hands still in her lap

"Go on, ma'am."

"They said they wanted to ask me some questions about what went on that night at Barbetta."

"What type of questions?"

"They asked me where I was, what I had heard, what I had seen. I told them very basically what had transpired, but I was in no state to … well, I was not lucid at the time."

"Not lucid?"

"I was ill. I had taken to my bed in shock."

"And so, then?"

"Well. It is even now hard for me to recall. They told me a version of events they wanted me to say. They wanted me to say that I knew for certain that it was Sean who did it. And that I knew why he did it."

"And so you …"

"I said what they wanted me to."

"And you told the truth?"

"I said what they wanted me to."

"Luna, are you a religious woman?"

"Excuse me?"

"Are you Catholic?"

"I … yes."

"Do you speak to your priest and make confessions?"

"I-I …"

All at once the blood stopped flowing to her head, and the courtroom, with all of its hushed thumbprint faces turned toward her … the ceiling fan turning, and a faint breeze stirring the papers stacked on the judge's desk ... all of it went dark around the edges, like the framing of a daguerreotype. Her eyes fluttered and she saw the scene, neon-lit, on the back of her eyelids, even when they were shut. No escape. Encroaching doom. *Who am I? What is this? How did this all come to be?*

And then, quick as an exhale of breath, consciousness slipped away entirely, and the policeman leaped up to prevent her body from spilling onto the floor.

Forty

That night. The night of the shooting.

It was the night that her life, that had been one thing before, entirely morphed into another

Curiously, she remembered a perfect sickle moon in the sky, clear and sharp edged as though the shape had been cut with a razor. Gauzy clouds had raced over it, obscuring it, and then revealing it again.

"Luna, several witnesses, diners at the restaurant, testify that when you came out to the garden and saw your husband's bloodied body, you sank to your knees and called out, 'My husband, my husband, my love!'"

"I ... don't recall."

"You don't recall?"

"No."

"Can you surmise who you were speaking of?"

"Excuse me?"

"Who was your love?"

"No. No, I can't say."

The man clasped his hands behind his back and paced. Then said,

"You are becoming a very well-known woman, Luna,

under your stage name … Blythe of the Gates, is it?"

"That is true."

"In fact, one can go uptown and see you on the moving picture screen for a nickel. I saw it myself. Very impressive. And the title card reads that you were the bereaved bride of Cosmos the Incomparable."

"Yes."

"Cosmos the Incomparable was the stage name of your husband, Jack Friday. Correct?"

"Yes."

"So he nurtured and guided you into the ways of magic?"

She didn't know what to answer. "I … in a way. I learned by watching him." She couldn't tell them the real source of how she attained her powers. The box of light, she felt, must never be spoken of. It loomed that powerfully in her mind. She longed for the comfort of its vibrant, thrumming power in that moment. But she couldn't feel it.

"So, Luna, you would say it was a strong marriage."

"How do you …I suppose … well. Yes. Whatever strong means."

"Well, on the moving picture screen, it implies a tale of a loving marriage. The tale is told at the beginnings of your stage act, as well."

"Well …"

"Is Blythe you?"

"Th-that is hard to say."

"Please try to explain."

"Well. She is based on me in the very least. She has all the best parts of me … but the same time I feel I created her."

"So she contains aspects of you. Based on you."

"Yes. She is me but … better. I would say she is regal.

Queen-like. And I …"

"Could you please speak up, Luna? The court can't hear you. You've gone a bit quiet."

"Yes. I simply said … yes."

The man looked down, nodded sagely several times. Then looked up at her, his head cocked to the side, as though something had just occurred to him.

"Please tell me, Luna. What is the nature of your relationship with Mister Sean Murphy?"

Startled, she glanced over at Sean. He had his eyes closed and seemed to be silently praying.

"Is that Mister Murphy that you are looking at now, Luna?"

"Yes. That is him. He, I mean."

"Please answer my previous question."

"Yes … I met him because he is a friend of my boy cousins."

"Please go on. Fill us in a bit more if you will."

"Well. I saw him at church. Family suppers and the like."

"So you saw him quite a bit, then?"

"I suppose so. I had just come to this country. I knew no one, except my family and my family's friends."

He strolled over to the large open window, acted as if he were casually looking out to the street below. "Would you say that Mister Murphy was in love with you?"

She moved her lips silently, but nothing came out.

"Well? Would you?"

She shrugged, mouth gone dry. "I d-d-don't rightly know how he felt about me. I don't know what goes on in other people's heads."

"But he was fond of you."

"I suppose."

"He was sweet on you? But you did not return his

feelings?"

"That I cannot answer. He was a friend when I needed one."

He left the window and strolled back, very close to where Luna sat. He looked her straight in the eye for some beats before asking, "Did Mister Murphy ever mention being a member of the White Hand Gang?"

"No. He never discussed such things with me."

"But you knew that he was? A member?"

"I had heard things, but they were second-hand."

"Who told you?"

Oh no, she thought. No way to back out of this without sounding a liar. "Well. I have heard of the gang, of course."

"And what do you know of them? And their activities."

"I don't know. I thought they just met at the pub and told stories and such?"

Some men in the courtroom chuckled at that. Her face flamed red.

"Did you know that the White Hand Gang members commit murders? Blackmail? Racketeering?"

"I don't know much about them, sir. I stay out of that stuff. It does not interest me."

The man looked at her again for a few beats, and then paced away again. Then, in a casual voice as though making small talk about the weather, he asked, "Did Mr. Murphy ever express a desire to harm Mister Jack Friday?"

Luna's heartbeat pounded in her ears, and the hiss of her blood. It took her some time until she said, "No, sir."

"Ever threaten to kill your husband?"

"I do not recall that."

"But your answer is not no?"

"My answer is that I do not recall."

"Did Mister Murphy ever express his love for you?"

"I told you already, I don't know what was in his head ..."

"But did he ever say the words?"

"I don't ... I ... well, he took interest in me like a family member, I suppose. He wished the best for me. He is a good man."

"A good man who goes around throwing people in the river with their hands and feet shackled?" He sallied this forth so quickly that it threw Luna's composure.

Someone called out "*Objection!*" But denied.

"Sean never told me of any such thing."

"But surely someone has?"

"Not that I remember."

"You go to confession, Luna?"

"What?" Not this again.

"Say the rosary?"

Now she was not just flustered, but angry. "What are you implying, sir?"

But he was done with her. He walked away, leaving Luna to stare mutely after him.

Interminable. A large wall clock with fleur de lys arms that scarcely moved as Luna was kept imprisoned by the round wooden gate. From the open windows came the sounds of autocars puttering by, horns squealing. Cries of vendors, cries of the paperboy, cries of the seabirds looking for the shore.

She thought she would never get out of there. That she would become so angry or frightened that her heart would thunder until it stopped completely, and this entire room of people would watch her die. The man would capture her death on his little sketch-board drawing and it would be on the front of the paper. Her hands and feet tingled as the next man approached the bench to ask her questions.

As he and the judge exchanged words, Luna glanced

again at Sean. He was looking right at her, his expression one of imploring, naked fear. But he also tried to smile at her, just a flash. In her nervousness she gave a stiff smile back, almost a grimace.

Her nervous system in such overdrive by that point, there was much she did not hear or register. This new man was different from the first, smaller. Rounder. He wore a pale lightweight suit that was small on him and strained at the seams.

The floorboards creaked under his feet as he approached her. He asked her different questions, too. General questions about where she was from, about her ocean voyage to America. Questions she did not see the relevance of, but she answered them.

He had a high, piping voice for such a heavy man. But quick, shrewd eyes. "So, Luna, would you agree that your transition to American life had its times of strife?"

"I suppose, sir."

"You came here for a better life, didn't you?" he asked sympathetically.

"Well, it wasn't that my life in Ireland was bad. It was just … it's a hard life, you know, just having our little patch of land and the chickens."

"Not enough to eat?"

"Food was scarce at times."

"And you had lost your mother."

She looked at him, stricken, unable to utter a word.

He went on, "It's okay, Luna. I just mean to say that it was a brave thing to cross the ocean that way and that you had already been through a lot."

"Y-yes, sir."

"So when you got here, who did you know?"

"Well, I already had an auntie and some cousins over

here. Living in Hell's Kitchen. We stayed with them in the beginning."

"So you knew your family members, and that's all? You knew Mr. Sean Murphy, too, right?"

"Yes, sir. He was a friend of my cousins. He was around the place quite a bit you could say. Church and at dinner, I already said before, though."

"So he was almost like a family member himself, then?"

"Something like that."

"Almost like a brother to you, would you say?"

"I don't know how to answer that. I've never had a brother."

There was a long pause of quiet in the room. The man looked down, then up again, and asked,

"Would you call Sean Murphy an honorable man?"

"That is fair enough to say. Yes, I think so." She flicked her glance over to Sean, who looked out of the window with a fixed gaze. He looked so pale.

"He came over on the boat himself, am I right?"

"Right."

"Left behind a mother and five sisters?"

"Yes. He was the youngest in the family."

"Did he ever discuss his family?"

"Sometimes. He doted on them. Sent money home whenever he could."

"So you would say he is a good man, then?"

"Yes."

"One devoted to family?"

"Yes."

"One devoted to the protection of ladies?"

Luna paused. "I believe he is an honorable man in many ways, yes. Even though he does make mistakes."

The man wore little steel-rimmed glasses, which he took

off and polished. "How would you describe your marriage to Mr. Friday?"

The sudden change in topic threw her. "Well. I guess it was a … short marriage."

"Short, yes. But was it a happy one?"

Her face flushed red, and there was that numbness in her hands again." I don't know how to answer that. It's all relative, I guess. Most people would say they have a happy marriage."

"But did you?"

"I don't know what to answer. Mister Friday was a complicated man."

"Complicated?"

"He was a very … driven man."

"I see. Yes, he became a great success at the end of his short life. Many would say due to much help and support from you, his wife."

"Well, yes, I did support his act. I was his assistant."

"Were you his assistant willingly?"

"Sir?"

"There are some who say you hated the role. That you felt humiliated and a spectacle."

"Well, that's show business, isn't it? Being made a spectacle?"

"But it has been said that you were forced against your will."

"I … well …"

"Did you feel unduly pressured to act as his assistant?"

"Well. We certainly were not wealthy when we married. I needed to contribute in any way I could. Most successful magicians have assistants. "

He crossed an arm over his chest, then propped the other under his chin as if to think deeply about this.

"You know, Luna, I can see now your difficult position."

"Meaning what, exactly?"

"Young. Naïve. In a new and frightening city. It must have felt as though you had no one."

"Well, that's not true. I had my family."

"Did you ever talk to your family about the beatings your husband gave you?"

"What?"

He pursed his lips as though it pained him to have to say it. "People have said that you sometimes had bruises. A black eye, once, I believe?"

"But that was just—"

"Lashes on your back and shoulders? They showed under your costumes. From your husband?"

"I don't know what … where did you hear of that?"

"Witnesses who made statements. People who were worried about you."

"Well, they needn't have been. I can take care of myself."

"So he did do it to you?"

"This is ridiculous."

"You told your sisters once, didn't you?"

"I don't recall."

"You told Mister Murphy too, didn't you?"

She had nothing to answer. Her nervous system so beleaguered now that her vision blinked and stuttered.

"He said that you confided in him more than once about your misery. He said—"

"I DON'T CARE WHAT HE SAID! WHY ARE YOU TORTURING ME THIS WAY?"

"We aren't here to torture you or humiliate you. We are presenting to the court the, um, context of the tragic situation here. We are helping the jurors to see the truth."

Luna no longer heard steam in her ears. It was more like

a roaring now. Silently, she cursed Sean for bringing her here, for making all of this happen, no matter what good had come of it.

Sean watched her, bit his lip, choked by his celluloid collar.

What would she do? What could she do? Lie under oath? Refuse to answer? Why did this have to happen?

Then for some reason, she remembered that strange bloke she had met the other night at the Purple Pup. What had he said? Neutrality. Accept the world with neutrality. Let the truth heal you. Then you can create with the world. Not against it.

Become the creator. And make something new.

Luna took a deep breath, and let it all out in a long exhale. Then looked into the eyes of the stout man before her and said, "Yes, Mister Friday sometimes hit me."

"Often?"

"Well, yes. Often enough."

"Can you say you were enslaved to your husband?"

"I would not say enslaved. Just caught up in an ... unfortunate situation."

"In which you were helpless."

Helpless. She had an impulse to shout at him, to say she was never helpless, to say she had merely made some poor decisions, for which she had paid the price already. Hadn't she already paid the price?

But she recovered herself, and in a steady voice said, "Yes, I was helpless."

"You, Luna, could have ended up the dead one, would you say?"

"I wouldn't say that anything is impossible."

"And Mister Sean Murphy knew of your plight. How do you think it affected him, this man who so cherishes his mother and sisters?"

"It made him very upset to know it."

"I know the court has heard things said of Mister Murphy being a hooligan. A thug. But would you agree that that is not the case? That what he is a chivalrous, protective man?"

Luna thought this over, and said, "A man can be both, can't he?"

The lawyer nodded, eyebrows arched, a slow smile spreading across his face. "Why, yes. Yes! Excellent point, Luna."

And like that, the questioning was done. And before long Luna stood upon shaky legs and an usher led her out of the courtroom. Heads swiveled to follow her retreating figure as she made her way to the doors.

In the right-hand back row, she didn't know if her eyes deceived her, but she could have sworn she saw the Magician, seated next to a man with a red nose checking his pocket watch. The Magician had his head facing forward, but his eyes spun to look at her, his face as fierce and resolute as ever, even in death. But a small, mischievous smile played about his still very red lips. As though they shared a secret between them.

She wheeled her head away as the bailiff opened the door for her.

MR. SEAN MURPHY ACQUITTED OF MURDER CHARGE. JURY OUT 3 HOURS

DECIDES IRISHMAN SHOOTING MAGICIAN A CRIME OF PASSION, TO PROTECT THE HOME, SAVE MRS LUNA MULKERRINS-FRIDAY FROM ABUSE AT THE HANDS OF HER SPOUSE

VERDICT REACHED IN THREE BALLOTS

Sean Murphy, 23, charged with the murder of Mr. Jack Friday, was brought into the courtroom by a bailiff. He was pale with excitement and agitation, and as he took his seat, moved and fidgeted about. His five sisters, who had traveled from Ireland to attend the trial, flocked around him, leaving their usual seats near the outer bar railing to be with the defendant.

The jury filed into the room, and Mister Murphy shut his eyes and appeared to pray until the foreman announced, "Not Guilty."

Mr. Murphy leaped from his chair and threw his hands up over his head, as his sister Oona Murphy collapsed from the excitement, while Colleen Murphy Mokler wept and murmured, "Praise be to God, praise be to God."

Luna sat on the roof of her building as the sun set, the newspaper in her hands, and read the story over and over again until the words blurred into meaninglessness.

It's over. It's over. I can't believe it's all over.

She read the part describing her, giving her testimony, the way she had grown emotional and agitated: Mrs. Friday at moments became overwhelmed with emotion, describing the violence she experienced at the hands of the late Mr. Friday. It is believed that it was this testimony that swayed the jury on Mr. Murphy's behalf.

Luna had washed her hair, and the afternoon breeze on the rooftop stirred her tresses around her shoulders, blowing it back, rippling at her silk robe. Somewhere, underneath the city sounds, was the sound of a single cooing dove, soothing and plaintive.

Well. I've saved Sean. But I have just killed Blythe of the Gates.

With regret, with wryness, with acceptance, she let the paper go from her fingers and let the hot wind carry it away, to wherever it may go.

Forty-One

As on most other Sundays, there was a family dinner. But the first dinner with Sean, released from Sing Sing was bigger, and much more festive. There was stew, as always, and soda bread. But there was colcannon with scallions, boiled bacon and cabbage, even a bit of poached salmon.

Dishes crowded the table in the Hell's Kitchen walk-up, the place crammed even more so with people. The cousins poured whiskey from great jugs. The party had spread to neighboring apartments, practically the whole building.

A small phonograph on a table in one corner, newly acquired, played the records of John McCormack. "The greatest singer ever to live," declared Luna's father solemnly. "Can sing sixty-four notes in one breath, he can, and he is a Westmeath boy." She was somewhat surprised that her plainspoken, working-man father had come to love a tenor, but stranger things had happened. He liked to sit in a chair next to the gramophone, head angled near the horn, and nod his head in stern approval at what he was hearing.

He played over and over a song called "The Happy Morning Waits." If anyone in the room realized that the

Irishman was singing Italian opera, no one mentioned it. Everyone was in too jubilant a mood.

Luna had not been to a Sunday meal in a long time herself, and it felt strange to be back. But it was not unpleasant. There was barely room to move, though. Family, friends, people she had never met. Everyone pressed together, talking and laughing and telling stories. The phonograph hissed away, but James had brought his fiddle and played a tune right over it. "I don't care a whit for canned music," he said in a mumble as his bow flew over the strings. "Gives me the mental indigestion."

The noise too overwhelming, Luna filled up her plate and took it down the stairs, where she spread a napkin on her lap and ate on the stoop with a group of others there already; her new brother-in-law Joseph and the old lady who ran the vegetable stand and some Irishmen she didn't recognize but who saluted her with whiskey and told her what a brave, wonderful girl she had been, and that she was a credit to her homeland.

They sat like that for a while, eating their meal, when James came out with his fiddle under his arm and sat next to Luna.

"How are ya holdin' up?" he asked.

"Oh, I'm fair. Glad it's all done."

"Aye. Ya did good up there with everyone lookin' at ya. Guess you're used to an audience, though."

She shrugged. "Well, I guess I'm taking a short break right now. Finding my bearings. By the way, where is the guest of honor?"

"Sean? Oh, he will be about, directly."

"Is he planning it this way? Dramatic entrance?"

"No. He was just out last night. I am sure he might be feeling pretty poorly this morning."

"Oh, really? You know this?"

"Aye. I was out with 'em."

"Doing what, God help me?"

James looked at her sidewise, a sly smile on his face. "Well, we all piled up in his autocar and went driving. Down to the shipyard and such."

"*James*. He just got out of jail!"

"Aye, that's why he misses his car so much! And his mates. Ya gotta go out and pay respects. Make some calls."

"But James!"

"Wot?" Still, with that mischievous grin, he stole the bit of soda bread off her plate and ate it with relish.

"Don't tell me he was with—"

"Never ya mind about it. He just got out from upstate and the boy needed to do a little cele-*bra-tin'*."

"Yes. I'm sure."

Just as she said this, as though on cue, Sean pulled up to the curb in his Model T, squealed to a stop and hopped the sidewalk the smallest bit with his front tire.

"Aye, Seanny boy!" James called.

"Brother!" Sean stepped out from his vehicle, and pushed his driving goggles onto his forehead; his cheeks rosy from the wind, and his reddish hair stood up all over his head as though he had just woken up.

The sound of his arrival must have carried through the upstairs windows, because Sean's sisters ran down the stairs and out of the door, where they ran to gather around him.

Sean's face registered a look of child-like joy; he shone like the sun itself as the sisters circled him, giving hugs and little pats and tinkling with happy exclamations.

"Did I actually hear them calling him Baby Sean?" Luna whispered to James incredulously.

"Well, he is the youngest." He shook his head. "Look at him. Blimey. He's still drunk."

The women, all five of them, seemed to be in their twenties. All wore up-country calicoes and high-necked shirtwaists. For a moment Luna wondered if they thought she was a loose-looking woman because she wore an embroidered peasant blouse that draped off the top of her shoulders, and her hair in a long messy plait down her back. But no, the women, so lively and open-faced with excitement over their brother's good fortune, seemed not to have an ounce of judgment in them. They were just happy.

Luna and James remained seated, watching, as more people came down to join what had turned into a block party.

James idly plucked the strings of his fiddle, goofing, and rocked back and forth as though he were playing a lute. But he paused for a moment, and looked at Luna seriously. "Ya realize it wont ya that saved 'em, right?"

"How do you mean?"

He flicked his head at the bevy of women. "T'was them."

"What?"

"T'was the sisters that swung the jury. How could they commit a man to death, with such lovely sisters who adore him so?" He fluttered his eyelids clownishly.

"Come now, James. I think it was I who did him the most good."

"Well, ya didn't hurt. But I would say, Mister Delmont, the lawyer? He paid out of his own pocket to get these women on a boat over here as fast as he could. It was the best investment he coulda made. He knew what he was doin'. Smart lad. He got all the sisters even though some got babbies at home."

Luna turned to look at him. She struggled mightily to maintain that *neutrality* that had seemed like such a godsend before. "James? Do you realize that I may have killed my career by taking the stand and saying the things that I did?"

"What do ya mean?"

She sighed. "I had an image. Lady Blythe had an image. She was powerful. She was a goddess. I took a long time to create her, to get into her skin. And now—"

"Why you talkin' *was*?"

"Huh?"

"Why was? She's not dead. She's you. She's right here."

"James. She wasn't me. And now all the papers are writing about me, about the truth. Who I really was. A poor battered wife to be pitied. They will see me as a fraud now."

"But ya weren't trickin' anyone."

"Well, not anymore I won't. How can I be her again now? I don't think I can. I am so embarrassed."

James turned on her fiercely. "Don't you be talkin' that way, girl. Ya go back out there and do ya magic. They can't take that away from ya. It's real. It may go against all God intended, but it's real."

"But James, in a way, even that was stolen. I mean, I stole something away that's not really mine." She thought of the box of light, under her bed. She hadn't looked at it since the trial. She couldn't bear to. Could she?

"But it doesn't matter how it all came about. It's yours now, and that's just a fact, is all." He shrugged. "A fact. You'll be back on that stage in no time."

"Well ..." She stared ahead, lost. She had thought she had lost her magic in the courtroom, because she couldn't summon it up, no matter how hard she tried. Speaking the truth made her ordinary, mortal again. Leaden on the earth.

But if she concentrated hard enough, if she opened the box again, tonight, might it all come back again?

"I don't know, James. I just need some time to figure things out. For myself."

"That's a good girl, right." He patted her on the back, then picked up his fiddle again and played a jig.

Sean looked over and gave a little salute and started dancing, sending his sisters into fits of giggles.

"He sure doesn't seem to have noticed me sitting here. After all those passionate letters from jail," Luna said darkly.

"Oh, he's still sweet on ya. And he appreciates what ya did for him, truly. He's just not really focusin' right now."

"I can see that. And focusing has never been his strong suit."

"Oh, come on, cousin. Ain't ya already seeing someone?"

"Why? Did someone say something to you?"

"No. I just picked that up on my own. So it's true, is it?"

Luna flared up in shame, thinking of Jacob, and how she had treated him so badly and hurt him. And how he loved her so much more than she did him. A man in a trap. "I don't want to talk about it."

James slid into another tune that all the women apparently knew; they cheered and clapped and lifted their skirts to dance themselves. Sean took each and swung her around by turn.

"It's just that—" Luna tried to hold back her frustration, but it was impossible. "It doesn't seem fair, does it? That Sean walks away from this unscathed. Whereas I ... first I couldn't work because they all said I was a whore. Now I may not get jobs because I'm a poor, pitiful, abused waif. And neither one is me."

"Ya will come out a this the better."

"I know. But it's so much easier for *some* people."

James abruptly stopped playing and stood up. "I'm going to get me some food. Leave ya for a bit."

"Fine."

The girls, all rosy cheeked from dancing, applauded and followed him up the stairs.

"*Wot*? We're done?" Sean put his hands up in the air. He looked at Luna and raised his eyebrows.

Luna pursed her lips disapprovingly.

He walked over and squatted down, next to her, bringing his large face near hers, with the ridiculous driving goggles still propped on his forehead, like a second pair of eyes.

It took her some time to realize he was waiting for her to kiss him on the cheek.

"You have got to be joking," she muttered.

"Wot? Don't tell me that!" He snatched a kiss off her cheek instead, sat down, and grinned unabashedly into her face.

"Well, Sean, I heard *you* had a good time last night. Looks like you still are. I can smell the whiskey on your breath."

He looked puzzled for a moment, breathed into his cupped hands, and smelled it.

"Sean, I don't care. It doesn't matter. I don't see why you would risk getting into trouble again at a time like this."

"What trouble might ya mean?" He smiled engagingly.

"James said you were all cruising around down at the shipyard, making mischief. You know the police are watching you, right?"

"Why, Luna! Ya *do* still care for me!"

"No. It's not that. It's just …" She sighed.

He patted her on the knee. "Ya want to know one o' the things the boys and I did last night?"

"What?"

"Went to the Nickelodeon. Know what we watched?"

"*The Water Nymph*, I suppose."

"Wrong!" He slapped his knee in satisfaction. "It was *Blythe of the Gates* we watched. We watched ya!"

"Oh? And how did you like it?"

"I thought ya was the most beautiful thing I ever seen. In fact, we watched it twice, and caused such a ruckus to show our appreciation. I yelled out to everyone, 'That's my girl up there!' And all the fellows yelled back and stomped their feet, and we made such noise that they asked us to leave. But it was worth it."

After a long, thoughtful pause, Sean asked, "How did ya *do* those things, though? How did ya dance through the air that way? How did ya make a flock of birds pour out of ya hands? I been puzzlin' over that. The fellas asked me your secrets, and I did not know them."

"Well, I'm not telling you."

"Oh, come on, love. Well, ya looked most fetchin' in that sort of gypsy, spangled sort of thing that showed ya, um, midriff." He looked down shyly.

She did not say anything; the silence stretched on and Sean did his best to catch her eye, giving her little touches and swinging her long braid.

"Hey, now, hey," he said softly, anxious when she did not respond.

"What?" Luna said testily.

Sean's face wore a hurt, woeful expression, eyebrows

puckered up. "What is the matter, Luna?"

"I just have a lot on my mind."

He stared at her for a few moments, looking more and more distressed. "Please don't be mad at me," he said and reached out to give her another pat, but thought better of it and drew his hand back.

"I'm not mad."

"Well, please, please just … I can't bear it if ya hate me."

"I don't hate you, Sean."

He looked down, as though screwing up his courage, and then looked at her again, an uncharacteristically serious expression on his face.

"Luna," he said softly, "If ya want me to marry ya, I will."

"*What?*" She couldn't believe what she'd heard, and inadvertently laughed. Sean, red in the face, said nothing, as the iceman's cart rattled by on the sidewalk, and from the upstairs window, the aria playing on the phonograph hissed and skipped, playing the same soaring declaration over and over, like a hiccup.

Sean took her hand. "Listen, I appreciate what ya done for me. And … and I know I may have ruined your reputation, and I …" His lips trembled, and his eyes shifted to different parts of her face. "I know it would be the honorable thing. So I will. Marry ya." The last bit was spoken in a whisper.

She had never seen him so frightened, or so earnest before. In that moment she felt sorry for him, in spite of herself.

She took him by one of his large, pink freckled hands. "Sean, do you even *want* to get married?"

He tried to straighten himself, to look strong. "Of course I do," he said in a faltering way.

"Do you even … I know you wrote me a lot of things from prison …"

"And I meant them. Then."

The word *then* hung heavily in the air between them. Sean tore off the driving goggles from the top of his head, and flipped them around, not looking at her.

"Sean," she said. "When I said I had a lot on my mind, I didn't mean I was waiting for you to propose."

"Well, I would," he muttered at the ground, "if ya wanted me to."

"I think whatever we had between us is over. And that's okay."

"Really? I mean, I still love ya, but I, well." He smiled at her. "I understand what you're sayin'. It's just … being shut up in jail, livin' in one small room, everything the same day in, day out. Thinkin' of ya kept me goin', ya know?"

She smiled back. "I know."

"But now I'm out now and everything," he shrugged, not knowing how to end the sentence.

"Sean, will you promise me something?"

"Sure I will."

"Will you call off the fellows from the White Hand from watching me all the time?"

"How do you mean?"

"I mean I don't want to be FOLLOWED AROUND anymore by men with GUNS and PIPE WRENCHES in their pockets."

"Oh, but hey, I thought I was helpin'!"

She put her head in her hands.

"I was helpin' ya! I got ya started, didn't I?" He looked at her beseechingly.

"Okay. Yes. I must concede that you got me started. But I don't need that anymore."

"Okay."

"Tell them I'm not your girl anymore."

"Okay. I will. As long as ya promise not to be mad at me, ever."

"I told you I wasn't mad to begin with."

"Then what's *wrong*, Luna? Something is different with ya. Ya've changed!" His left knee pumped up and down in a spastic way.

"Can't you ever sit still, Sean?"

"No," he admitted softly, though with effort, he stilled his knee. Then, in a low breathless rush, he said, "It just seems I always get the tail end of wild ideas, and then I can't let go to save my life. I just get pulled along whether I like it or not until I'm bruised and bloodied. That ever happen to you?"

She paused. "No," she lied.

"Ah," he said sadly, then looked at her anew. "Ya was always are so smart about things, and always doin' the thing that's right."

"I can assure you, I don't."

"Ya are the best person I know. The most good—"

"I am not always so good. I've done things this year I'm not proud of, if you must know the truth."

"It couldn't be anything *that* bad?" A pleading lilt to his voice.

"Oh, it's pretty bad. Sometimes I don't even know myself anymore." She looked into her lap, she couldn't meet his eye. "Can I tell you something, if you'll keep it secret?"

Now he smiled broadly. "I can keep a secret. Everyone knows that. Can't make me tell if there is a boot to my neck!"

She doubted this very much but went on anyway.

"Well, I have been thinking about moving somewhere else for a while."

"Why?"

"Well. I just want to get out of New York, mostly. Too much has happened here, to me. Sometimes it makes me feel I can't breathe."

"I told ya I would call my boys off from protectin' ya! I mean it!"

"I know, I know, I believe you. But it's just that I want to see more. I think I want to go to California."

"But that's so far!"

"They have trains, you know."

"But ya have no family there!"

"That's sort of the idea. Look, I've seen the place in the picture shows. Big, rolling hills. Lots of sun. I'm tired of buildings crowding in and shutting out the sun."

"But what will ya do there?

"Well. To start with, they need a lot of seamstresses. In Hollywood."

A look of dawning comprehension came over his face. "Right. *Riiiight!*"

"That's just so I can get my feet, though. I already have sort of a connection there. In the business."

Agnes had given her the name of her old agent on the west coast, "But Luna, I don't think you'll like it there. It's not like New York. It's harder to find a community. It's lonelier. That's why I switched coasts and joined the Follies."

But Luna had said, "I'll take my chance, then. I've been alone before."

Sean sighed. "Well. If that's what ya want. I just want ya to have what it is ya want."

"I think I do want it. Very much."

"Well, then ya have my blessing, then, dontcha."

"Thank you." But part of her for some reason felt wounded. *Aren't you going to beg me to stay?* "But, please, don't tell anyone yet."

He tapped the side of his nose with his finger and winked broadly.

By and by they went back up to the apartment so that Sean could make his grand entrance. More food and drink, more phonograph records as Sean told rambling tales of life in Sing Sing. Luna sat on a sofa with her sisters tight on either side of her. They spoke of Luna's tour and the places she'd stayed, Lil's honeymoon trip to the Falls.

They spoke of Pa, of Ma, of news from Doolin.

"You know, I can barely remember it anymore," Luna mused. "I know in my mind what it was like. Green fields, the pebbly gray beach. I know we had a little white house with a stone wall and chickens. But that's just it. I see them and name them, but don't feel them anymore."

"Oh, but ya will," said Lil, her gray eyes strong and steady on hers. "Those things are all there. They're just asleep right now. You're dreaming the dream of America. One day ya will awake."

"That sounds rather foreboding," Luna laughed, nervously.

"I don't mean it to be, sister. All I mean is that when a place births ya, it always lives inside ya."

And as the day passed by into early evening, Luna relaxed more and more, and laughed, and stroked Mary Catherine's hair fondly, and drank tea from a teacup with a bit of the whiskey splashed in. How nice it all was, really, to be tucked into this very full room with these friends and family, the people she had known longest in her life. It had been too long, not being with them this way.

The city sounds changed; the autocars were fewer and the night breeze drifted into the windows. She at last stood up to make her way home.

"But stay, Luna! You can sleep in my bed!" cried Lil.

"Darling one, it is not so very far to my flat. Why don't we all get a good night's sleep, and you can come there to see me if you want?"

"Oh, well. Okay. I just don't want you to go."

But she moved around the room, hugging her goodbyes, and given a loaf of barmbrack wrapped in brown paper to take with her.

Very last, she came to say goodbye to her father, who still sat in his place, the wooden chair next to the phonograph. Though he had been drinking all through the night, he sat as upright as a tin soldier.

"Goodnight, Pa," she said, and bent down to kiss his cheek.

She tried to look into his eyes, small squinty eyes, gray like pebbles. Eyes that had seen so much, but divulged so little. She tried to will those eyes to look into hers, to see her.

But again, they did not. They looked right past her. They kissed each other on the cheek, and he nodded curtly, and then acted as though she had already gone.

Oh, well. She had tried, hadn't she? "I'll see you soon, Pa. At church. I will be coming back to church, I promise."

And then she was gone, down the steep dark stairway, out of the door, into the city streets. She stepped up onto a streetcar, and let its swaying movement put her into a kind of trance.

What am I doing? I can't lose my family. Maybe it's true, that family is all you have. So what happens if you lose them? I'm going to break poor Lil's heart …

These and other thoughts churned through her brain even as she got off at her stop. It was a balmy evening, and music drifted from the doorways of dance halls. Children still played restlessly in the streets, running by in their high dark shoes like swarms of angels or demons, indifferent to the adults in their fancy night dress, out for a meal or a drink or a dance or whatever people look for when they go out into the night in the city.

But in her street, oddly, there was no one.

Darkness had fallen entirely, and the lamplight was weak. It was hard to see except for the couple of feet in front of her.

Since she was alone, she sang to herself, to keep herself company. A song she could remember being sung around the bonfires when she was a girl.

"In Dublin's fair city
Where the girls are so pretty
I first set my eyes on sweet Molly Malone
As she wheeled her wheelbarrow
Through the streets broad and narrow
Crying 'cockles and mussels, alive, alive-o
Alive, alive-o
Alive, alive-o...'"

Her voice quavered, small and alone in the darkness, and at the same time, Lil's words came back to her: *You're dreaming the dream of America. One day you will awake.*

And then it all *did* come back. Those bonfire nights on the moors, the way the cinders carried on the wind, and if you listened, the hushed roar of the ocean in the distance. It was all so vivid. So real. She even felt her mother there, holding her as she had on those nights, wrapping the afghan tighter around her, drawing her close.

Alive, alive-o ...

But as soon as she tried to grasp too hard onto the memory, it disintegrated into the ether again, slipped through her fingers, and she was back, alone, on a city street in a country that was not hers.

Ah, well. At least singing the song had brought her to the entrance of her building. *Ah, well.*

Up the stairs, twenty-four of them, because she had counted them before. This time she counted them backward, twenty-four, twenty-three, twenty-two …

I don't know what I'm doing. I know no one in California.

Eighteen, seventeen, sixteen…

Maybe they are all right. Maybe I should just stay in New York, not rock the boat.

Twelve, eleven, ten …

Although my life is quite the mess here and I can't bear it.

Six, five four …

Why is it that no answer seems the right one?

Three, two …

As she stepped onto her landing, she was startled to see someone sprawled across the floor next to her door. Inadvertently she let out a little cry. A drunk? A homeless man? She'd seen enough of them in this city that she ought not to be surprised. But at *her* door?

She cried out and the form stirred and awoke, blinking up at her from the hallway gloaming.

"Jacob! What are you doing here?"

She laughed, no longer afraid. Quiet, mild-mannered country boy that he was, he looked even more startled than she had been.

"I'm sorry, Lady Blythe. I guess I just got tired."

"How long were you here?"

"Not that long, just got here." He stood up, unfolding his long limbs, brushed off his trousers.

"Really, Jacob, you looked quite dead asleep."

"Well. I guess I've been here since sunset?"

"But why?"

"I wanted to see that you were home safe from the party. And I didn't want to be intrusive and let myself in like last time."

"But how did you *know* I was at a party?"

"Oh, there's an Irish stagehand who knew all about the big welcome home party for Sean."

He said the name offhandedly, but she could see the hurt in the set of his mouth, the way he turned his hat in his hands without looking at her.

"Well, let's not stand here in the hallway. Come in."

She turned on the table lamp with its rose silk shade and swaying fringe. Jacob took a seat on the couch and folded his hands in front of him. It had been days since they had spoken. She had thought he had left her for good after the way she had treated him.

"Would you like some tea?"

"N-n-no thank you. I don't mean to stay. I-I-I …"

The expression in his eyes was pained, and he struggled to get the words out. She knew him well enough to know that the stutter came when he was overwhelmed with emotion.

"Say it like you're on the stage," she reminded him. "It always helps, doesn't it?"

He looked up at her all at once, the directness of his gaze boring into her soul. He cleared his throat. "I just would like to know what your intentions are."

"I am not seeing Sean, if that's what you're asking."

He looked at her fixedly. Some of the anguish drained from his eyes, his stiff jaw and shoulders. But still searching for something in her face. What?

"I mean it, Jacob. I went to the party mainly to catch up with my family."

"But did he p-propose to you?"

Shocked by his prescience, she took care not to show it in her face. "Why would you think he would do that?"

"Because it is what any honorable man would do in this situation."

Luna sighed. "Jacob. *You* are the most honorable man I know. You read too much goodness into others."

"I see what I see."

"But it's not always accurate."

"I see you. And I like what I see."

"But there's a lot you don't know about me."

"But that's okay! I don't need to know everything. I would allow you to be who you are."

"You're committing to more than you know." She smiled, as though it were a joke. The smile died when she saw his face.

He gazed at her with perfect, poised focus. With his curly dark hair rumpled and damp looking, he resembled a drawing she had once seen of a young Christopher Columbus, on the deck of his ship, feasting his eyes across the water at the new world that lay just ahead.

I am truly being seen, for the first time in my life, praise Mary.

It made her joyful, exhilarated. But also frightened. There was so much she hadn't told him. The ambition that lived in her heart. Her visions of the future. California. Crisp blue sky, orange groves. The land of the moving pictures. It was the future, and she would be there, living it.

Could he ... was it possible that he might share that future with her? Her heart thrashed in her chest like a trapped bird. It was all so alive inside her. To speak of it could be to kill it.

"Luna. Please. I would like to have an answer from you. It is only fair."

"And what was the question?"

"I am asking if you would agree to marry me."

"I-I guess I wasn't expecting this." She got up and busied herself with the tea things. She brought him a cup, filled high to the brim, sloshing over the edge.

He ignored the tea, too intent on her face. "I didn't mean to catch you off guard, but I made up my mind about this some time ago."

In a daze, she stared into space. Her lips twitched. Without thinking she drank from the cup she had poured for Jacob. Too hot.

"You don't have to answer me this moment, Luna. But I would be happy if you considered it."

"Of course, I will consider it," she said in a tremulous whisper.

He at last broke his gaze, looked away, and gestured with his large hands. "You see, it won't be a typical marriage. I would not impose any old-fashioned ideas. I will allow you to be who you are."

"But who is that? Even I wonder," she laughed ruefully. *A modern woman*, she answered herself in her mind.

"I see who you are. I accept you. And I love you unconditionally."

For some reason, these words, the kindest words anyone had spoken to her, made her flame red, kicked up sparking energy in her limbs as though she could run. As though she could scream. She did not understand herself. She made no sense.

"Well, I, well, Jacob … I'm sorry if I'm feeling a bit weak

right now."

"Darling, are you feeling faint?" He moved up from the couch. "Lie down here, put your feet up."

But it wasn't faintness she was feeling. Just the opposite. "No, I will be fine. I just need … maybe you should go home now."

"I can see I've overwhelmed you. I'm sorry."

"I think maybe you should just go home now. It's late." She took his hand, and kissed him on the cheek, trying to soothe away his concern. "Can I give you an answer in the morning?"

"Of course. Take as long as you want. I'm not going anywhere. I'll wait all the time in the world."

That's the problem, she thought.

She handed him his hat and walked him to the door, and kissed him on the lips.

"I will talk to you in the morning. Goodnight," she whispered in his ear.

She listened as his steps echoed down the stairwell, until they were gone. Then there was absolute silence, a rarity in the city. She sat for a while until she felt as though she were the only living thing awake in the heavy summer darkness.

Whenever she felt confused, or afraid, or lonely, she was able to turn to the box of light. And it was right there, under her bed. So close. Right there.

But things, from now on, would have to change.

She was a small woman, and it was a high shelf. But if she stood on tiptoes, she would be able to reach it. She knelt and pulled out the box from beneath her bed, and her fingertips felt those comforting textures, the hammered brass tacks, the cracked leather. She carried the box to the closet.

Funny, it used to feel heavy to her. Now it didn't weigh a thing.

She stretched up and slid it onto the high shelf, pushing it back, back, until she could not see it. Her oldest friend. She resisted the urge to pull it down and open up the lid just one more time, to hear the hinges squealing, releasing those ancient smells of old newsprint and dust and old lives that had passed before hers. How many people had owned it before her? How many people would after her? She was too tired then to wonder.

She imagined basking in its luminous light as bright as the sun. Even now she felt that deep electrical hum permeating her veins, her bones, waking her passions, making her feel alive.

But for just that moment, all she did was reach up to the shelf again and stroke its surface one more time. Almost like an elephant's hide, every crease and wrinkle as familiar to her as her own face.

And as she closed her eyes in anticipation of all that would come next, she knew one thing was for certain. *I will let him go.*

Acknowledgements

Much gratitude to my publisher and my intrepid editor, Jayne Southern, and for the support of my family and friends.

About the Author

Leah Erickson has been published in many journals and magazines, in print and online, including *The Saint Ann's Review*, *The Fabulist*, *Eclectica*, *Pantheon*, and *The Coachella Review*. Her debut novel, *The Gilded Lynx*, was published in 2016 by Kraken Press.

She lives in Newport, Rhode Island with her husband and daughter.

Also by this author …

The Brambles, The Gilded Lynx.

And for more from this author …

Please turn the page for a preview of *The Brambles*

The Brambles

One

THE GIRL IN THE TREE

The dead girl haunted the minds of the townspeople like a half-remembered dream, a tune once well known, the words vanished into silence.

Many times they had seen her over the years, riding past on her bicycle or walking on foot, dreamily, down the road's dusty shoulder. Often her skirts were long and dark colored, crinkled cotton or crushed velvet. A colorful yarn Guatemalan bag hung with its long strap crossing her chest. She was like a figure from another time, though it was hard to say *which* time. Dressed like a sixties flower child, but with her long dark hair pinned up primly from her pale neck, she looked more Victorian, like a girl from a cameo. A silhouette of yellowed ivory, distinct in its delicate lines, but at the same time featureless.

One remembered *seeing* her, but the girl was always in the peripheries of inner vision, just at the edge of consciousness.

Summer or winter, there had always seemed to be an air of remote *coolness* about her. As though she hadn't much to do with the roads, the landscape, the town and its people. On her way to the library where she sat alone at a study desk. Or going to the market to pick up some things for *the mother*. (About whom much was whispered. Thought to be a solitary and odd woman who had homeschooled her daughter, though the public schools were excellent …)

The girl's name was Elizabeth, though few had called her by her name. She had lived in the town for years, and though seen by many, she was known by few. Seventeen years old at the time of her death, according to the news reports.

An elderly man, Ernest Stevenson, who suffered dementia and sometimes wandered around, lost, found her hanging by her neck from the limb of a white oak tree, deep in the woods that rimmed the edge of her backyard. At the moment in the early morning when the girl's mother first realized that Elizabeth was not in her bed, Ernie was outside in his striped pajamas and bare feet in the woods, like an apparition in the mist and the ferns; he stood looking at the girl's lifeless form as she swayed from a creaking rope in the soft early light, an expression of stunned wonder on his face.

Once the police came, news traveled fast.

What was there to say? People shook their heads. The girl must have had troubles that no one knew of. She and the mother kept to themselves, living in a house of a modern, Japanese design, with siding made of blackish charred cedar. The windows, irregularly sized and placed, had panes of frosted glass that looked like rice paper, impossible to see through. They obviously had *money*, because the mother had had the chic house custom designed. But no one had ever visited the house. If the girl was suffering, how could it be anyone else's fault?

A polite girl. Her voice was deep and level when she spoke to say please or thank you. Adult in her directness. No trace of an accent, though she had something vaguely foreign about her. Dark hair and eyes, dusky voice.

The more people tried to remember details about Elizabeth, the more elusive she became, as though in the mind's eye her identity was *pixilated*. She had died in the autumn, a time of year when she walked down the road and the sun burned low and golden behind her, turning her into a silhouette. She had lived among them, invisible, for so long, that no one could agree on exactly what she had looked like.

Except for the girl's eyes; penetrating, strange and feral looking. She'd suddenly turn to look back at you as you drove past her and make your heart stop, as if a painting or statue had come to life and now saw *you*. No one could forget those eyes, which still seemed to hover from the shadows, watching them. Once seen, never again unseen.